BLUE EDEN

The Future
AFTER THE ICE MELT

By

Phyllis Kalbach

*To Nancy Graham
enjoy the adventure*

*Phyllis
Kalbach
2013*

Books & Scribes
2432 Blue Heron Loop,
Lincoln, CA 95648

PUBLISHED BY BOOKS & SCRIBES
2432 Blue Heron Loop,
Lincoln, Ca. 95648

Cover design by Lawrence Fox
fox@artfox.us

Book cover image: www.fotosearch.com

Editor: Sue Clark
SJ Clark Literary Specialties

Printing:

In the United States of America

I Street Press
CreateSpace

ISBN 13:978-0-9798570-1-0

I dedicate this book to my husband, Cyril. Thank you for your support, encouragement and advice.

A special thank you to: Nancy, Jeri, Emma, Joan, Irene, Marilyn, Nondra, and Tom.

TABLE OF CONTENTS

TABLE OF CONTENTS

PART IV
SEPTEMBER 1
ONE HUNDRED YEARS IN THE FUTURE

PART V
SEPTEMBER 2
ONE HUNDRED YEARS IN THE FUTURE

"The mischief springs from the power which the moneyed interest derives from a paper currency which they are able to control, from the multitude of corporations with exclusive privileges which they have succeeded in obtaining. . .and unless you become more watchful in your states and check this spirit of monopoly and thirst for exclusive privileges you will in the end find that the most important powers of government have been given or bartered away."

President Andrew Jackson, Farewell Address,
March 4, 1837

PREFACE

In the later part of the 20th century and the beginning of the 21st century, people on earth began to send exploratory missions to the planet Mars. Time and time again, the robots sent to explore Mars informed the scientists on earth that Mars was void of life. No evidence of life could be found. Yet, those robots did send information verifying that sustaining life on Mars was not impossible.

During a fifty-year span, scientists began to prepare for Project Blue Eden; a project they had developed to prepare Mars for human habitation. Indeed, the planet had all of the ingredients necessary for life, including; ice caps at both its north and south poles. Evidence also indicated that Mars once had an atmosphere thick and warm enough to allow for the flow of liquid water on its surface; the prerequisite for life. Scientists knew that once there was again an atmosphere that would allow the existence of water, there would be life on Mars.

Project Blue Eden was launched. Scientists called the creating of an atmosphere on Mars terraforming. This project began with a warming up and thickening of the existing atmosphere. That way, Mars could be habitable for the microorganisms that could prosper in a carbon dioxide environment. This transformation included changes in the soil, atmosphere and water, which would play a large role in the organization of the future biosphere. As a result, carbon dioxide breathing, oxygen emitting biological plants would be introduced into the inhospitable environment.

Once the project was implemented, life took hold and began to flourish. A process that had taken billions of years on Earth was accomplished within a time frame of less than a century. Seeds were transported to Mars and scattered in abundance across the planet where they took root. Forests grew and vegetation blossomed. Fish, animals and birds of every variety were released into the oceans, streams and forests where they multiplied and thrived. Blue Eden waited, ready and alive, but no humans came to claim their creation.

In the summer of 1999, fifty men and ten women met on a private island in the South Pacific. They came from America, Australia, Europe, Japan, the Middle East, China and Brazil, but they represented the interest of no country. Instead, they were businessmen, industrialists, political leaders and members of royalty, and this secret meeting was to discuss their personal interests.

Oil was the economic base for most of the world's population at that time and these people's fortunes depended on the control of that oil supply. They needed to ensure that oil remained the dominant fuel supply far into the 21st century. They realized that the world was changing, but they also knew that wealth was power and that those with the highest concentration of wealth would survive in the future world no matter what the situation.

As the ice sheets melted on earth, water levels and temperatures around the world steadily rose, ravaging populated areas of the earth with floods, droughts, uncontainable fires and violent storms which rendered most of earth's life sustaining land uninhabitable. Multitudes of homeless refugees fled north to the once frozen tundra of Europe, Asia and North America. Citizens of once prosperous societies now found themselves as unwanted migrants at the mercy of fragile governments buckling beneath the strain of nature's unyielding attacks and humanity's desperation. Multiple walls were built around communities in an attempt to protect and separate those inside with the wealth and power from those disenfranchised migrants outside. Earth was dying and Blue Eden waited.

Part I

August 29
One hundred years in the future

CHAPTER ONE
Joe Gage
Cork Harbor Ireland

Today he was in Ireland and there would be no killing. Joe Gage held a newly lit cigarette between his lips, his helmet beneath his left arm and a dirty brown duffle bag slung over his shoulder as he walked across the tarmac toward a row of hangars and warehouses inscribed with the World Tech symbol. Aircraft workers hurried toward his landed gunship, avoiding his hard, dark eyes as they hurried past him.

"Hey, Gage," one of the other pilots called to him. "Goin with us?"

Squinting through the smoke of the cigarette held between his lips, Gage, a tall mercenary dressed in a black militia flight suit with the gold, corporate emblem on his chest and sleeves continued to walk, not appearing to notice his colleagues. He pushed open a metal side door and entered one of the immense, air conditioned hangars, ignoring the no smoking signs mounted on the door and walls. A huge cargo plane, with engine parts stacked beneath its bulky fuselage, dominated the left side of the hangar. The steady click of his leather-cleated boots connecting with the concrete floor cast an echo as he walked.

Gage entered the latrine at the end of the building, relieved himself and then shoved his helmet into his duffle bag. After throwing his burning cigarette to the concrete floor, he moved to a row of stained, chipped sinks lining the bathroom wall. He turned on the faucet, splashed cold water on his face and massaged the refreshing liquid through his thick brown hair, digging his fingers deep into his scalp. "Today you are in Ireland," he whispered, "and there will be no killing."

Gage glanced at the mirror above the sink and met his disheveled reflection. His body remained motionless while his mind sought answers. Is there a soul in there? Or did it die a long time ago? Did it ever exist?

He needed to shave and he needed to get clean he thought as he ran his fingers across the bristles on his cheek and across his chin. Yes, shower away the dirt, the sin, the ugliness. "Maybe it's too late," he spoke aloud. "Is there a point of no return?"

Several young militiamen entered the room laughing and talking. Gage ignored them.

"Hey, mate," one called to him. "There's a van waiting. Get out of that flight suit will ya. Ireland's a bloody steam bath out there."

"Sure," Gage mumbled. "I'll be there."

After stripping off his flight suit revealing a light-weight, short-sleeved militia uniform underneath, Gage stuffed the discarded flight suit in his duffle bag and joined the other pilots in front of the building. Yes, Ireland was hot. Sweat drenched his light-blue uniform and rivers of perspiration streamed down his forehead. Heavy wet air choked his lungs until his body acclimated to the heat and humidity.

Two passenger vans bearing the World Tech symbol – a solid gold ball encircled by the bold, ebony letters spelling World Tech, Inc. – sat waiting in the narrow parking lot separating the huge warehouses from a park-like strip of grass, trees and flowers. Beyond this patch of greenery lay the World Tech garrison; a compound of modern glass and steel buildings, parks and well maintained streets. Solar panels designed as an appendage of each building, fueled the batteries that kept dwellings cool and comfortable. Additional batteries propelled the irrigation system keeping the vegetation lavish throughout this corporate metropolis.

"Hey, mate." One of the young militiamen spoke as he took a pack of cigarettes from his shirt pocket. "I hear that in ten – maybe fifteen years – this whole island will be one big block of ice. So they say will be all of Europe. One day a desert, the next an ice cube. Hard to believe, ain't it?"

"Ain't hard to believe that if you keep talking like that, mate, you'll end up on ice permanently," answered one of his young companions who seemed nervous while the rest of the group kept up their loud conversation.

"Yeah, keep talking like that," another said as the group moved across the parking lot toward the vans, "and we'll all lose our heads."

Five of the men jumped into one vehicle; six in the other. The air conditioning in the vans chilled their sweat soaked uniforms, but the young soldiers appeared to adjust quickly to the abrupt change in temperature. Gage lit a cigarette and settled back in his seat while his companions talked about the past missions and the battle just fought. They laughed and relayed details about near misses and hits. Nothing was mentioned about those who did not return.

The vans passed through the heavily-guarded compound gates and onto the city streets. Gage stared out the window, his troubled mind deep in thought. He wondered why this mission – this battle fought only days ago – was worse than any of the others. What was so different? Certainly, he had experienced far more ruthless encounters in the past where he learned to harden his emotions and swallow his conscience, but this time something was different.

For most of Gage's thirty-six years, he had been a fighter, a soldier, a warrior. Coming from nothing, Gage had been a slave. Four years ago he had earned a commission with World Tech, Inc., the most powerful and wealthiest company in the world. Simple work for the most part, he thought. Escorting caravans of ships across the globe could be dangerous, but few bothered a heavily armed World Tech convoy. Those who tried were dispatched with ease.

This time, it had been different and unsettling. Eleven cargo ships had been commissioned to transport goods from the Sea of Japan through the Bering Strait and across the Northwest Passage to Northern Europe making stops in Russia, England and finally Ireland. Gage had chaperoned those convoys on numerous occasions and knew better than to get sloppy or to let his guard down, especially in the dangerous waters of the Arctic.

The Northwest Passage was a treacherous seaway linking the Pacific and Atlantic Oceans. With the melting of enormous ice sheets in the Arctic Ocean, an array of immense boulders, islands of stone and huge land masses appeared above the water in what was once a continent of ice. Those patches of land, shrouded in darkness and twilight for half the year and habitual sunlight for the other half, seemed to be uninhabitable.

Yet, the outcast of the outcast, the pirates, renegades and unconscionable criminals flourished on those remote, rocky islands at the top of the world. This mysterious new land provided hiding for those nefarious outcasts in caves and beneath the continual blackness of the winter sky. Raids against the cities, refugee camps and against the merchant convoys increased as those desperadoes grew in number and in strength.

No one expected the attack that came on that brightly lit August evening. A World Tech reconnaissance plane spotted a fleet of fishing boats clustered five miles off the shores of Black Rock Island and seven miles from the caravan.

"A ragged group," the pilot reported. "Obviously illegal." Fishing, even in those waters, was permitted only by corporate employees working out of clearly marked corporate boats.

Gage, commanded to buzz the vessels, confirmed that the boats were old, rickety and ill-equipped. Barefoot fishermen,

men and boys, most stripped to the waist, attended their nets and stared up at the hovering aircraft.

"Fire warning shots. Make 'em scatter. Get 'em outta there," came Gage's orders.

"Will do," he replied opening his guns with the push of a button and circling the flotilla. Spurts of gunfire rained down onto the choppy sea sending the men and boys scrambling for cover aboard their floating targets.

As Gage pulled his ship north in order to circle for another attack, return fire rattled harmlessly against the sides of his aircraft. Explosions erupted from the fishing boats as other corporate airships joined the skirmish and blasted the small boats with volleys of fire and lead. Flames, debris and charred bodies rose upward, fanned out in mid-air and then tumbled into the murky sea. The flotilla was gone. Gage rolled his aircraft sharply to the left, just missing a flaming missile whizzing through the air from the direction of Black Rock.

Another missile, shot from the shore, sailed through the air clipping a hovering gunship causing it to ignite and then explode sending a shower of flaming wreckage into the water below.

Orders were swift and emotionless. Destroy the enemy. Make the way safe for the convoy. Like a flock of birds moving in unison, the dark, disk-shaped flying machines, guns protruding from their sides and bellies and with the gold World Tech emblem displayed with pride above the guns, turned toward Rock Island.

The killing began. Rock Island appeared like a black pimple rising out of the blue water. White caps lapped against its dismal existence, spraying the island's low-lying cliffs with salt water. Gage's radar alerted him to movement on one of the cliffs.

"It's mine," he radioed – his voice steady and assured. In a single smooth maneuver, Gage's gunship moved within firing

range of a group of human figures hoisting a hand-fired missile
to the shoulder of one of the persons below. The group's clumsy
efforts failed to secure a target and within seconds, Gage's
deadly sights selected, isolated and destroyed the unfortunate
renegades leaving a smoldering depression where the men once
stood.

Sounds of battle – gunfire, explosions and excited
chatter over the airways – pulled Gage toward the commotion.
Hovering warships fired their guns into a village of scattered
tents and cave dwellings carved into the dark, barren hillside.
Desperate women and children ran, seeking shelter from the
bullets, missiles and shrapnel. Tents disintegrated and cave
dwellings burst into flames.

Flying above the destruction, Gage spotted a woman
holding the hand of a young boy. Both were running toward the
interior of the island. Guiding his craft in their direction, he set
his sights on the pair. The woman, her brown tangled hair blew
in the wind as she ran; the child sometimes falling and being
dragged when he could not keep up with her long strides.

A bright sparkle of light distracted Gage for a moment,
shifting his attention away from the escaping pair toward a
narrow gorge running from the beach-cliffs toward the center of
the island. Turning his ship away from the fleeing mother and
child and into the rugged ravine, Gage spotted the reason for the
flickering rays. Several barefoot, scantly-clothed men were
frantically moving guns and ammunition out from a cave
burrowed into the side of the gorge and placing their deadly
cargo into a two-wheeled cart drawn by a single mule.

Without hesitation, Gage released a missile watching it
as it sliced the air, whistled past the surprised laborers and
entered the mouth of the cave. Within an instant of the missile's
entrance, the mountain erupted, ripping apart the hillside and
spewing fire, rocks, billowing black smoke and pieces of earth
high into the pale summer sky. A furor of wind from the

massive explosion caught the gunship sending it whirling, twisting and turning out of control.

Steady and competent, Gage regained control of his vessel and turned back toward the village. Torn and mutilated bodies – human and animal – lay strewn across the landscape while gunships soared overhead looking for movement. Gusts of wind blew pieces of canvas across the scorched terrain, but nothing lived. The woman and child lay dead; their fingers still entwined, her tangled brown hair matted with blood.

There was no victory that day. The fishing boats, the men on the beach and perhaps even the village were all decoys and martyrs leading the warplanes away from the intended prize. While the corporate mercenaries chased their phantoms, the convoy of eleven cargo ships and ten smaller fast moving gunboats slowed their engines not desiring to rush into an ambush. Unknown to them at the time, the real ambush lay in wait beneath the sea.

Gage's mind drifted from the present to the past and back again. As the van rolled through the city streets of Cork Harbor, Ireland, Gage shifted in his seat and inhaled smoke from his cigarette. He was exhausted body and mind and he knew he needed rest. A good night's sleep in a clean room would clear his mind, or would it? There were questions without answers haunting his damaged spirit. He knew that peace would not come easy. The gentle movement of the vehicle and the steady hum of the tires did not assuage his fatigue. Gage closed his eyes and shut out his immediate world.

The other soldiers were now quiet and within their own thoughts. The swirling smoke from their cigarettes circulated in the van and the bustling city of Cork Harbor appeared shadowy and muted through the vans shaded windows. Images of the destroyed village loomed prominent in Gage's memory; and then the fire. His mind drifted back to the battle.

Deep below the surface of the Ocean, silent and patient divers had been hiding while the caravan of cargo ships moved in a slow queue over their heads. When the signal to action came, they were prepared. Half a dozen small torpedoes left the underwater launching stations and blasted into the bottom of the Roslyn Lee, the next to the last ship in line. The torpedo pierced her outer hull spilling debris, fuel and ballast water into the agitated sea. Moments later, a second round was fired, shattering the inner hull, flooding the engine room and stokehold and leaving the vessel without power. Explosions ripped through the hangar amid ship, detonating stored ammunition, lifting the Roslyn Lee into the air, breaking her in half. Fire shrouded her in a veil of smoke and foul smelling gasses. Seawater poured into the ship's gaping wounds as 3,300 tons of oil gushed out into the sea and floated to the top creating a filmy rainbow of color as it spread across the ocean waves. The oil ignited. Pitch black clouds of smoke rolled upward. Bright red and orange flames skipped and danced as they spread and surrounded the ships in a terrifying inferno.

As a volcano of fire and black smoke separated the last ship, as well as two gun boats from the rest of the caravan, an army of divers dressed in black wet-suits and face masks rose up from the ocean like a single, multi-headed beast. Their oxygen tanks and face masks, glittering in the veiled sunlight were discarded.

Working in unison, each diver produced a hand-held grappling hook, tossed them aboard the two stranded gunboats and the cargo ship, Majestic Queen, which were now desperately maneuvering back away from the fire and from the rest of the convoy. Ascending the ropes and boarding the crafts, the barefoot intruders overpowered and disarmed the startled militia and crew members of the smaller gunboats. They dragged the captain and first officers from their quarters and brutally beheaded them before the terrified eyes of the captured crew.

At the same time, an armada of speed boats, rafts and fishing boats appeared upon the smoke veiled horizon and entered the battle. Ivan, the elusive chieftain and leader of this murderous ambush stood like a warrior statue in the lead boat. His near naked body, muscular and stocky was covered in multi-colored tattoos depicting scenes of battle and symbols of death. Slung across his broad shoulders was a light weight military assault weapon loaded and ready for use. Woven into his thick red beard and braided red hair were small mirrors, pieces of glass and red beads each capturing and tossing about the sun's rays causing his head and face to appear as though they were ablaze and thus sinking terror into the hearts of even the most hardened warrior. Fearless and without hesitation this gang of savage pirates turned their attention toward the Majestic Queen, the last cargo ship in the convoy which was now isolated from the rest of the fleet and partially surrounded by a towering wall of flames.

While the captured gunboats fired volleys across the bow of the Majestic Queen, the pirate army swarmed aboard the stranded cargo ship and joined in a ruthless slaughter of armed and unarmed crew. The wounded were thrown overboard into the burning sea while others were collected for future ransom. The Majestic Queen and her gun boats now belonged to the pirates.

Gage's thoughts jolted him back to the present, back to Ireland and the smoke filled van. The tight confines of the van

became stifling. His head began to throb. He needed fresh air.
"Stop the van," he ordered the driver. "Pull over."

Swerving through the city traffic, the van stopped on the
street next to a row of parked cars. Without saying a word, he
grabbed his duffle bag, threw the sliding van doors open and
stepped out. Gage took a deep breath, inhaled the sweltering air
and salty ocean smell. He stood immobile as the van drove away
leaving him alone amidst a bustling humanity casting distrustful
eyes downward as they hurried past him. Gage took a slow deep
breath.

Slinging his duffle bag over his shoulder Gage began to
walk, not caring where he was going. He just needed to move.
His long strides took him past stores filled with clamoring
shoppers seeking the luxuries and necessities of life. Gage
noticed several beggars, their eyes lowered as he passed them on
the crowded sidewalk.

He entered a brick-paved plaza framed by cafes, art
shops and street venders. A massive marble fountain occupied
the center of the plaza with a stern-faced statue of the governor
of Ireland in the middle. Water bubbled around the statue and
geysers rose and fell within the walled fountain reservoir.

Seated at tables that were scattered about the plaza and
surrounding the fountain, well-dressed diners laughed and
chatted while they sipped wine and savored the restaurant's
specialty dishes. Gage noticed a young woman who stood
watching the fountain. Her white button-down blouse pulled
tight across her full breast, a knee-length brown skirt revealed
ample hips and her tan hair hung loosely down her back and
across her shoulders. A slight breeze blew wisps of hair across
her cheek and she brushed them aside with her slender finger
revealing a gold band. Her large round eyes the color of her hair,
moved away from the water and to the opposite side of the
fountain where Gage stood watching her. Their eyes met
momentarily, curious and provocative. Then her gaze moved

from his face to the insignia on his uniform, paused and moved back to his face. Her full lips tightened into a hard line and a look of bold contempt stared back at him. Dismissing him with a slight lifting of her chin, the woman turned toward a curly-headed boy running bare footed across the plaza toward her.

"Mommy," the little boy called, his plump cheeks flushed and freckled, his blue eyes sparkling with excitement.

"Come, Mommy. Come with me." His short arms extended out in front of him as he ran, his chubby fingers reached for his mother's hand. The woman's face softened and her smile filled her face as her hand grasped the young boy's hand. Gage watched as the two of them turned their backs and walked away. There once was another boy, Gage thought as he watched them disappear into a busy shop – a child with outstretched hands and a mother.

Gage's mind and body snapped to attention. Someone was watching him. His hand moved to the gun holstered on his hip while his eyes surveyed the plaza. Nothing seemed suspicious and yet, the hair stood up on the back of his neck. He felt a danger and it was near.

Alert to his immediate environment, Gage left the plaza, moved onto the crowded sidewalks and walked for several blocks toward the beach. When he stepped onto the long wooden boardwalk, he surveyed the area, alert and cautious. Vender's booths and carts lined the uneven, unpainted walkway where food, trinkets, hats and lotions were sold. Sunbathers cluttered the shoreline while children ran about the sand. Murky waves rolled like a foul serpent upon the beach and then receded again into the harbor.

The aroma of sizzling meat and spices mingling with the ocean breeze reminded Gage he had not eaten since early that morning. After ordering a beer in a paper cup and a plump sausage from a small thatched-roofed café facing the beach,

Gage chose a wobbly metal table outside on the boardwalk. He slid his duffle bag from his shoulder to the ground.

Gage took a long drink from the bitter beer and then wiped the foam from his lips with the back of his hand. The beer was warm but it tasted good. The sausage, made of protein paste and spices, was at least hot and had some taste.

People seated near him began to gather their plates of food and move away from his table. Gage, mindful of the power and fear his uniform instilled in people, felt them surveying his attire. Yet, he felt another pair of eyes watching unafraid from somewhere in the distance.

Gage studied his surroundings. This was the public area where the lower classes played and escaped if only for a while, their lives of servitude. Further up the seashore stood the luxury hotels, casinos and private beaches designed for the world's powerful and privileged. From his seat on the boardwalk, Gage could see those splendid edifices rising in the distance like monuments to opulence and inequality. Later that night he would visit that world, dine in abundance and spend the night on silk sheets with a lady of pleasure. For now, he belonged on that section of the beach reserved for slaves and servants.

After draining the last drop of beer, Gage crushed the large paper cup in his fist. With his keen mind still focused on his environment, he allowed his subconscious to burrow into his soul. In reality, Gage belonged nowhere. Money purchased his freedom and the uniform gave him power, but his life still belonged to the corporate kings who employed him. Not a slave anymore, he thought, but a servant.

"Ha." He laughed almost out loud.

A servant who bows to no one – a servant with no place to run, no place to hide, he thought.

His muscles tightened. Was that danger he sensed? He knew he was being watched, but by whom and why? The answer came to him from out of the crowd in the form of a young, brown-skinned woman. She moved with assurance toward him, avoiding a collision with the barefoot children romping, pushing and shoving their way across the boardwalk.

The hem of her simple brown dress flowed against her thighs as she walked. Her sturdy shoes seemed out of place on that hot sandy shore. Her large dark eyes viewed him from a face framed in dark braids pinned in swirls on top of her head. As she came closer, Gage could see her full lips pressed together nervously. When she stood before him, she gave a slight curtsey.

"My lady wishes to talk to you, sir." She spoke with her head bowed.

Gage leaned forward. "Tell your lady I don't buy anything I don't see first."

The woman looked up and fixed her eyes on his face. "My lady sells nothing." As she spoke, she reached into her pocket and pulled out something she held in her tight fist. Holding her arm out straight toward Gage, she opened her hand revealing a folded piece of paper.

"My lady wishes you to have this, sir, and she wishes me to bring you to her."

Surprised, Gage took the paper from her hand and unfolded it. What he saw startled him. In the center of a blue rose was drawn three number 8s – the symbol of a dark, secret criminal organization known only as The Eight. Closing his fist around the piece of paper, Gage used his right hand to grab the women's arm. He pulled her toward him.

He hissed, "Who are you?"

A moment of fear passed across the woman's face, but she regained her composure. "I am nobody, but I assure you. If I am harmed, you will not live to see the morning. And you will never know the identity of my lady."

With reluctance, Gage released her and leaned back in his chair. A gust of hot wind tossed garbage across the wooden boardwalk. The laughter of children playing and waves rolling onto the sand seemed to fade into a distant void.

"A car is waiting for you," he heard her say. "On the corner of Tenth and Riley Street. A driver will take you to my lady." She turned and disappeared into the crowd.

Gage sprang to his feet. He looked at the paper, crumpled it into a ball and stuck it in his pocket.

"Tenth and Riley," he said. "Three blocks from here." He slung his duffle bag over his shoulder and began to walk. In no time he was standing across the street from a gray limousine parked on the corner of Tenth and Riley. A uniformed chauffeur leaned against the passenger side of the automobile. The young driver looked up, nodded at Gage and then opened the back door of the car. Gage crossed the street and stepped inside.

They drove for about twenty minutes before stopping in front of an ostentatious hotel and casino. The driver pulled the door open and Gage stepped onto an immense, covered driveway. He was not sure what he was supposed to do next until he noticed the young, dark-skinned woman entering the hotel lobby. She paused for a moment, looked over her shoulder and motioned for him to follow. After leading him through the lobby and into an elevator, she inserted a key card into a slot and pressed the button for the penthouse.

"Do you have a name?" he asked as the elevator sailed upward.

She ignored him. When the elevator jolted to a stop and they exited through the open door, the young woman gave a slight smile and said, "Patricia."

Stepping out of the elevator, they entered a plush carpeted hallway from which Patricia led him through double doors and into a penthouse apartment. Floor to ceiling windows with panoramic views of the harbor filled the far wall. Sunlight showered across the spacious living room where two curved white sofas sat facing each other in the center. To the right was a formal dining room complete with a polished mahogany table and a sparkling chandelier. To his left a spiral staircase curled upward to a landing.

Patricia removed her shoes and motioned for him to do the same. She led him to the sofas in the living room. "Please be seated and wait," she said and then proceeded up the spiral staircase leaving him alone. A rectangular coffee table, set with small pieces of cake and sweet breads, stood between the two sofas. Paintings and sculptures decorated the entire living room and dining area. Gage thought the pieces of art, no doubt, came from the Louvre. The beauty and serenity of the room served to heighten Gage's curiosity and sense of danger.

Five minutes passed before an Asian man and a woman appeared at the top of the stairs and began to descend. The man, perhaps six-feet, dressed casually and wore slippers. The slender woman beside him wore a simple white, button-down blouse and a light-blue skirt falling just below her knees. Straight black hair fell to her shoulders and a fringe of bangs rested above her dark eyes blazing with light. She was about thirty, he thought. A calm gentle exterior appearance, but her eyes displayed a powerful energy within. Like a waterfall, he thought – roaring, twisting, splashing within the confines of a quiet, serene forest.

Gage rose as the two approached him. "Officer Gage," the man said, extending his hand. "I am Robert Sato and this is my daughter, Rebecca Montoya. Please be seated. We have a lot to discuss."

The two sat down across from Gage. "I hope you have tasted our treats we have selected." Sato gestured his hand toward the food on the table. "Perhaps you would like a cold drink?"

"Got any beer?" Gage was not expecting that beer might be available in a place of this caliber.

Sato smiled and nodded his head. A servant appeared from a doorway off the dining room, walked to an ornate bar in the corner and produced three, frothing cold beers in tall classes. The servant set them on the table.

Gage took a drink and set the glass down. "Unless you're impostors," he said, "you're Robert Sato, the ex-prime minister of Canada."

"Yes," Sato nodded. "And my daughter here is the wife of. . ."

"The wife of Anthony Montoya," Gage broke in. "Without question the richest most powerful man in the world and my employer."

"You are exactly correct, Officer Gage," Rebecca replied with a slight laugh. "And I assure you we are not impostors. We brought you here for a specific reason."

Gage studied her face. "Go on."

"That piece of paper my servant handed you. You've seen that symbol before, haven't you?"

Shocked, he answered her. "Many people know that symbol. Not many know what it means. I don't associate with people familiar with that symbol."

"Perhaps not, Officer Gage," Sato spoke. "We have investigated you thoroughly. We know things about you that you do not even know about yourself."

"I've had enough of this." Gage jumped to his feet. "Why have you brought me here?" He demanded. "What do you want?"

"Please sit down, Officer Gage." Sato remained calm. "We have much to discuss with you."

Gage glanced at Rebecca, her tense face and those magnificent dancing eyes. He sank back down in his seat. "Go on," he said.

"You work for my son-in-law, Rebecca's husband," Sato began. "We want you to continue to work for him, but. . ." He paused a moment. "We also want you to work for me. . .for us. . .for my daughter. Ahh. . .I can see we are beginning to interest you, Officer Gage," Sato said before taking a sip of his beer and setting his glass back down on the table. "My daughter needs a new bodyguard and we have decided that person will be you. Rebecca's husband keeps her bodyguards on his payroll, and you will stay on his payroll. You will also be on my payroll and your compensation from me will be three times what Anthony pays you."

"Okay," Gage leaned forward and clasped his hands together. "So what's the catch? What do you really want from me?"

"In a few days," Sato said with a smile of satisfaction. "Rebecca will be traveling to Tennessee. She will be visiting friends in Oakbourgh."

"Oakbourgh." Gage sat up, his eyes wide. "That's a hellhole. A dangerous hellhole. Last I heard migrant raids were so bad they were expecting the walls to fall any time. I don't believe you're sending your daughter into that mess and I don't believe her husband would allow it."

"I go where I please." Rebecca's words shot at him like gunfire. "This visit will be short. We're bringing someone back with us. You will choose four others to join us. They will be under your command and on my father's payroll. Only his payroll. My husband will know about my trip. As a matter of fact, he will also be in Oakbourgh. We have a retreat there. My husband says he goes there to relax." Rebecca shrugged her shoulders. "You will meet him and you will be introduced as my new bodyguard. My husband will not, however, know about my father's payment to you and he will know nothing about the others."

Gage clasped and unclasped his fingers while he listened. "Who is this person who's coming back with us and might I ask, is this person coming willingly?"

Rebecca smiled and caught her father's eye.

"She is a girl," Rebecca said. "A teenage girl. Her name is Hannah and we are going to kidnap her."

CHAPTER TWO
Annie Miller
New Town, Canada

"Annie Miller, you stand convicted of treason and heresy. What do you say for yourself before sentencing?"

From his dais, the stoic judge peered down at the diminutive prisoner shackled about the ankles and wrists. Standing before him in her loose-fitting yellow prison shift, she looked more like a child than the twenty-eight-year-old woman she was. Her reddish-brown braids fell across her breasts, which rose and fell with each slow controlled breath. Annie placed a steady gaze on the stern-faced magistrate.

"I want my children," she told him with an unwavering voice and with her eyes from behind her wire-rimmed spectacles focused on his face.

"What will become of them?" Her voice trailed to a soft whisper and her eyes moved from the judge to the long narrow face of her young attorney. He placed a strong arm around her waist as he moistened his thin lips before speaking.

"Your Honor. The defendant has no relatives. She has three children. They will be put to the streets. They are but babies." His voice was monotone as though reading a script. Nevertheless, the audience in the courtroom gasped at his words and a murmur rose toward the high ceiling of the courthouse.

Annie was only mildly aware of her surroundings and of the selected assemblage of onlookers who came to witness her punishment. No audience was permitted in the courtroom during her trial. She was alone during that time with only an inexperienced counselor to speak on her behalf against a powerful team of corporate attorneys and a judge employed by the corporation. Spectators, however, were invited to witness the sentencing.

Someone gave Annie new glasses to replace her broken pair and make-up to cover, as best as possible, her physical bruises. Although no one could see her broken ribs, surely someone had to notice her broken nose and black eyes. Some curious spectator must certainly have seen her swollen face and broken teeth. Someone must have known that her slow, painful-looking movements could not be attributed just to the heavy chains wrapped about her body.

Of course no one notices, Annie thought, and it doesn't matter anymore. The scars from her beatings are just as invisible as the scars from the humiliations she endured from her captors during the past few weeks. No one came to help her during those jailhouse beatings and interrogations. No one was left to help her now and no one would help her children. Annie turned toward the dais and leveled a cold, dark glare upon the dispassionate magistrate.

The judge shifted in his seat, peered down at the prisoner and cocked his head to the left. For a moment, Annie noticed a look of curiosity cross his face. He saw me, Annie thought, and it rattled him. He actually saw me and he sensed the difference.

The metamorphosis was immediate. Seeing the transformation from a trembling, confused, sobbing girl to a woman who read and judged his soul must have been disconcerting to this experienced executioner. Indeed, he must have seen this phenomenon before in prisoners, but to watch the change occur before his eyes obviously disturbed him.

Annie's epiphany came like morning sunlight on a soft, lace curtain. Shadows evaporated into the sunlight and Annie knew the truth. This trial was not about her. It was about them, the corporate kings – the employers. The secrecy, the torture, the walls were all barriers between the lives of those in power and the truth. This proceeding was about their survival, not hers;

about their lives, not hers. Yes, in their eyes she was not just invisible, she was already dead.

Annie was not innocent. She had gone to that meeting of her own free will just as she chose to befriend Tanika. Was it really Tanika, Annie wondered, who led her to that first meeting and to disaster, or was it her own flawed soul? Would she have time to find the answers to those questions? Maybe not.

Although Tanika was a woman no one ever seemed to notice, Annie did notice her. The night they met Tanika was sitting on the edge of a metal framed bed in the school dormitory. She had her back to Annie, humming an old ballad. Annie recognized the tune, but could not quite remember the words. As Tanika hummed, she held a young boy in her arms while caressing his blond hair with a rough, work-worn hand. The boy appeared to be about three and Annie assumed he was the woman's son. Tears flowed down his pale cheeks and soft sobs drifted from his lips. His slender arms encircled his mother's neck and his small fingers played with her long unkempt hair hanging unfettered down her back.

"Don't cry golden boy," the woman sang to the child, her lips close to his ear. "Close your eyes and fly to the stars. Don't be sad brave boy. Close your eyes and tomorrow is ours. Dream your way to the stars and I will follow you there. Look toward the stars my brave little child. See how they shine, see how they shine."

Annie sat on the bed next to Tanika, surrounded by her own three children. Her twins, seven-year-old Greta and Gilbert, shared her lap. Nine-year-old Alex sat with his right arm draped over his mother's shoulder.

"He always cries," Alex said, gazing at the little boy. "He's new here."

Greta turned her blue eyes toward her mother's face. "I think he's lonely," she said. "He doesn't have anyone like we do."

"Yes, and Mrs. Hull puts him in the crying room. That only makes him cry harder." Gilbert's freckled brow wrinkled with concern as he spoke. Annie ran her fingers through his thick red hair. "Maybe you can help him," she told Gilbert. "Maybe you all can."

The children nodded in agreement. "And when Dad comes back, we'll all go home," Alex spoke with assurance.

"Yes." Annie smiled, nestling her children closer and placing her chin against Greta's golden curls. "When your father comes home, we'll have a party. And we'll all sleep in our own beds for ever and ever."

Annie held her children close while her body absorbed the soothing tune the woman was singing. Her eyes perused the long, aseptic room lined on each side with ten, metal-framed beds each attached on the right side to a tall metal cabinet used for a closet. In each bed rested a child either alone or with a single parent. A pristine bay window framed the far end of the room through which they could see a round, white, winter moon.

Footsteps moved down the stone aisle between the rows of beds and Annie felt a firm hand on her back. "It's time to go," Mrs. Hull spoke with authority.

Annie recoiled from the cold touch and looked up into the pale face of Marjorie Hull, the proprietor of the prestigious World Tech Boarding School. Dressed in black, Marjorie and her two daughters moved about the room advising parents to leave.

Although this was the boy's dorm, Greta was allowed to sit with her mother and two brothers for a short time before saying good night. The girl's dorm was across the hall. With reluctance, Annie placed Gilbert and Alex in their beds next to each other and carried Greta across the hall to the girl's room, which seemed to match the boy's dorm in every way.

She left her daughter after telling Greta goodnight. Annie walked to the entrance of the girl's dorm and then turned back to blow a kiss toward the small bundle wrapped to her chin in a lightweight, navy-blue blanket. Golden curls spilled across the child's pillow as she watched her mother go to the door. "Goodbye, baby," Annie mouthed before stepping out into the main corridor of the school.

For Annie, the long hallway was cold and empty. It ran the entire length of the upper floor housing the various sleeping quarters of students and staff. Most of the other parents had left, not wanting to be on the streets so late. By leaving late, Annie always ran the risk of being stopped and questioned by the corporate patrols. Curfew was 2:00 a.m. giving workers time to visit the pubs and theaters and to return to their homes or back to their factory dorms. The night shifts worked until morning; therefore, would not be caught on the streets during curfew.

Margie Hull's son, Able, stood at the top of the wide sweeping staircase that connected the upper floor to the downstairs lobby. Annie quickened her step as she approached the stair landing, bowed her head and curtseyed before the tall slender figure of Able dressed in a somber, long-sleeved, black suit.

Before Annie could straighten herself, the woman with the long, wild hair and the sweet voice strode between Annie and the stone-like figure of Able. As she descended the staircase, her cadence caused the hem of her black, ankle-length skirt to sway and dance. The fringe on the white shawl she wore tied around her waist bounced with each movement of her body.

Annie cast a sidewise glance at Able whose doughy face remained emotionless. He seemed to stare ahead as though he was looking at nothing. Annie shivered, untied the shawl about her waist and hurried down the staircase. She adjusted the wool wrap over her head and around her shoulders.

When Annie stepped out from the foyer through the heavy front door and onto the empty city streets, a brisk wind caught her skirt and blew it up to her waist. "Damn wind," she cursed as she attempted to hold it down, at the same time attempting to keep her scarf upon her head and around her shoulders. That wind is forever, she thought, and tonight it seems to be worse. Annie looked up at the round, glowing moon casting a pale, shrouded light upon the sleeping city. She could smell the fish foundries a few blocks away and heard the faint thump, thump of the distant factories.

Scouring the deserted streets, Annie caught the figure of the sweet voiced woman a block and a half away moving fast and with a purpose. Annie ran to catch up with her. There had been another murder last night, the fifth in six weeks. The victim had been a factory girl, only nineteen. A rumor spread that the girl was selling her body. Others said she just got caught after curfew and could not make it back to the dorms. Annie did not care about the reason the girl was murdered. She was terrified to be out alone, although staying late to visit her children always made her forget about the long walk home in the dark. The chilled wind and the veiled moonlit night reminded her of the danger. Annie did not want to be alone.

"Excuse me," Annie called as she ran to catch up with the woman. "Please wait," she shouted, while the wind muffled her words and scattered them into the cold air.

The woman slowed her pace and glanced back over her shoulder. Annie quickened her step and was soon walking beside this unconventional stranger.

"I'm Annie," she said out of breath. "I hope you don't mind if we walk together. I work in the thread factory and I live in the dorms there. Are you going in that direction?"

Emotionless brown eyes rimmed in light-yellow looked at Annie from a long, thin face with a square jaw and a rough complexion. Annie thought she had seen those eyes somewhere in the past. Maybe in a picture, she thought; perhaps a picture of a wild animal. Annie lowered her eyes and turned her head away.

"Yes," the woman spoke with a hint of distain while giving a slight snort through her nose. "The one who likes to grovel. I wonder what it is about a person that makes her want to grovel?"

"Excuse me? I'm afraid I don't understand." Annie, confused at first, remembered this slight woman was the same woman who stepped between Adam and herself as they stood at the top of the stairs. Without giving a bow, this woman had rushed passed the two, her head held high as she hurried down the stairs and out the door.
"Well, I don't see anything wrong with showing a little respect," Annie responded.

"Ah, yes." The woman's lip turned upward into a half smile, half smirk. "And when was the last time anyone bowed to you. . .um? Annie. You said your name was Annie?"

"Yes, Annie." She broke into a broad smile and then into a nervous chuckle. "No one has ever bowed to me and I can't imagine them ever doing so. Well, except maybe my husband." They continued walking, but at a much slower pace.

"I had a husband, too." The woman's voice became soft and tinged with bitterness. She turned her head to look Annie in the face. "When my husband was killed, I went to work at the gun factory. I make guns for the company goons." Her voice was flat. She shrugged her shoulders with indifference. "My name's Tanika."

"Wait. Listen." Tanika grabbed Annie's arm and pulled her roughly into an alleyway. The wind whistled loudly through the narrow passage, tossed a piece of crumpled paper into the air and rattled against a metal dumpster. The whirl of an approaching engine merged with the night noises.

The two women crouched in the black shadows of the alleyway and watched as a World Tech military vehicle glided through the dusky streets. Floating only inches from the ground, guns protruding from its cigar-shaped frame and with the World Tech label embossed on its side, the gunship instilled fear rather than a sense of protection.

"We haven't done anything wrong," Annie whispered while clutching her wool wrap closer to her body. Fear chilled her blood, but a strange sense of excitement warmed her again.

"Yea, well, if you're questioned by the militia, you'll be on their list." Tanika said "We gotta get outta here. I've got a place we can go. You can come with me, or you can stay here. I don't care." Tanika turned and disappeared into the shadows of the narrow lane leaving Annie alone. A rat scurried across her foot. Human whimpers mingled with the whining wind that swirled about her head. Thieves, muggers and throwaway people lingered in the crevices of the city, hiding from the goons as they waited for prey. Annie's trepidation evaporated into a heightened sense of urgency. She chose to follow this intriguing woman whose silent steps took her in the opposite direction from the factories and the dorms.

In a matter of moments, Annie found herself walking in silence beside Tanika. Moving like two spirits through the darkness, each not saying a word, they passed through the outlying industrial area, past dark, unoccupied warehouses and narrow alleyways and into the market street. As they walked, the click of a boot or the whirl of an engine would cause them to crouch, like cockroaches, in cracks or crannies or behind discarded garbage or debris.

Farther away from the safety of the dorms and into the darkness of the unknown, Annie walked willingly beside Tanika. Thoughts of her responsibilities vanished. The boredom of the factory, the emptiness of her future, the yearning for her children's smiles and the gentle arms of her husband all evaporated, replaced instead with the mysterious fervor of this unplanned journey. Annie was exhilarated.

Then they came to the corporate neighborhoods: small, hurriedly built, family houses made of stucco with metal roofs and front porches; identical square houses with families sleeping inside; children with mothers and fathers, grandparents and safety.

"And the corporation will keep us safe," Annie whispered.

"Did you say something?" Tanika turned her face toward Annie.

"I was just thinking," she responded. "This place is so peaceful." Her eyes followed the long sidewalk decorated with street lights. "Loyal workers really are taken care of, aren't they?"

Tanika stopped walking and looked at Annie with those strange, yellow eyes. "Yes," she said. "They live in company houses, buy their food in company stores, send their children to company schools. They learn what the company tells them to learn, speak company dogma and everyone is grateful for their jobs. Everyone worships the hand that feeds them." Tanika's body seemed to tremble slightly.

"I used to live here," Tanika said with a sigh. She pointed to a long row of company owned houses lining both sides of the street. A sudden gust of wind blew a strand of hair across her face and she brushed it away with a chapped and calloused hand.

"Come. Let's not stand here," Tanika said while pulling Annie into the shadows between two houses. "The moon is pale, but it casts a light across the neighborhood. And there are street lights here."

The two women stood close together, cradled by the blackness. Tanika leaned close to Annie's ear, her voice barely audible. "I'm a citizen," she continued in a whisper, her face veiled in shadow. "So I was allowed to live here. My husband was not. He was an illegal."

Annie could feel Tanika's warm breath on her face. Tanika continued. "I was born in Montana and when the state joined the Canadian Union, I was automatically granted citizenship. My husband was not so lucky. He was from Nevada." Her words became louder, then trailed away to a sigh. "He entered the country illegally, so he joined the militia in order to gain his citizenship. My citizenship was not enough to help him. Being married to a citizen was a start, but he needed more. He needed to prove his loyalty to the corporate kings. It is the way for all illegals."

"My husband and I are also illegals," Annie told her companion, surprised by the ease in which she divulged this information. "The corporation brought us here from Oakbourgh. They needed young strong bodies to build. . ."

Tanika interrupted. "They needed serfs to build the new cities and to cultivate the new lands that thawed after the ice melted."

"We're lucky," Annie said. "We'd be starving with the masses on the other side of the walls if it weren't for the corporations – our employers."

"Why did you come with me?" Tanika asked.

"I was afraid," Annie admitted. "I stayed too long with my children. I was afraid to be caught out after curfew."

"Ha!" Tanika replied. "Were you really afraid of being out after curfew, or were you afraid of going back to the factory dorms? Do you fear that hopelessness, that constant responsibility to the corporate kings? Yes," she shook her head as she spoke, "and what do you get in return? Food? A roof over your head and what else? A few hours a week with your children? So which is it, Annie? What are you really afraid of?"

"But, I do need to go back to the dorm," Annie spoke; now feeling quite nervous. "Shouldn't you be going there, too?" Annie adjusted her glasses and peered through the shadowy darkness into Tanika's face.

"I already told you. I have a place to go. You can come with me if you want, or you can stay here. I don't really care." Tanika turned away from Annie as though she were leaving.

"Where are you taking me?" Annie called louder than she should have.

Tanika turned back toward her companion. "I'm not taking you anywhere. You choose to follow me. It's your decision."

A cold gust of wind bashed against the women, tossing their skirts and whipping their shawls against their arms and faces. "Annie," Tanika spoke while grasping her shawl tight beneath her chin with both hands. "Your husband is alive. He was with my husband Kyle when Kyle was wounded. Those wounds killed him."

Annie sucked cold air deep into her lungs and coughed. Tears formed in her eyes. "What are you saying?" She gasped.

Tanika moved closer to Annie and leaned toward her. "Why do you think our children are allowed into that prestigious school instead of being thrown into the streets or into work houses? Do you really think it is because our men were killed while working for the corporate militias?" Tanika laughed through her nose. "Oh, Annie, no, no, no. Thousands die working for the corporations. No one cares. Your husband was working for the employers just like mine was. Theirs was a mission so secret that even when it was finished, or if it was never finished, no one would hear of it.

A worried Tanika looked around, and then continued. "Rumors began to spread that a piece of Blue Eden was buried in the desert somewhere near the Rocky Mountains. Yes, I know. There are always rumors, but there was something different about this story that caught the imagination of the masses more than the others did. These stories had to be put to rest or," Tanika gave a slight sigh, "disproved. There are corporate kings who believe their own lies because lies keep them in power. But, there are powerful people in the World Tech Corporation who do not really think Blue Eden is a myth." Tanika stopped and moistened her lips. "They want to find it as much as The Eight. If they find Blue Eden first, then it will be their property to do with as they please. They will exploit it just as they have exploited our own planet and everyone on it."

"You're speaking treason." Annie stepped backward.

"Maybe," Tanika said. "But don't you want to know what happened to your husband?" Tanika smiled and Annie moved closer.

"Our husbands," Tanika continued, "along with a small platoon of militia, were sent to search the desert near the Rocky Mountains in the hope of finding the secret of Blue Eden. Most believed they would find nothing. Still, the gamble was worth it for the corporate kings to investigate this new rumor.

The corporate kings believe that our husbands died somewhere in the desert on a fools mission looking for a myth. But unbeknownst to the kings, your husband and mine survived to find the secret. Your husband is still alive. Mine is dead. But the corporations believe them both to be dead. Our husbands found the secret, but they did not give it to the corporations. They gave it to us."

Annie opened her eyes wide in astonishment. "What are you talking about?" her words came in gasps.

"The corporate employers keep our children in that school, Annie, because they want to keep us happy. They want to keep us from asking questions. They want to keep us well fed and our children brainwashed so we will not ask about how our husbands died or where their bodies are. In truth, the corporations don't know where your husband's body is and they don't even care."

"How do you know these things?"

"I know these things because Robert is with us."

"Who is us?" Annie asked.

"I had orders to bring you in," Tanika continued, ignoring Annie's questions. "I didn't want to. I'm still not sure you...well, it doesn't matter. The others want you to join us and I know your husband does"

"Are...are you with the subversives?" Annie stammered. "Robert would never..."

Tanika laughed and shook her head. "The subversives, the unions, the radicals? Oh, of course we support them. But no, we do not join them. We give our allegiance to something much bigger and more important." Tanika leaned close to Annie's face. "We, Annie are The Eight." Tanika's lips twisted into a grin. "Yes, the Society of The Eight. We hold the secrets to Blue Eden and we protect those secrets with our lives. Come with us, Annie and learn our secrets. There is a meeting tonight and you will be welcome."

Annie accepted the invitation with excitement, not fear. She embraced the danger rather than the boredom of her own reality. All of a sudden, Annie's spirit was free.

Now, Annie stood before her judge, confined in shackles and waiting his decision. She knew her fate. Lifting her chin, a soft smile on her lips, Annie awaited the verdict. She was not innocent.

"Death!" The judge's voiced roared in unison with the crack of the gavel. "Death," he said again in a softer voice. "And may God have mercy on your soul."

CHAPTER THREE
Hannah Merrick
Oakbourgh, Tennessee

In a tiny attic room above a two-story brick house, a teenage girl stood like a silent wraith by an open window looking down on a dark alleyway separating the back of her house from the rear of a neighbor's home. The stench of rotting garbage and human waste permeated the hot night and drifted into her sparsely furnished quarters. In the distance, a baby's piercing wail mingled with the arithmetic hum and thumping of a factory, but Hannah's intense focus was on the blackness of the alley. Her eyes searched for the flickering of a light.

Wind rattled the rainspout and the old house groaned. Hannah did not make a sound. Her once long, light-brown hair was now cropped short and her stepbrother's blue, cotton shirt covered her small bound breasts. Since Hannah was 14 years old, her freckled face and slim hips would pass for those of a young boy. She waited patiently and without doubt. Bobby was her best friend. He would not fail her tonight.

Last week Hannah's father signed papers giving her in marriage to a man who, her father explained, was a loyal employee and a good Christian. Sam Peter's wife of ten years failed to bear him a living child and Sam Peters wanted children. A young healthy wife would give him the sons he needed to provide income for the future. Signing the papers meant that the marriage was legal, but they would not live together until after tomorrow's ceremony. Hannah would not be there.

While holding on to the rough, unpainted windowsill, Hannah leaned out the window to search the narrow dark alleyway for movement. A splinter pierced the palm of her hand causing her to gasp. Blood trickled down her wrist. She removed the long sliver and threw it to the floor. Hannah walked barefoot across the rough wooden floor, sat on a rickety double bed, pulled her knees up to her chin and folded her arms around her legs. She rubbed her cheek with her knee, wiping away beads of sweat. Still early, Hannah thought, after glancing at her grandmother's old clock sitting on top of a dusty dresser. In another ten minutes it would be past midnight, the factories would let out and Bobby would come.

The young girl lay down on the thin, worn mattress, pulled a rumpled sheet to her face and inhaled the scent of cinnamon. Only those behind the inner wall had cinnamon, but Hannah's grandmother somehow had always managed to acquire it. Hannah remembered the small packages addressed to her grandmother, Maddie, which had appeared without notice on the back porch.

While she waited for Bobby, Hannah's memories took her back to a time when her grandmother was still alive. "Don't ask questions child," her grandmother would say, her dark blue eyes shining with hidden secrets from behind wire-rimmed spectacles. "These are not the times to ask questions." Then she would give Hannah a plump warm biscuit covered in cinnamon and together they would savor the flavor for as long as possible.

The packages continued to come even after her grandmother was too old and sick to leave her attic room. Hannah would collect the packages, bake the bread and take the precious treat to her grandmother's bedside. They spent their stolen hours seeking comfort in each other's companionship, reading forbidden books, studying history, ancient literature, math and astronomy. There in that tiny attic sanctuary was where Hannah first heard the stories of Blue Eden.

Of course, when her mother was alive, Hannah heard whispers of a prohibited place and illegal gatherings, but such talk was for grown-ups and certainly not for her young ears. She was three and her mother still worked at the museum when Hannah's father was given a promotion to supervisor allowing him a larger three-bedroom house closer to the factories. Hannah's father was elated. He promised they would all soon be sleeping behind the third wall. Hannah became happy in her new environment.

Bobby lived two houses away and his mother and Hannah's mother became close friends. Both women worked and Maddie cared for both children. As they grew, each attended segregated schools – one for boys and the other for girls. After class, the two were inseparable. He in his short pants and blond hair shaved close, she in her long cotton dress and braided hair.

They spent their days chasing brown lizards through the alleyways and collecting insects. They played soldier and factory worker with a small group of their barefoot, bedraggled friends. When the killing heat rose to over 135 degrees Fahrenheit, they remained inside sitting close together in front of a small electric fan, watching company television and sharing sips of rationed water. Hannah and Bobby's childhood ended at the age of ten.

It was the day of the march. Both Bobby's parents were attending as were his two sisters and his widowed aunt, but Hannah's father forbade his wife to attend. Arguments boiled. At first, hushed whispers could be heard, but soon the whispers changed to loud and threatening words.

"Participation in this protest will destroy our lives," her father shouted. "I will lose my job, the house. I could even be ordered to leave the protection of the walls. How could you do this to us?" her father thundered. He clenched his fist in his wife's face and backed her against a wall. "How could you do this to your daughter, your child?"

Maddie grabbed her son-in-law's arm trying to pull him away from her daughter, at the same time, pleading with him to stop. "I'll go in her place. Please, Jim, I'll go in her place."

With a single backlash of his arm, Jim sent Hannah's grandmother tumbling to the ground, her eyeglasses sliding across the floor. Maddie's long white braids, once pinned in swirls upon her head, fell loose. Grabbing his wife by the hair, he threw her to the carpet beside her mother.

"No one leaves this house" he shouted, his hand shaking as he pointed his forefinger at them.

Hannah watched her mother's face form a white mask of defiance. "We are already dead." She spoke with teeth clenched, her eyes dark pinpoints. "This march gives us hope and hope to our daughter. I am doing this for her."

He glared down at the two women, his voice softer this time, but as defiant as his wife's. "No one leaves this house."

Hannah's mother did attend the march as did thousands of other workers. Hannah's father was called to work that day, but the factories shut down. That day the employers were to hear the voices of the workers and the women imploring the corporations to end their oppression and brutality. They sent a list of grievances to the ruling corporate kings demanding better working conditions, better living conditions, a return of full rights to women and complete personal freedom for everyone.

Enthusiasm impregnated the air that day. Bobby and Hannah wanted desperately to be a part of the excitement, but they were ordered to stay with Maddie and forbidden to leave the house. Hannah remembered standing at the window watching as Bobby's family and Hannah's mother joined the march participants already filling the streets. Men dressed in shorts and thin shirts and women dressed in long, dark veils were all walking as one body toward the third wall. Hannah's mother turned her enshrouded face back toward the window and waved. It was the last time Hannah saw her mother or Bobby's family.

Word of the massacre traveled with great speed. The slow and peaceful procession of men, women and children had moved through the city streets. In some instances the mood was even festive with children prancing and darting about between the adults, skipping over litter scattered about the roadways. The adults, breathing in the still, heavy heat and the smells of perspiration, garbage and human waste, became more solemn as they walked over the uneven, broken pavement.

Helicopters hovered above the assemblage and followed the marchers on their trek toward the third wall. Apprehensive militiamen cradled their guns and watched the protesters. Although aware of their ominous presence, the congregation seemed not to notice.

Upon reaching the gate of the third wall where podiums were erected, the crowds began to chant the names of the corporate rulers. "Kessler, Lister, MacAfee, Winslow. Come out. Come out. Kessler, Lister, MacAfee, Winslow. Come out. Come out."

The protesters waved their arms, undulating with the rhythm of each syllable. Their shouts became louder and louder, erupting into a chorus of thunderous cheers and applause when five women, shrouded in veils stepped onto a high platform and faced the crowd. The women raised their arms, saluted their audience and then after removing their veils, let their long dark clothing fall to the floor of the podium. They stood dressed in short-sleeved, knee-length dresses of a light-blue color. Each dress was covered in a print of bright blue flowers and their short hair was decorated in blue paper flowers.

The women in the gathering began to remove their veils. Some tossed them in the air toward the helicopters and others threw them at the militia. "Join us," they shouted. "Come down. Come down."

The attack was swift and barbarous. A fleet of armed gunships rose up from behind the third wall and swarmed over the people. Blasts of deadly projectiles blazed from cannons attached to the flying gunships. Several stunned militiamen froze in disbelief while others began firing their weapons. Parents fell to the ground bleeding and torn. Their children's bodies were ripped and severed.

As panic ensued, terrified survivors scattered, taking shelter in alleyways and doorways only to be pursued by the air born killing machines. Many who escaped were later arrested, questioned and released while others simply disappeared. Still, others fled to their homes and lived to remember.

Statements from corporate representatives blared from television screens and were posted on flyers throughout the city. "It is always the duty of citizen workers to sacrifice personal rights for the survival of the companies that protect them and civilization itself. Each day brings more attacks against our city walls and against our way of life and each day those attacks are becoming more violent."

Employees were reminded that a family member who acquires work at a corporation and is loyal to that company will be supplied food, shelter, medical care and protection for them and their family members. Those who resist the authority of the employers not only commit treason against society, but also endanger the lives of every loyal worker within the city walls. "To question your employer is treason. Your employers protect you."

Hannah's father came home late that night, his posture stooped, his eyes cold. He spoke to no one. Three weeks later he brought home his new wife and her two young children. Amanda had been his mistress and had lived in a shantytown behind the outer wall. She came with a stilted smile and gleaming green eyes and immediately took charge.

Her daughter was to share Hannah's bedroom while her
son took Grandmother Maddie's room. Maddie was assigned the
attic. Bobby, now orphaned stayed with them, but after a month
had passed, Bobby was given a position of employment behind
the third wall where the corporate rulers lived. Hannah's heart
broke.

Each night Hannah's grandmother climbed the steep
wooden steps leading to the attic, and each morning she
descended to prepare the meals and do daily chores. Hannah
helped her. Grim and mournful days followed, but life was not
without some joy. In the evenings when they finished their
work, Hannah and her grandmother climbed the steps together
and found solace in each other's company. Soon, Hannah began
falling asleep in the attic and as time passed, she moved her
sparse belongings to the tiny room designed to store discarded
treasures.

Two and a half years passed before Hannah saw Bobby
again. A young delivery boy came to the kitchen door and after
asking if she were Hannah, he pressed a note into her hand. The
note read, "I will see you Wednesday after the factories let out.
Wait for me in the alley. B."

Hannah's spirits soared. She hummed as she
accomplished her household chores and cast her grandmother a
sly smile. Maddie, aware of the clandestine meeting, was
supportive and supplied her granddaughter with a small alarm
clock that would awaken her with a soft musical tone if she fell
asleep while waiting.

Although her grandmother fell asleep, Hannah stayed
awake trying to be quiet while she paced the floor in her bare
feet from the window to the bed and back.

Hannah dressed in the proper attire for a young girl her
age – a long black skirt, a white blouse and a white scarf over her
head – stepped out through the attic window onto the roof of the
house. Using a flashlight she had tied to her waistband, Hannah

searched for movement. There was none. She sucked in her breath, bit her lower lip and moved barefoot toward a drainpipe running from the roof of the house to the ground below. Grasping the metal pipe with both hands, holding the pipe between her knees, Hannah started to slide down. Not thinking to wear gloves, her hands and legs began to bleed, but it was too late to stop. As she reached the rough pavement, Bobby appeared out of the darkness.

They embraced like old friends and then marveled at how each had changed. Bobby was taller and leaner, his face longer and more narrow than when she had last seen him as a ten-year-old boy. His blond hair smelled of soap and his clothes were new, but his dark blue eyes revealed a spirit that seemed older and more mature. But, he was still Bobby.

"I only have a few hours to stay with you before I have to leave," he told her. "My master likes to visit the houses on Tenth Street where the ladies live. He comes after dark and leaves just before daylight. This time I was able to hide in the trunk of his car and if I'm careful, I can do it again."

Hannah and Bobby sat down in the shadow of the back porch and leaned against the wall of the house. Hannah listened while Bobby, in a whisper, told her about his life behind the third wall.

He sniffed and rubbed his nose with the back of his hand. "Everything is green," he began, "and there's flowers everywhere. Most of the time it smells beautiful, but sometimes when the wind is right, I can still smell the odor of this section behind the second wall."

Hannah started to giggle, but covered her mouth. "Grandmother always tells me that walls never keep anything out. They only keep things in. Tell me some more."

"The roads are paved to perfection," he continued, "and everyone rides around in solar powered and electric cars, not bicycles like here. The people eat in little cafes, or nice restaurants and they sit at tables and other people serve them their meals. Everyone wears jewelry and the women don't always wear veils. They have fashion shows and wear colorful clothes"

"Do people serve you your meals?" she asked him.

"Of course not. I live in a room over a garage that's attached to a big house and I share the room with three other guys. They're all older than me, but they're teaching me to be a mechanic and a driver. I wash cars and mow lawns for the employers. Sometimes the owners of the big house fly to other cities in small airplanes and someday I might get to go with them. Maybe sometime. . .maybe someday, I'll learn how to fly airplanes."

"You seem so happy," Hannah said with a hint of jealousy

"Ah, it ain't everything, Hannah. Don't go thinking it is." His eyes took on a faraway look as he squeezed her hand. "Someday you and me are gonna get out of here." He turned to her, his eyes full of hope. "We'll go north to Canada. My cousin, Annie Miller, lives there. Her husband's with the militia up there and Annie and her husband will help us. Wait and see. I feel it."

The clock on the dresser played a soft, musical tune pulling Hannah away from her memories and back to the present. She sat on the rickety bed in the attic with her arms folded around her legs. In a few days, she and Bobby would be in Canada. Hannah sat up and put on her stepbrother's work shoes. Since they were a size too big, she had stuffed paper in the toes to make them fit. Hannah walked to the window, picked up her backpack from the floor and stepped out into the hot night air. So many nights in the past she had climbed down this drainpipe to meet Bobby. Tonight would be the last.

Flinging the backpack over her shoulders, Hannah grasped the metal drainpipe with both hands and while holding the pipe between her knees, began to slide down. Before reaching midway, two massive explosions lit up the night, shaking the house and ripping the pipe away from the wall. Hannah managed to swing her feet over to the roof of the porch just as another blast erupted bringing the metal pipe clattering to the ground. Lights came on in the house and she heard her father's voice.

Stranded on the rooftop, Hannah searched the alley for Bobby. "Down here. Jump." Bobby's voice came from the same direction as a flickering light.

Squatting down on the roof of the porch, Hannah could see Bobby standing in a shower of light filtering down from a top story bedroom window. His arms were stretched up and he motioned for her to jump. After throwing her backpack to Bobby, Hannah flipped onto her stomach and while holding onto the roof tiles with her hands, she dangled her feet over the edge. Standing on a rickety metal chair, Bobby grabbed Hannah's legs and guided her as she dropped first to the chair and then to the ground. Sirens wailed and the blare of helicopter engines mingled with the sounds of more explosions. Hannah and Bobby held each other, hopeful and unafraid.

Part II

August 30
One hundred years in the
future

CHAPTER FOUR
The Escape
Oakbourgh, Tennessee

"Annie and her husband will help us," Bobby said moments before the ground shook and black plumes of smoke, originating from the direction of the outer wall, rose again into the night sky. "We're going to Canada." Bobby gathered Hannah into his strong, young arms, lifted her off her feet and swung her around in circles. He pressed his lips close against her ear and spoke in a hushed voice, "We're going to freedom Hannah. . .freedom in Canada."

"And my family is waking up," Hannah said breathlessly. "Put me down. They weren't supposed to miss me till morning."

"And maybe they won't." Bobby spoke while setting her down with care. "Do you really think they'll check the attic? Even if the house crashed into a heap, they would never look for your body." He gave a quiet laugh and rubbed his hands through her short-cropped hair.

"Not bad," he said. "You're cute with short hair. And, you look great in your stepbrother's clothes."

Hannah pushed him away, shot him a look of pretend annoyance as she said, "The migrants are attacking again." She picked up her backpack from off the ground and slung it over her shoulders. "We need to go. It's after midnight. We'll discuss fashion later," she said, taking note that both she and Bobby were dressed in the same short-sleeved, blue shirt and tan trousers worn by all the city's male factory workers.

With his eyes bright with excitement, Bobby picked up his own over-stuffed backpack and threw it across his shoulders. He then slipped his hand in Hannah's, gave it a squeeze and led her down the dark alleyway toward the main boulevard.

Streetlights flickered. Their illumination vanished as the rattle of gunfire intensified. Frightened voices floated out from open windows of brick row houses and the smell of gunpowder filled the sweltering, smoggy air.

Bobby and Hannah paused a moment and looked upward. Above the city, gliding like strange creatures of prey, sailed a fleet of corporate gunships. Hannah moved closer to Bobby as they watched the black silhouettes of the flying machines float above them. Hannah shivered.

"Are you afraid, Hannah?"

"No, I'm not afraid," Hannah answered with confidence. "Nothing can hurt us today. But I can't help but wonder. . ."

"Wonder what?" Bobby asked, still looking toward the sky.

"We want out so badly," she turned her eyes toward Bobby. "Freedom for us is out there. What out there is so bad that the migrants risk death to break down our walls?"

"Freedom is in Canada. The migrants can break down all the walls they want, but we won't be here. Come on. I got something hidden over here." From out behind a dumpster, hidden in the back-street shadows, Bobby wheeled a sturdy bicycle.

"You'll have to ride on the carrier," he told her. "It'll be uncomfortable, but it's faster than walking."

"Where did you get this?"

"Don't ask me questions," Bobby told her as he straddled the bicycle. "Just get on. We have a rendezvous to attend and we can't be late. Someday, when we are safe and when we are old, we'll talk about all this. Now get on."

Hannah swung her legs over the carrier and balanced herself on the back of the bicycle. She leaned against Bobby's backpack and wrapped her arms around his waist.

They began to move, slow at first and then faster. The explosions and gunfire had stopped. The city lay in darkness.

Guided by the single light on the front of the bicycle, Bobby peddled down the main boulevard of the city. Several cyclists passed by them in the darkness. Perhaps, Hannah thought, the other riders think we are, like them, two young men getting off from the late shift at one of the factories. The darkness and the uniform she wore made her feel invisible and safe.

Soon, they passed through the section of the city lined with theaters, cafes, brothels and honky-tonks. Loud music and laughter spilled out into the street where groups of people milled about holding flashlights. Talking and laughing, they seemed unbothered by the darkness or fighting at the outer walls.

Some people were used to the daily insurgencies while others lived in constant fear. Hannah had always been afraid, but that constant pounding of terror against her being soon numbed her senses to the constant danger. At times, she ignored the menace of gunfire and explosions. In doing that, life seemed to be normal and more comfortable.

Those outside the walls wanted the riches of Oakbourgh and waged constant assaults against the walls of the city. The prosperity of Oakbourgh was enormous, an oasis in the desert sitting atop a wealth of deep-water wells. Those wells not only quenched the thirst of the residents, but also served as a profitable source of revenue. Each day, valuable barrels of clean, uncontaminated water were shipped from the city by train and sold on the open market. The corporate militia not only protected those transports, but also protected the city from any perversity from either the migrants or locals.

Maintaining order within this wealthy desert outpost meant the necessity of the population to adhere to strict rules of governance. It was illegal, Hannah knew, to leave the city without proper papers, but that was what she and Bobby were doing tonight. Yet, at this moment as she sat balanced on the back of the bicycle, Hannah was not afraid. Her lack of fear was not the consequence of suppressed emotions, but instead the result of a new awareness of wondrous possibilities.

In a few days, maybe a week, she and Bobby would be in Canada. To Hannah, Canada was the Blue Eden that her grandmother had always spoken about to her, a place where everything was green and the air smelled like cinnamon and oranges.

The world behind the third wall where the corporate kings lived was filled with real flowers and shimmering fountains. People who had never been inside the protection of the third wall, called that area Canada. Yet, Bobby, who had lived inside the privileged circle, insisted that beneath all the beauty, light and elegance, life was dark and cold. Life there was Blue Eden for some, but many preferred to be somewhere else. Would it be the same in the real Canada, she wondered?

The bicycle bounced over broken pavement, but somehow managed to stay upright. Bobby turned down the Avenue of the March, the unofficial name of 17th street. As always, blue paper flowers were strewn along the city's main artery that led to the gates of the third wall. Although the law prohibited the distribution of those flowers along the street, somehow, new flowers appeared every day. That day of the march, Hannah remembered, was the day that the heart of the city stopped beating. Hope became fear and acceptance became hate.

On the day of the march, Hannah's mother had told her father that joining in the protest gave her hope. Hope for what? Hannah had always wondered. The protest killed her mother and in killing her mother, a piece of Hannah died as well.

"You must never give up hope," Hannah's grandmother told her after her mother died. "Once the hope is gone, your life slowly slips away from you. And, it is not just the dream of hope that keeps you alive. You must actively pursue those dreams. No matter the cost. To do nothing bankrupts your soul. That is why your mother had to go on that march, even if it killed her."

Hannah did not understand, nor did she even want to understand. "I know how hard this is for you," her grandmother told her one evening as they sat together in their attic room. "You are so young," she said as she cradled Hannah in her arms and spoke softly to her. "Child, the time has come for you to be entrusted with a secret so important that you must protect it with your life."

"What are you talking about?" Hannah wiggled free from her grandmother's embrace and looked up into her tired, drawn face.

Hannah's grandmother rose from the bed and shuffled across the room in her bare feet. The hem of her thin white nightgown swayed against her frail body. After stopping in front of a small wooden dresser, she pulled open the middle drawer and took out a leather bound book. Sighing, the woman held the book against her breast and in obvious pain walked back to the bed.

"This is for you," she said after sitting down and placing an old book encased in a thick leather cover with dog-eared, yellow pages in Hannah's lap. "The Secret Garden, Frances Hodgson Burnett," Hannah, read out loud. She and her grandmother had read this story many times, not this exact book, but the same story about a secret garden hidden behind walls, untended and left to die until found and restored to life.

"Thank you for the present, grandma."

"This book," her grandmother began, "was placed into your mother's safekeeping. When she died, I protected it. Now…" she paused and pursed her lips together. "Now, I must pass this book to you. Listen child and don't speak," she said, placing her fingers over Hannah's lips.

"I have little time to speak. Your mother discovered this book buried deep within the archives of the museum where she worked. More important than that, she also discovered the secret hidden within this book. Hannah, there are people who will kill to get their hands on that secret. Listen carefully. There will be many people who will come to you and try to take this book, but you must only give it to the person who will use it correctly. When that person comes, give it to no one else. It is the secret hidden inside this book that people want and nothing else."

Hannah's eyes filled with tears. "Grandma, I'm scared. How am I to know who this person is? And what is the secret?"

"Oh, sweet child." Her grandmother pulled Hannah against her body and held Hannah's head against her heart. "There are others out there who will help you. There are groups of people who are gathering information. One day they will need the information you have and they will come for it. Others will also come for the secret this book contains, but keep it safe for the right person. What you have here is only a piece of what is needed. It is, however, a very very important piece."

"A piece of what, Grandma?

"A small piece of Blue Eden, my dear. An extremely important piece. Now, you must protect it."

"But why, Grama? Why must I protect it?"
Hanna's grandmother brushed the tears away from Hannah's cheeks.

"Responsibility comes even when we think we are not ready, even when we think we don't want it. But it comes. You have the strength and the courage my dear. You will know what to do when the time comes."

The old woman took Hannah's face between her gnarled and work-worn hands and looked deep into the girl's eyes. "I promise you. You will know what to do."

Her grandmother died that night. Today the leather bound book rested in Hannah's backpack as she and Bobby began their journey toward Canada.

"Are you okay?" Bobby asked while looking over his shoulder and slowing the bike.

"I was just feeling a little sad."

Bobby stopped the bike and got off. "We can't be sad today," he said. "We will talk about this when we are safe."

"When we are safe and when we are old," Hannah laughed.

"Get off the bike. We have to walk now," Bobby told her while starting to dig through his backpack. He pulled out a flashlight and turned it on. "Leave the bicycle here," he said. "It will get back to its rightful owner soon enough. Come on. We don't have far to go."

They began to walk; neither saying a word. Miles of warehouses stretched before them, crisscrossed with deserted streets and alleyways. Although the street-lamps were out from the attack, the steady glow of Bobby's flashlight led the way through a maze of unoccupied, industrial buildings. Workers had gone home for the night, but would return at dawn to continue processing a profitable accumulation of merchandise waiting transport from Oakbourgh.

The night was still and hot. Not even a slight breeze cooled the sweat that stained their clothes and trickled down their foreheads. The insects slept, no doubt afraid of exerting the slightest bit of energy in this oppressive heat. Hannah and Bobby walked together in silence. On occasion, their fingers touched.

From out of the darkness and without warning, a man wearing the uniform of the militia appeared before them. He

leveled a machine gun in their direction and ordered them to
stop.

"Turn your light out." the man demanded, his voice an
almost unintelligible growl.

Bobby quickly snapped off the light.

Another man stepped out from the darkness and aimed
a beam of light at them.

Hannah turned her face away from the glaring light and
would have run if Bobby had not placed a firm hand on her arm.

"What are you doing here?" the first man commanded.

"The lobo sent us," Bobby answered.

"And what else did the lobo tell you?" the voice came
through the blackness from behind the other flashlight.

"Twenty-eight. . .fourteen. . .seventy-five," Bobby
responded.

There seemed to be an indefinite silence while the man
with the flashlight moved the stream of light from Bobby to
Hannah and back to Bobby. "You're late," he snarled and then
without warning switched off the light. "Follow me!"

Huddled together, Hannah and Bobby stumbled along
behind their churlish leader while the man with the machine gun
trailed behind. As they moved down a narrow alleyway, street
lights flickered and power returned. Hannah and Bobby were
ushered through a sturdy, unlocked wooden door into a dimly-
lit warehouse filled with stacks of barrels labeled water.

"Keep moving." The man with the gun shoved them
from behind. Now that there was some light, they began to walk
faster. The sound of their cautious footsteps on the concrete floor
hung on the thick hot air as they quickened their pace along
narrow aisles meandering through stockpiles of crates and
barrels. A closed door appeared. One of the armed men knocked
four times and the door opened. The men ushered Bobby and
Hannah inside a small room. The door closed behind them.

The room, a small, unfurnished office, was better lit than the warehouse. Twenty-five people filled the room, four of whom including the two guides, wore the uniform of the World Tech Militia. A group of teenage boys and young men, ragged and exhausted looking, squatted along the far wall. A veiled woman sat against the right wall. A small child slept in her lap. Another young boy lay asleep on the floor beside her. In the center of the room, a man, a woman and four children sat together, their bulging suitcases scattered around them. An older couple stood in the corner holding hands and keeping watchful eyes on their luggage. Hannah and Bobby joined the group.

"That's everybody." A stocky militiaman standing at the front of the room spoke as he looked over the gathering.

"Yes, these are the last," the guide with the gun said, nodding his head toward Hannah and Bobby.

"Then we'll get started." The thickset man, a rifle slung over his shoulder and with holsters containing pistols strapped on each hip, paced the floor a few times before speaking. With each step, his scuffed leather boots made a heavy thud against the concrete floor. "We don't care why you're leaving here," he began. "We know some of you are running from the law, some from a husband. Some of you are escaping your debts. We don't care."

Hannah watched this man as he spoke. His thick lips drew out each word. His piercing dark eyes darted about the room, sometimes stopping to glare at one person or another. His bloated face seemed to have no neck attached to it, so that instead of turning his head in any direction, he turned his entire body.

The man continued. "You each came up with half the money needed for this trip. The rest will be owed to us when you get to Canada. We are going to make sure you get there safe. You are now our investment. When you get to Canada, you will have jobs waiting. When you get paid, you will pay us."

He paused a moment and perused the crowd. "You will do everything we say. Your lives depend on that. Once you leave these walls you are a migrant, homeless and dispensable. There's nothing but desert and walled cities between here and Canada. Those cities are walled because they don't want the likes of you inside. There's barely enough supplies for the citizens of those cities let alone the likes of you. You are not welcome. And there's another thing."

He stood, feet apart, his thumbs crooked over his gun belt. "Those migrants out there are not anything you want to come up against. Whatever they used to be, civilized folk with families from towns with churches? Well, that's all gone, swallowed up by nature. Their homes are either under water, or just dried up and blew away. They're on the move now; just trying to keep ahead of the next dust storm. They're looking for food, water or a habitable piece of land. They're all moving north. Just like you. The only difference is you have the money to buy protection."

Hannah noticed that the other three soldiers were passing out small paper cups filled with liquid.

"What we're passing out now is a little tranquilizer," the stocky spokesman said. "We found out things work better when you are more relaxed. Go ahead, lady. Take it. And give it to your kids."

Hannah and Bobby were each handed a cup. "It's okay," Bobby whispered. They lifted their cups and drank the bitter liquid. It may have been only a few moments, it may have been longer, but the room began to spin. Hannah tried to hold on to Bobby, but she felt herself falling backward down, down, down and then blackness.

CHAPTER FIVE
The Prison
New Town, Canada

Annie huddled in the corner of her cold, stark cell, her knees drawn up beneath her chin, her arms wrapped around her legs. A thin mattress lay on the concrete floor against the wall to the right. On the opposite side stood a metal toilet with a steel sink protruding from the wall. The cell had no window. Instead, a heavy steel door with a small barred opening separated her 5'x 8' living area from the long corridor that ran between the rows of cells. A veiled light filtered through that small opening, filling the room with a dim haze that deprived Annie's mind of the peace and comfort of darkness. Days and nights merged.

How many times had a plate of protein paste been shoved through the opening in the thick door? She lost count. Annie ate the food without tasting and when finished, pushed the empty plate back through the portal. The rattle of keys, the shuffle of a guard's shoe, the hollow wail of a prisoner were sounds that faded into the fetid air never to be acknowledged.

Annie awaited her fate alone in the harshness of her surroundings and with no regrets. Everything dies. Every person dies her thoughts told her. Even our planet dies. However, to know the truth and to turn away from it was the worst kind of death. The shame of turning away when you have the ability to help, stabs a hole in your soul that throbs like an infected wound for the rest of your existence. Annie was not innocent, but she was at peace. So, she hoped, was her husband, Robert. An agreement was made that if she were captured, The Eight would protect her children and they would be taken to Robert.

Annie shifted her position. Her body trembled with pain. She bit her lip and closed her eyes. Her mind took her soaring back to the time of her innocence.

Robert had been seventeen, she just sixteen and married four months when they accepted employment in Canada, an exciting time for Annie and Robert. The melted glaciers had opened vast new lands for settlement in the far Northwest Territories, requiring skilled and unskilled laborers to plant new forests and to build new cities. Walls were built to enclose those new settlements and to protect those who lived inside.

The great migration north had begun decades before they were born. When the snows evaporated across the mountain ranges around the planet once fertile land became desert wastelands unsustainable for all life forms. But, when the rising temperatures melted the glaciers, a new wilderness in the far north opened for settlement. That land, however, was precious and available to only a fraction of the displaced populations.

Wealthy corporations were quick to develop those new northern territories. Businessmen with the most money and greatest political clout staked their boundaries and established control over their property. Workers lucky enough to establish employment with those companies were ensured food, shelter and security while those without proper corporate acceptance were forced to sustain themselves on earth's expanding wastelands. When Robert and Annie were brought north under the protection of the corporations, they were delirious with hope. How could things have gone so wrong?

Memories of those dreams flooded Annie's head making the reality of her imprisonment just a nightmare. In the morning she would wake and she would again be with her children and Robert. The pain in her body faded as her mind took her back to Oakbourgh, Tennessee where Annie's first memories began. Oakbourgh had water. Although the earth's water supply was evaporating exponentially, the city where Annie lived sat atop fresh streams buried in deep underground caverns. There were many such havens around the planet surrounded by walls, weapons and militia. But, as the precious liquid evaporated from those desert oases, the corporations abandoned them without hesitation. The lack of water made those sites unprofitable and thus useless to the corporate employers. The once protected citizens of those enclaves found themselves unemployed and eventually homeless migrants left to fend for themselves in a hostile and unforgiving environment.

Still huddled in her cell, Annie curved her lips into a sweet smile as she remembered the day she and Robert left Oakbourgh for Canada.

"Canada is green, they say," Annie had told Robert's sister, Kerry. "And the sun shines all day and all night." Annie had thrown her arms up toward the ceiling of the bedroom, stretching her fingers wide apart while twirling in circles, her long skirt swishing as she turned. Her reddish-brown hair fell loose from its bindings and tumbled unfettered down her back.

"And when we come back," Annie said after stopping and taking Kerry's hands, "our pockets will be filled with money and we will buy a house behind the third wall." She tilted her chin into a haughty pose.

"When you return," Kerry told her, unable to control her giggles, "you will have a cart full of children. . .and," she continued speaking after bursting into full laughter. "Pockets full of money."

"Pockets full of money and a cart full of children," The words spun in Annie's mind and seemed to echo against the cell walls. Now Kerry is dead, she thought and so are Kerry's daughters and husband. All killed in the massacre. Her own family also perished in the massacre, except her cousin, Bobby. Maybe Bobby is dead too, she thought. He was only a baby when she left Oakbourgh and now he might as well be dead. After the massacre, all letters from home stopped. And what about her own children? She had to believe that The Eight took her children to their father as they promised.

Annie heaved a deep sigh and shuddered. Tears flooded her cheeks and she brushed them away with her hands. "No, no, no," she sobbed. "Not now. Please not now." Robert is alive, she told herself. Tanika had told her and the others had, too. But, after all this time, Annie had heard nothing from him. Not even a small message. She so wanted to believe he was alive, to feel his arms around her, his breath on her face, his kisses. "Just come home, Robert," she whispered. "Just come home."

But where is home now, Annie wondered. Today, she belonged to The Eight. Her home was a cell.

"We hold the secrets to Blue Eden," Tanika had told her that night they first met. "And we protect them with our lives. Come with us, Annie, and learn our secrets. There is a meeting tonight and you will be welcome."

Annie was more than welcomed. She was embraced like an old friend. The room where they took her was hidden beneath the floor of a pharmacy building. They entered first through a back door and then into the pharmacy storeroom. A tall figure, clothed in black and wearing a dark cloth sack over his head, approached them. Holes were cut for his eyes, nose and mouth.

"You brought her." He spoke in a husky whisper.

"She came," Tanika whispered back.

Annie could see the man's lips curl into a smile. He nodded. "Come," he said. "Everyone is waiting." He flipped on a flashlight and started walking toward the far wall where a door stood partially hidden behind stacks of boxes. After opening the closet door, the man bent down and pulled open a trap door revealing a wooden, spiral staircase leading down into darkness.

Shining the flashlight on the two women, he motioned for them to enter the stairwell. Tanika obliged. Annie hesitated for a moment, but then stepped calmly onto the first step. She was not afraid. For some reason that Annie did not understand, her spirit embraced this mysterious place.

Down she stepped, holding on to a metal railing. The trap door thudded closed over her head and the beam from the stranger's flashlight bounced along the stairs as they descended. A veiled light came into view and when she reached the bottom step, a strong, yet gentle hand took Annie's arm and guided her to where a group of about fifteen people were sitting quietly on the floor. Each person's face was covered, the men with black sacks, the women with either veils or shawls. She felt their eyes staring at her, but no one spoke. Annie wrapped her shawl around her face and sat down.

Three people, a man and two women sat facing the larger group. One of the women removed her veil with stiff, claw-like fingers and spoke.

"Welcome Annie Miller. We've been expecting you." Her voice was frail, her face narrow and wrinkled. Although her white hair was pulled into a tight bun, a few stray wisps escaped to fall across her high forehead and across her gaunt cheeks.

"We are The Eight." Her quavering voice floated above the silent congregation.

"We are The Eight," they repeated in soft unison. "We are the keepers of the truth," she chanted. "We are the protectors of the truth."

Annie kept silent while the others whispered the chant.

"We have come here to seize power and to deny it to others," the old woman continued "Our leader, El Espiritu, tells us that our plans are falling into place. Our need for patience is coming to an end and we will soon come out of the shadows. This earth will no longer belong to the corporate kings. Humanity will again walk free and with dignity.

Blue Eden awaits, ready and alive," the old woman spoke to the hushed audience. "And the time is very near."

The old woman closed her eyes. Her breathing seemed labored. Annie watched with fascination as another woman slipped off her veil revealing a young face, but with the right side twisted and scarred from a brutal injury. A patch covered her right eye. She began to speak. The dark basement held a hushed audience.

"Blue Eden was created," she said.

"Yes. Yes." The audience chanted.

"It was a gift of life given to humanity, but those in power had a dilemma," she continued. "They had gained their wealth and power by plundering the earth's resources and by convincing humanity that this plundering was necessary in order to ensure continued existence. Blue Eden represented life and proved the power mankind possessed enabling us to restore life to a dying planet. However, admitting the existence of Blue Eden would expose the corporate king's deception and undermine their power."

The audience swayed and clenched their fists.

"It was decided by the corporations that Blue Eden would be kept a secret until those in power were ready to use its resources. Citizens were taught to look within themselves and not outward toward their neighbors or their environment. Curiosity became treason. Science became heresy. Soon, even the powerful began to believe their lies. Blue Eden became a myth."

Her tone was calm and steady as she spoke.

"When the oceans washed across the lowlands and the rivers ceased to flow, fear grew like a wild fire that wanted to rage against its masters and against each other. But it was too late.

"The corporate masters had built walls, smashed computers, executed the outspoken and filled libraries with dogma. The surviving population laid down in submission." Her voice rose and then trailed to a whisper.

A moan came from the veiled listeners as they rocked and swayed. The woman's disfigured face glowed with conviction.

"The Society of The Eight was formed in order to gather and protect as much information as possible before that information could be destroyed. Books, computer disks and film were collected and hidden. Those hiding places have been forgotten for decades, until now. They have at last been discovered. Now, The Eight holds proof that Blue Eden exists. We are keeping it safe until the time when we can use its knowledge to restore life to our earth and freedom to earth's people."

The group became agitated. They rocked back and forth and moaned. The woman waited until they calmed themselves and then continued.

"The time is close. The first set of instructions to finding Blue Eden was discovered buried in a museum storeroom in Oakbourgh. Today, all the segments of information for Blue Eden have been discovered and we are ready to put them together. Yet, it is far more dangerous now. The corporate kings are also gathering information. There are spies everywhere. If they accumulate all the information first, then Blue Eden will belong to the corporate kings. They will take control, destroy The Eight and our freedom will be lost. We must work fast, but with care. The Eight must get to Blue Eden before they do. People with secret identities have been given the responsibility of protecting this knowledge. When the time comes, this knowledge will be assembled in one place and Blue Eden will be ours."

Annie listened in amazement. Her mind raced with exhilaration. Robert was alive and working with The Eight. Joining The Eight meant finding Robert. Her spirit burned with a new energy and wrapped itself in the hope of a new future.

Hope mocked Annie from the shadows of her prison cell and spit on her courage. Hope had abandoned her. She was alone.

The cell door rattled and swung open. The silhouettes of two guards stood dark and threatening against a backdrop of bright light.

"Get up, Annie," one of them said. "It's time to go."

Annie rose to her feet and allowed the guards to cuff her hands behind her back. Strong hands held each of her arms and guided her forward.

The cell door slammed behind her.

Part III

August 31
One hundred years in the future

CHAPTER SIX
The Third Wall
Oakbourgh

Gage took a long slow drag from his cigarette, savored the taste of the fine tobacco and exhaled the excess smoke into the stifling atmosphere. From his position on a hill, safely within the confines of Oakbourgh's third wall, he leaned back in his cushioned, patio chair and gazed out over a plush, corporate golf course decorated with desert plants – sage, cactus and Bougainvillea. Gage wondered how much precious water it took to keep this golf course so lush and green in Oakbourgh's ferocious desert heat. Still light, the early evening temperature was a suffocating 120 degrees. Several foursomes moved their carts from hole to hole while their caddies offered them cold water from ice chests and held umbrellas over their employer's heads to protect them from the blazing sun.

Gage wore his civilian clothes – slacks and long-sleeved shirt made from a thin synthetic fiber called Tyson fabric, designed to offer protection against ultraviolet rays. The material also functioned as a thermostat keeping the body cool in extreme heat. Gage had exchanged his leather boots for a pair of Tyson loafers – closed-toed, cloth shoes with synthetic soles.

His dark eyes alert, he surveyed the imposing estates perched upon rolling hills surrounding the golf course. Each estate was on an acre of land and each belonged to a corporate executive or a corporate senator. It was the executive's job to make sure the factories ran smoothly and the workers were compliant. The senators, chosen by the corporate kings, made the laws ensuring that money flowed into the hands of the correct people. It was their job to inform the corporate employers of problems arising within their assigned district.

If there were strikes or general uprisings as there were on occasion, private soldiers like Gage were employed by the corporation to keep the order. Such violence seemed light years away from this tranquil existence. Yet, concealed beneath the long tale of his shirt was his holstered gun.

A servant approached Gage while he sat perusing the peaceful surroundings from the backyard of Sato's residence. A young serving boy placed a warm cinnamon roll and a crystal goblet filled with orange juice on the small glass top table in front of Gage. After bowing, the boy hurried away.

Picking up the goblet of orange juice, Gage held it in front of his face for a moment and took a sip. The taste was tart, sweet and cold all at the same time. He felt the roughness of the pulp on his tongue, swished it around in his mouth and swallowed. At $200 a glass, Gage knew he should relish each sip. Instead, he lifted the glass to his lips, tilted his head back and drained the glass of its expensive liquid. He smelled the empty glass and savored the aroma of oranges which somewhat camouflaged the acid-like smell of smog hanging low in the yellow sky.

The sound of women's laughter diverted his attention toward his employer's house. From across an expanse of manicured lawn on the other side of a Grecian style swimming pool, he observed a crew of servants setting up tables with white linen coverings, candle centerpieces and porcelain place settings. Cooks attended to a free-standing barbecue that contained two sizzling, well-browned roasts turning on rotisseries and emanating the aroma of savory beef. Real beef, Gage thought, not that protein paste designed to look like real food.

Four women dressed in short skirts and low-cut blouses, each laughing, talking and holding a drink, came onto the patio. Rebecca Sato was with them. They walked across the patio and when they arrived at a white canvas canopy erected next to the pool each woman, except Rebecca, peeled off her skirt and blouse revealing a one-piece swim suit made from Tyson fabric.

The elite enjoyed a rich variety of fashion made from the fine quality of Tyson material, but work uniforms and the general attire for peasants were made from a genetically engineered cotton plant. This plant was designed to need little water and grew in abundance across the dry hills and planes of Montana and Southern Canada.

Gage noticed Rebecca excuse herself from the ladies. She began walking in his direction. Her long graceful strides exuded confidence as she moved across the lawn, her knee-length white skirt swirled with a quiet energy about her slender legs.

"I see you are enjoying yourself." Rebecca's voice drifted through the still parched air. She pulled a chair out from the table and sat across from Gage. "I hope you found your travels here comfortable," her voice held a soft and warm tone.

"Did I once say Oakbourgh was a hellhole?" He raised an eyebrow.

Rebecca gave a slight laugh. "Well, it is primitive here, but World Tech provides as many luxuries as possible. The golf course, as you see, keeps our corporate senators occupied and the shops, theaters and restaurants keep their wives happy.

"What else do the corporate senators have to do except play golf," Gage said coldly, then nonchalantly took another drag from his cigarette. "When they're not playing golf," he continued after taking the cigarette from his lips and placing the burning stub in a crystal ashtray on the table. "They're following orders from their corporate bosses, or writing laws to ensure the citizens are kept quiet and the money flows in the right direction. Then they hire people like me to enforce those laws. For them, it's a few years in Oakbourgh and then it's back to Canada or Ireland and a private estate in civilization. For the rest of us. . .well. . .it's on to another job." Gage gave a chuckle. "I can see I'm boring you," he said.

Rebecca had looked away from Gage and seemed to be watching the three women at the pool. "You've finished your orange juice," she said. "Would you like some more?" She took a small gold case from a purse she carried, opened it, took out a slender cigarette and placed it between her lips.

Gage looked at her with interest. The pink blouse she wore highlighted the slight blush on her cheeks and on her lips. Her black hair fell loose, framing her face and brushing against her slender shoulders. She held the cigarette by long delicate fingers tipped with red-painted nails.

"Real orange juice, warm cinnamon rolls. I could get used to this kind of life." Gage picked up his fork and knife, sliced off a piece of the hot roll and put the sweet pastry in his mouth. "Perfect," he said. "Just like everything here. As a matter of fact, I don't think I've ever had a real glass of orange juice before; always just that chemical stuff. And most people can't even afford that."

Rebecca placed her cigarette in the ashtray. "We hire the very best," she told him. "Our pollinators take very good care of our plants. They know which flowers to germinate. Always the strongest, the sweetest." Rebecca smiled showing a row of perfect white teeth. "I'll show you our greenhouses later. I'm sure you'll be impressed."

Gage sat studying her face as she spoke.

"We produce enough fruit to supply almost everyone behind the third wall," she continued, "There was a time, I'm told, when insects pollinated the flowers." She leaned back in her chair and sighed. "Can you imagine?" Her silky black hair swayed with the movement of her head as she laughed. "How sloppy. Insects flying around providing our food supply."

"Maybe it's a myth," Gage said while tapping his cigarette on the edge of the ashtray. "But, now let's get down to business. We need to talk about this mission you're paying me to do. Let's talk details. My men will be here in a few hours. What am I going to tell them?"

"Yes. Your mission," Rebecca's eyes narrowed. She glanced toward the women now splashing in the pool. "Hannah Merrick is fourteen-years-old. She lives behind the second wall in one of the company row houses on Garret Street. Her father is a factory manager. She lives with him, her stepmother and her stepmother's two children. Hannah's been married, well. . .on paper anyway. They haven't had the ceremony yet. But that's not our concern."

"So, what is our concern?"

"You," Rebecca continued, "and the four commandos you hired will go to her house after the party here tonight. You will take her from her house and go to the airport where a private plane will be waiting for you. Board the plane and wait for further instructions."

Gage sat with his hands clasped together, resting on the tabletop. When Rebecca finished speaking, he rubbed his fingers together, placed his elbows on the table and leaned toward Rebecca.

"Tell me," he said. "Why do you need four war-hardened commandos to kidnap one little girl? Is there something you're not saying?"

Rebecca's eyes narrowed and her face hardened. "Are we not paying you enough, Officer Gage?"

"There's never enough money, is there, Mrs. Montoya?" He leaned back in his chair. "So far," he continued, "I have only been able to recruit two of your commandos. Not the four you requested."

Rebecca's eyes opened wide in surprise. "Two?" Her voice was strained and cold. "You're already disobeying orders."

"Not at all," Gage told her. "You wanted men I could trust. I'm afraid that narrows it down to two. These men I trust to cover my back and they are as good as ten. They will be here this evening as planned. They will arrive as businessmen and check into the Edmond Hotel in the factory district. I will meet them there tonight after we leave this dinner party. We will coordinate our plans, pick up the girl and rendezvous at the plane. And now. . ." Gage glared at Rebecca. "We will need to trust you."

Rebecca stiffened.

"We will bring you this girl and we will meet you at the airport. But, you have to understand. . .I am a survivor and so are my men. Whatever happens at that airport, we will walk away alive. You have paid me half the money for my men and the other half is due when the mission is complete." Gage leaned forward. "We will collect."

Gage watched as Rebecca shifted in her seat, her face locked into a dark frown. "I am fully aware of your talents on the battlefield, Officer Gage." She paused for a moment "You are now my body guard and you will understand that there are more dangers here behind these walls than you will find on any battlefield." She wet her lips and fixed a steady gaze on him. "I want you to pay close attention to those women over there."

Gage diverted his eyes toward the pool.

"I'd rather put my attention elsewhere," he said with caution.

Rebecca ignored his remark. "Those women over there are corporate wives, married to some of the most powerful men in the world. . .the corporate kings. Those women may look harmless, but they are extremely dangerous. Of course, so are their husbands. Those ladies are full of gossip and they report everything to anyone who will further their family's power. Angie, the tall blond getting out of the pool, is the wife of World Tech's information director."

Gage watched Angie untie her long blond hair from a ponytail and sit down on the edge of a lounge chair. A servant, waiting with a towel and a beach robe, covered her long, lanky body.

"The short, thin brunette, Michelle, is the wife of the defense director." Rebecca gave Gage a sideways glance as she spoke. "He is responsible for our militia."

Gage watched as Michelle climbed out of the pool, collapsed onto a patio chair and took a towel from her servant.

"And the most dangerous of all is Miranda."

Gage turned his eyes to the plump, curly-haired woman lying in a chaise lounge and slowly sipping from what appeared to be a glass of orange juice.

"Her husband. . ."

"Yes, I know," Gage interrupted. "Her husband is the second in command to your husband. Together, they run World Tech and most of the civilized world itself. The king of kings."

Rebecca gave a tight-lipped smile. "A young woman was sentenced to death two days ago in Canada. She was an important member in a secretive criminal organization that has a lot of well. . .shall we say, moral support from the workers."

Gage cocked his head and narrowed his eyes. "The Society of The Eight. You asked me about that organization before."

"Yes," Rebecca continued. "This gathering today is about what is happening in Canada. It's about the situation the arrest of this woman has caused. There's a lot of unrest in the factories and in the mines. Capturing this woman in some ways may be productive for the corporation, but it could also be disastrous. The corporation wants to kill her, but I'm not sure the workers would stand for that. We don't want another uprising on our hands."

Rebecca took a deep breath and wet her lips. "The woman was tortured, but what she told her jailers can never be trusted. She told them what they wanted to hear, but . . ." Rebecca shrugged her shoulders. "If she told them what they thought they already knew – what's the point?"

"So, what is your point?" Gage said. "This is somehow tied in with this girl, Hannah, isn't it?"

"All in due time, Officer Gage. Right now it is time for me to play hostess and for you to pay attention. Come with me, but before you do," Rebecca rose from her seat and stood over Gage. "Start thinking of two more names to join this mission. Give me the names and I will make sure they meet up with us. Have them before you leave here tonight." Her eyes turned hard and seemed to peer through him. With an abrupt turn, she walked back toward the house.

Gage crumpled his cigarette into the ashtray. This is going to be interesting, he thought, as he got up. For a few moments he watched Rebecca as she crossed the lawn toward the pool. When she joined the women at the pool, she sat down in an empty chair beneath the huge canopy and began, what seemed at first, to be just chatter. Gage followed her and stood a few feet away, close enough to hear the ladies' conversation.

He felt uncomfortable as he listened, but Gage understood patience. In more than one case, his life had depended on his ability to listen, learn and take action only when necessary.

"My dear," Angie leaned toward Rebecca and spoke in a hushed voice. "You must come with us tonight after dinner. Michelle and I are going to the theater district behind the second wall. It's great fun. Miranda won't go, but you must."

Michelle giggled and clapped her hands together while Miranda shook her head and scowled.

"We were there two nights ago when the migrants attacked. Rebecca dear, you have only been back here in Oakbourgh for a few hours so you probably know nothing about this, but. . ."

"The migrants broke through right into the residential area," Michelle interrupted with excitement. "They actually broke into some of the houses and terrified the workers living there."

"It was like they were looking for something or someone," Angie brushed another lock of wet hair from her face. "They went through several houses poking around with their guns but took nothing."

"Well, I did hear a rumor that a girl disappeared," Michelle reminded Angie. "Of course, we have no way of knowing if that is true or not, or even if it had anything to do with the attack."

"I can't imagine migrants wanting to take those people," Angie shuttered. "That story is just ridiculous. Well," Angie said to her companions. "Michelle and I were downtown when the lights went out and the explosions started. It was all very exciting. You really must come with us tonight, Beck. Bring your new security man with you." Angie waved her hand toward Gage. "Of course, we'll all have our guards with us so no one bothers us."

"Unless we want to be bothered," Michelle added and then laughed.

"You'll have to excuse me," Rebecca said with a strained smile. "Some more of my guests have arrived." She stood and walked toward the house. Gage walked beside her.

"And now you'll meet the husbands, including mine." Rebecca glanced up at Gage. "He may seem like a lovable buffoon, but don't believe it. He is shrewd, devious and he will cook you for dinner if he chooses."

"Thanks for the warning." Gage replied while keeping a watchful eye on the casually dressed men congregating around the patio tables. They all wore shorts and brightly colored shirts. Anthony Montoya, Rebecca's husband, a tall, thin man with salt and pepper hair and dark brown eyes, waved at Rebecca.

"Hey, Becca come on over here and sit down." He motioned with a wide swing of his arm. "Bring that new security man with you. Sit down both of you." He looked around and called to one of the young serving boys. "Bring these two some vodka and orange juice."

Gage and Rebecca sat at one of the tables. Another of the many poolside servants sat drinks in front of them. As Rebecca spoke, Gage took note of each man. Mortal men he thought, weak in appearance, yet wielding more power than a monsoon. All assets on earth belong to them. The world is their personal property including every tree, every building and each human life.

Winslow, the bald, fidgety man with the skinny legs and potbelly was the company's defense director. He ran the militia and the justice system. MacAfee, the heavy-set blond with a mustache, was the senate prime minister and the second in command in the World Tech Corporation. Kessler, the old man with glasses and the bushy white hair, was the one who signed the checks, both corporate and government. Anthony Montoya, CEO of World Tech, Corporate king and Rebecca Sato's husband, laughed and joked with his guests. He guided each of them to a seat around a large, round patio table.

An older woman, dressed in a floor-length black dress and holding onto the arm of a younger, stone-faced man, took a seat at one of the tables. "Adam and Margie Hull," Rebecca whispered. "Our company's education gurus."

Gage glanced at the pair. So these two are the perfect example of pure thought, he told himself. Their job is to make sure young minds are submissive and fearful. Education was strictly controlled and the Hull's were a part of that process of control. Although some public schools operated in the factories and admitted worker's children up to the age of eight, private schools for the elite were run by the corporations and religious institutions. Admittance to those schools was dependent upon test scores, family or corporate or religious affiliation, recommendation and tuition. Military service, Gage knew, was one way to bypass the tuition and exams, however, each applicant still had to receive a recommendation. The Hull family supplied honored recommendations, often with a price. Why were the Hulls at this meeting, Gage wondered?

"No, no, no," Montoya got up. "Make room for the Hulls over here. We have lots to discuss." The men rearranged the chairs to seat the eight people around a single table.

"The ladies can have the other tables when they're ready to eat." He winked in Rebecca's direction. "Except for you, Becca and you, Mrs. Hull, you can stay."

Gage's adrenalin raced, but his mind was calm and alert. The Sato's respectable name was an important piece of the power puzzle. The Sato family was old, wealthy and powerful and that name helped Montoya maintain his corporate throne. Montoya had money, but the Sato family had both money and name.

"Hey, how's that dinner commin." Montoya hollered over his shoulder to the servants. "Let's eat"

Servers placed large platters of food on the table, each filled with grapes, strawberries, carrots, celery, cucumbers and tomatoes. Slices of warm bread and creamy butter were placed in front of each guest. Montoya filled his plate first while the others waited. Rebecca nodded to Gage to take what he wanted when the others began selecting from the delicacies. Real fruits and vegetables, Gage thought, not the protein paste eaten outside the third wall.

"So, what's this fuss I hear about this factory girl in Canada?" Montoya spoke, then filled his mouth with grapes.

"She confessed under interrogation that she belongs to The Eight. She would not say, but we believe that she's working for the leader of The Eight – this person they call El Espiritu." Kessler mumbled through a mouthful of bread.

"Yes, but she changed her story when she talked to the priest," Winslow interjected. "Is this a person who lies to her tormentor or one who lies to her God? We need to find out. The problem is that she has been sentenced to death. If this sentence is carried out, we may lose valuable information. You may need to commute her sentence, Mr. Montoya. Right now she's sitting in a cell in Tent City, Canada until you make a final decision. She was moved to the coliseum yesterday."

"Wait a minute, wait a minute," Montoya said. "Tell me more about her. Is she really so important or is she just saying what we want to hear? If she's really so important, does anyone know why? Does she really work for this. . .El Espiritu? This spirit person who is the leader of The Eight. This spirit person who no one has seen?"

"This Annie was invisible until we captured her about two weeks ago," Winslow said. "They picked her up after curfew with some of those union troublemakers. Normally, she would have been fired and deported if someone hadn't noticed where she worked." He paused a moment, buttered a slice of bread with a silver butter knife and then continued without taking a bite. "If someone had not noticed who she was . . ."

"Well, just spit it out," Montoya said, waving a fork at him.

Winslow continued. "This Annie had transferred from the thread factory to the munitions plant. Took a job as a scrubwoman, but it paid more money. Not anything to notice except . . ." He picked up his bread and took a bite.

"Except what?" Montoya spoke with agitation. "Get on with it."

"Except for the job she was doing. She was a scrub woman in the offices at night with complete access to the destinations of all munitions shipments. Not that she had legal access to this information, but she was in a position to get her hands on it."

Now servers placed platters of barbecued beef on the table along with bowls of mashed potatoes, gravy and more orange juice. After filling his plate, Winslow continued. "Raids on our shipments have been running high over the past six months. Even when we put out false information about destinations, the convoys were still attacked. We knew we had a mole in the works, but didn't know who. . .until we got Annie.

Winslow continued. "She is a simple girl, or so it seems. She was raised here in Oakbourgh. Where she was born, we are not sure and neither is she. We think it was in a coastal migrant village where her family was caught up in one of those pirate raids. Most of the men of her family were either killed or captured. Annie and her mother survived somehow. The mother had family here in Oakbourgh, so this is where she and her baby daughter, Annie, settled"

Gage shifted in his seat, feeling uncomfortable as he listened. Why did this conversation suddenly cause him to smell the salty ocean? What are these images of a village and a boy he was seeing in his mind?

"Annie and her husband were brought to Canada to work in the fields and to build the walls. They could read and write, but neither of them was ever documented. They remained illegal. Her husband later joined a corporate militia in order to gain papers and to find better and legal work with the corporation. Both were on their way to gaining respected membership in Canada and World Tech.

"So what happened?" Montoya leaned back in his chair placing his hands behind his head.

"Her husband was killed." Winslow told him, "Fighting the migrants in the American desert. She was given a factory job and her kids were allowed to attend Mrs. Hull's academy. Then, somehow she got involved with The Eight. But, there is more to that story." The defense director took a long drink and wiped his lips with a cloth napkin.

"Robert Miller, Annie's husband, was part of a team commissioned by World Tech to parachute into the American desert and find any evidence of this Blue Eden rumor. As you know, gossip is strong that the proof of this Blue Eden is hidden in the desert."

McAfee laughed. "Peasants are always looking for some paradise. They wouldn't know what to do with it if they found it."

Winslow leaned forward, his body tense. "According to our records, Miller and the team found nothing. Miller sent a message that they were under attack by migrants and needed backup. When rescue arrived everyone was dead, including Miller."

"Oh uh," Winslow said. "Well actually, one corporal survived long enough to tell us what happened. We buried them all in the desert. We let Miller's kids attend the school so that his wife would not cause trouble. She would not ask questions about her husband's death."

"Yes, but something is going on in the desert." Winslow interrupted. "Migrants are now moving toward the Rocky Mountains instead of moving north. Even workers are leaving the compounds and going south. How they are surviving out there is anyone's guess. They must have found water, but I can't imagine where."

"It's more than that," McAfee stated coldly. "Two days ago one of our cargo ships was taken in the passage by pirates and most of the crew is being held."

Kessler leaned forward and slammed his hand on the table. "Another one of our ships was completely destroyed in the same battle. The attack was brazen and bloody-well organized. These pirates are costing us a fortune."

"Yes, Winslow continued, shaking his head. "And the pirates are asking for Annie's release. Well, they're demanding it." He sighed. "This so-called simple factory girl is anything but. We need to find out who she really is and Mrs. Hull, here, is going to help us."

Mrs. Hull, a tight smile on her lips, nodded.

"This Annie woman," Winslow said, "Has three children and they are in the care of Mrs. Hull. Annie has information and we have her children."

"Okay," Montoya said and then belched. "So let me get this straight. This Annie Miller has information, but she won't talk. We have her children and we have some strong rumors about this Blue Eden." Montoya sighed and drummed his fingers on the table.

"We have spies in the field and we have an army moving across the desert toward the Rocky Mountains so we can discover exactly what is out there. If there is an Eight stronghold out there, then we will take control of it. Rebecca, your cousin Buzz Mullans, is heading the military expedition. He's got orders to rout out this Eight Society and destroy them. That leader of theirs, El Espiritu they call him, will cease to exist. That is if he exists at all." Montoya leaned across the table and clasped his hands together.

"I will tell you this. Whatever this Blue Eden is, whether it's rumor or reality, it belongs to me. If it's real, we will find it." He paused and took a drink of orange juice. "I see no reason why we need this Annie insurgent," he continued. "Make a public spectacle with her death tomorrow morning. Let our workers know that we are in charge." His eyes were cold and dark. Those at the table grew silent.

Gage felt his blood turn cold. He had seen men dispatch death with ease and indifference, but it was chilling to watch a king wield his power without wisdom or compassion.

Gage's eye caught Patricia, Rebecca's private servant, moving unnoticed across the patio. She stopped beside Rebecca's chair, leaned over and whispered in her ear. Gage watched the color drain from his employer's face. She held her breath for a moment and then seemed to compose herself.

"Gentlemen, would you please excuse me," she said. "I have a call from my mother and as you know, she has not been well."

The others at the table nodded toward her and Montoya waved permission for her to leave.

"Officer Gage," she said softly as she rose from her chair. "Please come with me. I'll finish showing you the grounds after I check on mother."

Gage, Rebecca and Patricia walked together toward a two-seated golf cart parked close to the patio. "Please get in, Officer Gage," Rebecca said. "I'll drive."

Gage climbed into the cart, but Rebecca and Patricia walked a short distance from the vehicle engaged in an intense conversation. When they finished, Gage watched Patricia walk back toward the house. Rebecca climbed into the cart beside Gage and placed her hand over a scanning screen. The cart's engine began to whirl. "Take us to the greenhouses," Rebecca spoke into a speaker on the dash. Giving a bounce, the cart rose a few inches off the ground and began to float.

Gage sensed Rebecca relax as she leaned back in her seat. She looked down at her hands, her jaw tightened and her eyes concentrated on some deep far-away thought. When she spoke, she said "I'm afraid our job just got a little more difficult, Officer Gage. Hannah has disappeared. We've got to find her."

CHAPTER SEVEN
The Train
The Desert

Hannah slept a dreamless sleep. The peace of oblivion enveloped her in the blackness of her hiding place. On occasion, an unidentified sound invaded her serenity. Did a child cry? Did someone moan? Silence comforted her again and she slept.

Dark exploded into colors. A brilliant, dancing kaleidoscope pierced her subconscious and Hannah screamed. She was moving, tumbling, falling.

Dust filled her nostrils and her mouth. She coughed and then began gagging. Hannah fought to open her eyes and when she did, she discovered that she was lying face down on rock-littered ground. Attempting to push herself up, Hannah noticed a trail of blood oozing from a small puncture wound in her right arm. She perched on her knees and vomited.

Sick with pain, fear surged through her body as her mind began to clear. A fiery sun showered her with blistering rays. Still sluggish and sick to her stomach, Hannah looked around her environment. It appeared she was lying amidst the wreckage of a derailed train. Several overturned box cars, twisted track and spilled cargo littered a desert landscape. Black smoke billowed upward from out of a deep gorge.

Someone screamed for help and a plane's engine whirled in the distance.

"I drank the liquid." Hannah spoke out loud, her voice raspy. "Where's Bobby? Bobby." she called.

"Shut up, boy." A hushed voice spoke close to her ear and a hand covered her mouth. Another arm encircled her waist and began yanking her backwards.

"You're going to get us all killed."

Hannah, too weak and disoriented to resist, felt herself being dragged across the ground and pulled through an open door of an upside-down boxcar.

"Don't say a word," the voice told her as the hand was released from her mouth.

Hannah, on all fours and still disoriented, crawled away from the stranger. Hollow metallic sounds echoed against the walls of the stifling boxcar as she moved. A sudden burst of gunfire caused her to stop and peer out the door through which a white film of morning sunlight streamed.

Outside, the landscape was strewn with broken, twisted railroad track and train cars. Smashed water barrels and boxes of merchandise lay tangled in the wreckage and strewn across the desert. An explosion erupted, sending shock waves through the boxcar where Hannah hid. A plane's engine hummed overhead.

"Get back you fool." the voice spoke to her again. "I should have left you out there."

Looking in the direction of the voice, Hannah recognized one of the men who had taken the drink with her and Bobby in the warehouse. His face was covered in blood from a gash on his forehead. However, his black-rimmed glasses were not broken. A woman sat in a corner, her face smeared with dirt and tears, her eyes frantic. Two small children cowered in her lap. Hannah remembered this mother from the warehouse. She had four children, Hannah thought. Where were the other two?

"My name's Dennis," the man said, his face pale and tense. "This is my wife, Carla and my two children."

Hannah heard his words, but said nothing.

"The Militia is surveying the situation from the air," Dennis said. "They're looking for saboteurs and they're shooting anything that moves. They must have thought you were dead. You were lying out there in the open and not moving for so long."

"But we're not saboteurs," Hannah said.

"We're migrants." His words were sharp, his eyes cold. "We have no papers. Besides, they won't rescue us. It's not the militia's job to rescue. The militia can't discern between survivors and saboteurs, so everyone is the enemy. The job of the militia is to protect the merchandise, not the passengers."

From their hiding place in the boxcar, Hannah and Dennis watched as a child emerged from the train wreckage and stumbled into sight of the circling plane. Hannah noticed Dennis' muscles tighten. This child, Hannah remembered, was not his and Carla's. Their two missing girls were still somewhere in the wreckage.

A frantic voice called to the disoriented child. A terrified woman attempted to pull the small boy to safety, but a flying, killing machine circled the confused and frightened mother and child, leveled its guns and sprayed them with deadly metal. As the bullets fell, the woman threw herself over the boy in an attempt to protect him. There was no protection this day as the gunship continued its ominous search for looters and saboteurs.

A soft wail came from Carla. She held her two children as she looked at her husband in desperation.

"We'll find our two girls," Dennis told her. "The planes will leave soon and then we can go out. We'll find our girls out there and help the others. Whoever caused this disaster won't be around here now. They'll come back at night to loot the wreckage and the mercenaries know this. When the planes leave, we have to leave, too. They'll be back when it gets dark. We can't be here."

I won't leave without Bobby, Hannah told herself. Where is he hiding? I know he's alive. Her eyes peered out the opening in the boxcar and searched the wreckage.

"Why do you think someone did this?" she said." Maybe the bridge just fell."

"I can't be sure," Dennis said "But, I got a good look at the mess out there before I hid in this boxcar. There's a bridge over a ravine that the train was crossing. It looks like explosives were placed on each of the bridge towers. All of the towers have been ripped apart and I think the explosions must have caused the fire in the gorge. We're lucky." Dennis paused, looked at his wife and two children and continued. "We were in the last boxcars and the last three cars were blown away from the rest of the train. Luckily, they didn't fall with the bridge. Our boxcars stayed above the gorge. Everything else went down into the ravine."

Hannah glanced upward as a fleet of gunships took one final sweep over the wreckage and then flew away from the devastation. She watched the planes grow smaller and smaller in the morning sky until they disappeared from sight.

"It's safe," Dennis said. "We can leave here."

His wife shook her head no, and continued to hold onto her two children.

"All right then," he said. "You can stay in here for a while. Come on, boy. We have to see what our situation is."

Hannah, still dressed in her stepbrother's clothes minus her floppy hat and backpack, followed the tall, thin Dennis out of the boxcar. A seemingly endless desert scattered with rocks and scrub brush surrounded her. Toward the west and in the shadow of rolling hills, sprawled the skeleton of a silent, decaying city. Beyond the city rose the massive Rocky Mountains, barren of vegetation or life.

Only a few yards away from where Hannah stood, a bridge spanning a wide ravine had collapsed plunging railroad track, bridge towers and train cars nearly one hundred feet into what was now a dry river canyon. Most of the passenger cars were at the front of the train and had fallen first into the ravine. The cargo cars at the train's rear had tumbled on top of them. Within the gorge, fire rapidly consumed the fallen wreckage sending black, choking smoke into the atmosphere.

From a ridge above the ravine, Hanna could see an expanding fire leaping across the disaster below, incinerating cargo boxes and debris with each touch of its flaming tentacles. Broken barrels, once containing precious water were everywhere but the liquid did nothing to slow the inferno. Bodies were lying in the ravine, but none of them moved.

Still in a dream-like trance, Hannah looked in the direction of excited chatter. With the impact of the explosion, a lone passenger car decoupled from its adjoining car, slid on its side and had come to rest with the front one-third protruding over the precipice. Passengers were escaping out of windows and handing children into the arms of frightened and disheveled rescuers.

Stunned and injured people began coming out from hiding places within the wreckage and some of the bodies lying near Hannah began to move and moan. She noticed a dark-skinned man appear amidst the rubble holding the hands of Dennis and Carla's two missing daughters. They ran to their father sobbing, and it seemed both joy and fear crossed their faces.

Where is Bobby? Hannah scanned the wreckage. She recognized some of the same immigrants who were with her and Bobby in the Oakbourgh warehouse. Hannah realized that after they drank the liquid, they had all been concealed in empty water barrels with air holes drilled around the tops, then placed

in boxcars like everyday freight. Each person had been drugged
and kept asleep with an IV line supplying them with a
continuous sedative. Hannah rubbed the puncture wound in her
arm. She and Bobby were supposed to wake up to a new life in
Canada.

"Hannah, you're alive." Hannah turned toward the voice
to see Bobby emerging from the wreckage. He hurried to her
side and held her in his arms. "We're alive. We're together," he
said as he held her. Tears filled her eyes and flooded down her
cheeks. Bobby was alive. They touched each other's sunburned
faces and examined their cuts and scrapes. For a few moments,
there was no one else but her and Bobby. She felt his breath blow
through her hair; his hands press her head to his shoulder. They
were safe.

"My name is Dennis MacIntire." A commanding voice
startled Hannah. "We need to go through the wreckage." The
voice continued. "And collect water, food and any supplies we
can find that we can carry."

Hannah and Bobby joined the group of survivors who
had gathered around Dennis. Each person seemed relieved that
someone knew what to do and they appeared eager to follow his
instructions.

"I can see a city over yonder." Dennis pointed toward
the west. "I think it is. . .I hope it's abandoned. We can take
shelter there, but we're going to have to hide until we can decide
what to do next. The militia will return as will bandits and other
migrants." He paused a moment and surveyed the group. "You
know. . .we are all migrants now, too."

"We're no migrants," a balding man, wearing a business
suit called out. "We're paid passengers. We were in the
passenger car and we all work for World Tech. And we have
papers."

The man who spoke sat down in the dirt, his face ashen. "Look," he said. "I think my ribs are busted. And this lady," he nodded toward a young, blond woman dressed in a long black skirt and white blouse. "Her arm's injured. There's a lot of injured people here. We're going to stay here and wait for rescue."

"No one is going to rescue us here," a man called out from the crowd.

Mutterings of protests and denials circulated among the survivors. Hannah moved closer to Bobby. She looked into his face, afraid to say anything.

"Don't worry, Hannah," Bobby said. "They don't know what they're talking about. We'll figure this out. It's going to be okay."

Hannah swallowed a lump in her throat and her body relaxed.

"He knows what he's talking about," another man shouted, startling Hannah with his agitated tone. "I was in Oakbourgh with a group of accountants," the man continued.

"I'm an accountant. I know the profits coming out of Oakbourgh are diminishing. Underground earthquakes have changed the water flow and the mining operations are becoming more expensive. Within the year, two at most, the city will be abandoned by the corporations."

The small assemblage of bruised and bleeding people listened. No one spoke. Hannah knew, as did the survivors, that the abandonment of communities around the world by the employers was a very real and constant occurrence.

"So, what's that got to do with us?" Someone asked

"I've heard the corporate discussions," the accountant continued. "I can tell you, no one is going to come here to repair this damage. No one is going to rescue anyone. Oakbourgh is one of the last outposts in the desert. Getting water and merchandise to the far north has become more expensive and dangerous. These railways are constantly attacked by bandits and migrants." The man, nervous now, paused and looked around.

"This desert is crawling with criminals and desperate people," he continued. "Somehow, they're acquiring weapons making the attacks more deadly and costly. It is now cheaper and safer to take the merchandise to the coast and transport by ship. I'm telling you. No one is going to fix this rail line. No one is going to come here. It just isn't worth it anymore. There's no profit."

The group of survivors included those traveling with legal documentation and those, like Hannah and Bobby, who traveled without permission. Fear, confusion and exhaustion darkened their faces. Hannah, like the others, stood in stunned silence.

"Our best bet is to stick together." Dennis told them. "You've seen what the militia does. They shoot first and ask questions later. Anyone else we meet out here ain't gonna be that friendly either. We have to find some place to take shelter from the sun. It's hot now, but it's not even noon yet. Maybe we can find some shade in those hills over there. We'll have to try." He sighed and then looked at each person. "I was a school teacher in Oakbourgh. I taught English. Has anyone here any medical training?"

A plump, middle-aged woman raised her hand." I volunteered at the clinic. I can bandage simple wounds."

"Good enough," Dennis said. "The rest of us will gather supplies including any medicine or medical supplies we can find. Those train cars are filled with merchandise. We'll make some sleds from the wreckage and fill them with water and any food we can find. We'll make some litters. If people can't walk, we'll have to carry them."

"He's right." An older man spoke out. "We have to leave here, but my wife did not survive. I will bury her first. I don't think the planes will come back until dark. They won't be expecting any of the saboteurs to be out in this heat. We have time."

"My brother, too," a dark-skinned man with a thick accent and a soft voice said.

"Okay." Dennis sighed then surveyed the skies. "You two work fast. Dig a grave. The rest of us, including the kids will gather supplies. Also, find anything that will serve as a weapon."

Reluctantly, the dazed and frightened survivors left the group and began to sort through the debris. They collected bottles of water and containers of protein paste and put them in a pile. Hannah joined them, glancing at the sky from time to time as did the others. Each person, Hannah noticed, doused themselves with water and drank freely from the bottled water found in the overturned boxcars. Hannah, and most of the survivors, retrieved pieces of clothing from luggage and used the clothes to cover their heads. The sun was growing hotter.

It appeared to Hannah that everyone who had not fallen with the train into the ravine or been killed by the mercenaries, seemed to have sustained cuts and abrasions. Many of the cuts were bleeding and had to be bandaged with pieces of clothing found in the suitcases. The pretty blond woman with the injured arm sat beside the man with the broken ribs. Her body trembled and her wide open eyes revealed her fear, however, these two seemed to be the only survivors seriously injured.

Hannah retrieved a bottle of water from a large box and took a long drink. As her mind started to clear from the drug induced sleep, she became more alert to her surroundings. Although the temperature was rising making it difficult to work, almost everyone appeared to be working. Two of the mothers, who were dressed in burkas, carried infants in a carrier strapped to their backs while their older children followed along behind. Even the well-dressed women who seemed to be unaccustomed to physical labor, shuffled through the debris finding items of use.

There appeared to be about thirty people who had escaped from the last passenger car, including several businessmen, three families with children, a young couple and a train porter. The rest of the group had been hidden in the barrels. Those were the people traveling illegally – an act of treason against the employers.

Most of the young men seemed tough and stoic, Hannah thought, used to hard work. Their skin shades went from dark brown to fair and to Hannah, their eyes held secrets she hoped to never understand. She and the others carried salvaged supplies to where Bobby was helping to assemble two sleds from flat pieces of wreckage. Since no one had discovered any real weapons, several survivors began fabricating spears, clubs and sharp hand-held instruments from pieces of wreckage.

Two of the men, Hannah noticed, worked together to dig a long shallow grave for their loved ones. Bodies found in the wreckage above the gorge were buried. Hannah and Bobby stopped working and gathered around the gravesite with the rest of the survivors. A hot wind scattered loose dirt against her ankles and tossed the ends of the cloth hanging over her head. She sensed an apprehension and uncertainty in almost everyone's attitude.

After a few moments, someone said a prayer and several of the women cried quietly. The old man, whose wife died, was trying to be stoic, but tears filled his blue eyes and flowed down his withered face. Some of the young men knelt, gave the sign of the cross, and prayed in silence. Hannah and Bobby stood together at the edge of the group, their hands touching. The funeral seemed to take only a moment before Dennis gave instructions to go back to work.

As Hannah returned to searching through the wreckage, her eyes scoured the debris for her backpack. The bag containing her grandmother's book was gone. The smugglers had not put it in the barrel with her. Where did they put it? Her head began pounding from the sun and a sense of panic began to envelop her. Her stepbrother's shoes rubbed blusters on her feet and her stomach churned.

"What if I lost it?" She said out loud. "What if I lost it? Lost it. Lost it?" The sky started to spin and her legs buckled.

"Hey, watch it," someone said. "You need some rest. Take some water." One of the migrant boys grabbed Hannah's arm and guided her to sit on the ground. He knelt down beside her. "You're little and skinny," he said, "You're dressed like a boy, but you ain't no boy. I've been watching you. Here, you need some water." He held a bottle to her lips and she gulped down the warm liquid. Hannah looked at the tall, rawboned boy with the brown eyes and deep tan.

"Thank you," she told him. "I can't find my backpack." Her head throbbed and her skin stung from sunburn. She began to feel nauseous.

"Drink some more water," the boy said, "but don't drink so fast. You'll get sick. Here comes your boy friend."

Bobby hurried to Hannah's side and sat down beside her. She took another drink, slow this time. "It's just the heat, Bobby. I'm okay. I can't find my backpack. I've been looking everywhere for it. I can't lose my grandmother's book," she said.

"Grandma gave it to me to protect. I've been looking for it, but I can't find it. What did they do with our backpacks?"

"I found them," Bobby told her. "I put them over by the sleds." He pointed toward the two sleds piled with food and water supplies. "The smugglers went through our packs after we went to sleep," he said. "They stole all the cigarettes and marijuana and all the money I had packed." Bobby sighed. "That was supposed to help us when we got to Canada."

"But my book," Hannah said looking into his eyes. "Did they take my book?"

"I don't know, Hannah," Bobby answered. "I only noticed what was important. Tell me what is so important about that book?"

Hannah struggled to her feet with Bobby holding on to her. Not answering him, she moved as quickly as she could to the two backpacks lying together near the sleds. Kneeling on the ground, Hannah rummaged through her knapsack and retrieved her leather-bound book.

"It's here," she said, pressing the book to her breast and sitting down. "Thank goodness."

"What do you have there?" A woman spoke from above Hannah's head. "It looks like you have a story book."

Hannah looked into the face of Dennis' wife, Carla. "My children like storybooks," Carla said while leaning forward and rubbing her work-worn hands. She pressed her thin lips together and peered at the cover of the book. "Maybe, you will let me read it to my children."

Hannah looked at the woman's dark, aquiline features. Dirty, black hair streaked with gray framed her face and fell lose over her shoulders.

"When we are safe," Bobby answered her. "You can read it then."

Hannah gave Bobby a slight smile before placing the book into the backpack. Slipping the backpack over her shoulders, she stood up. People were starting to congregate in a group preparing to leave. Several young men began pulling on ropes attached to the sleds stacked with supplies. The sleds started to move, scrapping furrows in the landscape.

Hannah and Bobby followed behind the procession of vagabonds as they proceeded west toward the abandoned city. Everyone was a migrant now, Hannah thought. Even those with papers would have to prove they were legal and that could be difficult or impossible. Hannah looked back over her shoulder for a last look at the wreckage

The man with the broken ribs decided not to leave the wreckage. Even after taking morphine, his pain was still too unbearable to be moved. He lay in the shade of one of the boxcars and watched his companions turn their backs and walk away. A vast desert surrounded them and a blazing sun hung directly over their heads. Bobby took Hannah's hand and gave it a gentle squeeze.

"When we are old," he said. "We will talk about this. And when we get to Canada, everything will be green."

"And Annie will help us," Hannah told him. "Annie and her husband and her children will help us." They looked into each other's eyes, and there was hope.

CHAPTER EIGHT
The Garden
Oakbourgh

"You are a dangerous woman, aren't you, Mrs. Montoya?" Gage spoke in a matter of fact tone as he sat beside Rebecca in the golf cart as it floated a few feet above the ground. They had just left the barbecue and were on their way to the greenhouses. Darkness was falling and the disappearing sun sent streaks of magenta, yellow and orange across the western sky. The air was still stifling hot. Rebecca looked at Gage and he noticed her expression change from deep concentration to one of curiosity.

"You pointed out to me," Gage said. "About the danger our corporate wives present. Might I remind you that you are the wife of the king of all corporate kings? That would make you the most dangerous wife of them all."

"Fear of danger has never been one of your weaknesses, Officer Gage." Rebecca faced forward as she spoke. "Actually, you have very little weaknesses that I can see." She turned her head toward Gage and cast him a sly smile.

Gage threw his head back and laughed. He shifted his position in the soft leather seat and stared straight ahead.

"I'm used to danger." Gage weighed each word as he spoke. "I'm even use to battlefield politics. But this palace intrigue is way out of my league."

"I doubt that anything is out of your league, Mr. Gage." Rebecca's eyes danced with amusement. "World Tech wants this girl, Hannah." Rebecca leaned toward Gage, her voice calm and serious. "A few days ago World Tech organized a, shall we say, phony attack on Oakbourgh. Our corporation hired militiamen to dress as migrants and to set off explosions within the second wall. . .in the area where Hannah lives. Their goal was to enter a few houses, rough up the people, rob them and take Hannah. The plan worked in scaring the daylights out of the workers, but Hannah was nowhere to be found. Even her family was surprised she was gone."

"So, World Tech wants this girl," Gage said. "If they want her so badly, all you have to do is pick her up. The corporations answer to no one. Why all this game playing with explosives and pretend migrants? Why do you need me?"

Rebecca sighed, moistened her lips and then gave a verbal command for the cart to stop. She turned her body to face Gage.

"Ever since the massacre," she began, "Our corporate leaders have been a bit nervous. Not that we haven't had uprisings in the past, of course we have, but things are different now. The Eight is growing stronger. They have become highly organized and the support from the workers is growing. This phony attack will do two things. First, it will keep the workers more distrustful and fearful of the migrants. Fear is a powerful weapon. Second, World Tech could take Hannah and the kidnapping would be blamed on the migrants."

"Okay," Gage said. "So, what does The Eight have to do with this girl? She is only a girl."

"Hannah has something everyone wants. The Eight want it and the employers want it. Look," Rebecca said as she leaned back in her seat. "One of Hannah's ancestors was one of the original Eight. He was a biologist and a college professor and he worked on the Blue Eden project.

"So you and the corporations believe in the Blue Eden myth?" Gage said.

"It is only a myth until we have proof it exists," Rebecca told him. "When we prove a myth is real, the entire universe changes and that proof is what Hannah is holding, or at least that is what we believe she is holding. If there ever was a Blue Eden project, it was buried in secrecy a century ago. According to the myth, the governments had to stop the project because of what was happening here on earth. The ice sheets melted much faster than the scientists predicted and the migrations had started right away.

"Organized governments fell, and as you know, wealthy corporate leaders stepped in to fill the void. Resources became scarce if not impossible to obtain. Those with the greatest control of the remaining resources were the ones guaranteed to survive the longest. Natural resources fell into the control of corporations, not democratic governments."

"And your family was and still is on the top of that food chain."

Rebecca gave a slight nod of agreement. "My ancestor was one of the fifty people who met on a private island in the South Pacific in nineteen ninety-nine. Those people who came together that day realized that global warming was changing the planet, but they also knew that wealth was power and that those with the highest concentration of wealth would survive in that future world no matter what situation occurred. Those people knew that climate change was about science, but not just about science. It was about business and politics and wielding influence. Their goal was to ensure that there was no balance of power. All earth's resources would fall under their control.

Rebecca paused and continued speaking while looking up at the night sky.

"Corporations gained that control by denying science or at least spinning science to fit their interest. Think how the people would have reacted if they'd discovered our leaders had created a viable biosphere on another planet and at the same time allowed our planet to die."

"I've heard all of this," Gage said. "But it's only myth. You can't believe this?"

Rebecca looked at him and smiled. "The history is not myth," she said. "All documents concerning Blue Eden were either destroyed or at least they were supposed to be. Eight scientists began collecting information and hiding it. Those eight scientists grew in number and the society of The Eight was formed. The new corporate governments, controlled by the corporations, hunted those people down. When they were captured, they were publicly denounced as anarchists and then executed. But, other leaders stepped forward to take their place. The Society of The Eight became a criminal organization and was driven underground."

"I understand," Gage said. "There came a point when the corporate leaders started believing their own lies. But now, it is not just the peasants who are dying because of lack of resources, the lives of the corporate kings are also in jeopardy. This entire planet will become uninhabitable. If there really is a safe harbor somewhere, the corporate kings and their families will be the first to arrive there. Blue Eden will belong to them."

"Yes," Rebecca said. "But right now I want to show you the Montoya private gardens."

She started the golf cart and gave the command, "Greenhouses."

After about fifteen minutes, the cart came to a stop in front of a manned guardhouse beside a walled area and a closed gate. An armed sentential, after observing the occupants of the golf cart, bowed, pushed a button and the gate swung open. Rebecca manually took control of the steering wheel and navigated the golf cart through the huge compound filled with hundreds of large, commercial greenhouses stretching, Gage thought, for miles in all directions.

Floodlights mounted on poles lit the narrow arteries between the rows of huge glass structures, each numbered and labeled. Stopping in front of one of the greenhouses, Rebecca alighted from the cart, unlocked and swung open a door to one of the structures. She then guided the golf cart through the wide door and into an indoor citrus orchard covering what appeared to be the length of three football fields. A glass ceiling stood about 65 feet over their heads and the building appeared to be about 50 feet wide.

Gage choked and held his nose against a strong citrus odor that burned his nose.

Laughing, Rebecca said, "You'll get use to the smell, Officer Gage. I know you're not used to the smell of real citrus. This is real fruit, not the synthetic paste everyone else consumes." She smiled at him. "These are the Montoya private gardens."

Gage watched Rebecca's delicate fingers twist two oranges from a type of fruit tree that was now almost extinct. Gage realized that the only places these trees existed were in private collections like this one.

"We'll save this fruit for later," she told him. "Come on. There's a lot more I want to show you."

They boarded the golf cart again, left the citrus structure and wound their way through a maze of greenhouses each one functioning as a microenvironment, closed and self-sustaining, and unaffected by outside weather conditions. Each section of the enclosed arboretums contained a transplant garden area and lath house, growth chambers and walk-in growth rooms.

All the greenhouses were connected on one side to a common head house or narrow service building that included a small laboratory, work areas for potting, cold storage, offices and supply rooms.

Gage and Rebecca wandered through vegetable and flower gardens and fields of corn and grain, stopping on occasion to pick fruit or vegetables. Militia patrolled the outside perimeter and the greenhouse workers would not come to work until morning. Gage and Rebecca were alone amidst miles of privately owned industrial sized, enclosed gardens.

"We call this The Farm," Rebecca told Gage as they traveled through the uninhabited growing houses. "You know we grow crops on the outside between the first and second walls, but. . ."

"But," Gage interrupted her. "That food is for the peasants. Most of those fields are mined. They're really used as a barrier between the inner city and the migrants."

"Yes, you are correct, Officer Gage. We use those crops to produce protein paste. There are private gardens similar to this one in cities all over the world, but I'm sure you understand that Oakbourgh's water is amazingly clean and free from contamination. So, the food we grow here is safe. Our factories produce food that has taste and nutrition and is healthy."

Gage watched Rebecca's face as she spoke and sensed a sadness shrouding her spirit.

"My grandmother told me stories about a time when these trees and plants were everywhere on the planet and grew outside under a blue sky."

"A Blue Eden," Gage said. "Only a myth."

Rebecca sighed and the sadness lifted. She stopped the cart and turned toward Gage.

"Have you ever tasted a peach?"

Gage stared at her.

"I mean a real peach, not a manufactured, artificial peach, but a real one," she said.

Before he could answer, Rebecca picked up two fresh peaches and placed one in his hand. The peaches were round, firm and covered in thick fuzz. Gage glared at the peach. What was he supposed to do with it?

Rebecca laughed, then she bit into the fruit. Juice squirted out of the peach and ran down her hand and arm. Rebecca's expression of pure pleasure did not escape Gage. She took another bite.

"Try it," she said. An artificial peach has no juice, Gage realized before following her instructions to taste the real fruit. Soon both he and Rebecca were covered in sticky peach juice.

Laughing freely, they each consumed several more peaches carefully placing the pits in a box on a work table.

"There is one more place I want to show you before we have to leave." Rebecca said. "This is my special space, my private garden where I go to escape from everything." Gage allowed her to take his arm and she gave it a tug.

Gage and Rebecca left the cart and walked through the fruit garden into an adjacent greenhouse.

Before his eyes could adjust to the darkness, Gage felt a soft mist dance on his face and he heard the sound of a waterfall. Lights attached to 65' tall ceilings filtered artificial sunlight down through a thick canopy of colorful blossoms and giant leaves attached to massive tree trunks that rose upward to more than 50'.

Rebecca took his hand and led him down a dirt path overgrown with vegetation. They brushed aside hanging vines covered with fragrant flowers. The sound of the waterfall became louder as they entered a clearing containing a man-made pond. A waterfall tumbled down a rock embankment and splashed into the pond sending a spray of cool water into the air.

Rebecca smiled up into his face; her eyes so much like the dancing waterfall, Gage thought. He watched her walk to the water's edge, kneel and dip her hands in the water to wash off the peach juice. She splashed the water over her face and though her hair. Gage knelt beside her and did the same. The pond was cool as was the mist that continued to float on the air.

Rebecca kicked off her shoes and stepped into the water. She unbuttoned her blouse, allowed it to slip over her shoulders and tossed it to the ground. Gage's body tightened and warmed as he watched her remove her clothing and dive naked into the pond. His eyes followed her as she swam to the center of the pond and waved for him to enter. He stripped off his clothes and joined her. They swam around in circles and splashed the water on each other. Rebecca caught his face in her hands and kissed him on his lips. Gage felt her breast brush against his chest and he caught his breath. He questioned her with his eyes.

"Officer Gage, I am your employer and can do as I please."

"And I, Mrs. Montoya, am a man with needs from a woman whether she is my employer or my employee." He found her lips and she accepted his embrace.

There was another time when he had felt such peace, another place where his memories feared to travel.

"Why are you looking so pensive?" Rebecca said as they both lay naked by the water's edge.

Gage propped himself on his elbow and kissed Rebecca's face. "You're a married woman, Mrs. Montoya, and married to the most powerful man in the world."

"My husband cares about my money and my name. He has taken a second wife and she is pregnant. What I do is of no concern to him."

She sat up and her expression changed to one of urgency. "We have to go, now. We have to meet your two mercenaries. They should be waiting in the hotel room behind the second wall."

Rebecca stood and started to dress. Gage sat up and watched her.

"We'll go back to my house and pack our things," she said. "Our mission starts tonight. We still need two more names from you, Officer Gage. Men you can trust and men you can control. Our time is growing short. Hannah must be found."

CHAPTER NINE
The Ruins
The Desert

Hannah and Bobby had been walking for what seemed like hours. A shudder ran through Hannah's body as she looked over her shoulder. The train wreck was no longer in sight. Instead, all she saw was a vast desert of gray dirt inserted with an occasional clump of scrub brush. Was it her imagination that a trail of black smoke streaked across the cloudless sky? Was it a gun ship? A mirage?

Gritty dust stirred by a sudden breeze, swirled through the air, slapped against Hannah's sunburned face and invaded her eyes. Blinded by the dirt, Hannah stopped and placed her hands over her face. The straps from her backpack dug into her shoulders and muddy tears flowed down Hannah's face. She wiped the tears from her eyes with the end of the cloth hanging from her head.

Survivors moved past her, walking at a slow, steady pace, staring straight ahead. Behind the group of survivors came the men pulling the sleds through the dirt. Those men had stopped many times to change positions and sometimes had even hoisted the sleds onto their shoulders. Parents carried their young children for a while until they became too heavy. Exhaustion was epidemic. To Hannah, everyone and everything seemed to be floating in a lifeless ocean made of dirt and rocks. A sprawling city lay before her, appearing more like a neglected graveyard than a place of refuge. What would they find there? She wondered. A place to rest? Shade? Bandits?

"Don't be frightened," Bobby told Hannah. "When we get to Canada, everything will be green. And Annie will help us."

"Yes," Hannah whispered. "Annie and her husband and her children will help us and when we are old, we will talk about this adventure to our grandchildren." Hannah smiled, although her throat was dry and her cracked lips tasted of blood.

Bobby's complexion looked pallid beneath his sunburned and slightly swollen face. His nose had begun to peel. Hannah noticed him limping as he lifted a plastic bottle of water to his lips and drank, then handed it to Hannah.

"Wash your face with this," he said. "Get the dirt out of your eyes. You'll feel better."

Hannah took the bottle and was splashing water on her face when the sound of a crash and men yelling broke the silence of the desert. She and Bobby turned to look back at the commotion, but most of the migrants continued moving forward as though in a daze.

Behind the procession of migrants, a brawl had broken out between several of the young men who had been pulling the sleds. Three of them were now pounding their fists into each other and screaming obscenities. Two others, their hands locked around each other's throats, crashed together on top of a sled, rolled across it and tumbled to the ground. Bottles of water and boxes of food flew in every direction.

Children began wailing and someone screamed.

"I've been telling you and telling you," a woman's voice cried out. "There's a man out there and he's telling us to go away. We have to go back."

"I see water out there," a man said with excitement. "It's coming down from the sky. Can't you see it? It's a sign."

Two of the men began to wander away from the group, their eyes fixed on some distinct mirage. Their wives hastened after them, grabbing their arms to bring them back.

Dennis and two of the accountants were attempting to pull the combatants apart when the old man who had buried his wife, picked up one of the brawlers as though he were a rag doll and threw him away from the fight. Landing on the ground, the young aggressor attempted to get up, but instead fell backwards too weak and disoriented to stand.

Hannah plopped on the ground and watched the old man douse the combatants with water. Bobby sat down beside her, took a long drink from his bottle of water and then splashed the liquid over his face. Many of the migrants were also collapsing where they stood. Even though water at this point was in good supply, the blistering sun, blowing dirt and constant fear was taking its toll.

"We can walk another fifteen minutes," Dennis shouted at the depleted travelers. "Just fifteen minutes and we can make it to those ruins over there on the outskirts of the city. There's shade and we can rest." His eyes darted rapidly over the group of men, women and children. "We'll have to leave the sleds here. We can come back for them after nightfall. Take what food, water and medicine you can carry in your packs. We'll eat and rest when we get to the ruins." His words flew with the constant wind that was picking up speed and growing stronger. It tugged on people's head coverings and wailed like a phantom screaming warnings of what lay ahead.

"Don't let those people wander off," Dennis yelled, pointing to the men who were stumbling off into the desert. "Bring them back here. They're chasing illusions."

"But they can see water and trees out there." someone said. "I can see it too."

"It's an illusion," Dennis yelled. "The water isn't real. Not everyone sees the same mirage, but everyone can see those ruins and the city. They're real. But the water isn't real. Look. We have to keep walking. Only a little longer. When we get to the ruins, we'll be able to sleep. And don't take your shoes off," Dennis shouted, pointing his finger at a woman. "You'll never get them back on. Your feet will swell the minute you remove your shoes."

A plump woman sitting with her husband and toddler, glared at Dennis, but obeyed his orders. She retied her shoes and allowed her husband to help her to stand, her swollen feet still stuffed in her shoes.

"Come on, kids. We have to go." Hannah looked up into the bright, blue eyes of the old man who had buried his wife. Shoulder-length, brown hair streaked with gray framed his tanned, weathered face covered in whiskers.

"My name's Zack," he said as he held his hand out to help Hannah stand. "Girl, it's time to go. We can't stay here."

The exhausted survivors were starting to move again, their eyes stoically fixed on the distant city. Some looked back at the supplies they were leaving behind, but most shouldered their packs and stumbled forward. An ancient, asphalt road, broken and covered by the dirt and sand pointed toward their destination.

Hannah took the old man's large, calloused hand. He lifted her up in the air before setting her on the ground. "I'm Hannah. And this is Bobby," She said as her best friend rose to his feet. The old man nodded.

"The first rule of desert hiking is to walk slowly," Zack said to Hannah and Bobby as they joined the battered group stumbling toward the city. "You're going to have to force yourself to slow down because your natural reaction out here may be panic. Stay calm. This is your best bet to survive." Zack's low, gravel like voice soothed Hannah and urged her forward even though her feet were killing her.

"We couldn't walk fast if we wanted to," Bobby said.

"When we get to those ruins, there will be some shade." Zack said his eyes fixed on the horizon. "You can prop your feet up then and take your shoes off. It's important you only take your shoes off if you can find shade and elevate your feet. Otherwise, your feet will swell and you might not be able to get your shoes back on. Remember," Zack said. "You could die from heat stroke, so this is no time to save your water."

Hannah felt that Zack was talking to himself most of the time, but his voice comforted her and kept her focused.

"Apply water to your armpits and groin area," Zack said. "Those are two areas that will help most to lower your body temperature. Kids, we're almost to the ruins. We can take a break and rest in the shade. That will keep your spirits up."

Hannah listened to the old man's voice and felt the weight of fear loosen its grip. Straight ahead lay the city, beyond that the Rocky Mountains. Somewhere north was Canada and here, lost in this wind-blown hell was this tattered group of survivors.

As they walked, gusts of warm wind from the south stirred up frightening dust devils, sending dirt and small rocks rolling across the flat desert. Little vortexes of swirling air danced across the land like angry spirits pelting the exposed survivors with choking dust and stinging sand.

"Legend says that dust devils are the spirits of our dead ancestors walking the world once again," Zack said to those in the group who would listen. "If the spirit is good, its dust devil will rotate clockwise and if the spirit is bad, it will rotate counter clockwise. Some are powerful spirits that can even grant wishes."

"Then I wish we were in Canada." Bobby's voice rasped from his raw throat.

Hannah's heart almost stopped when loud gasps and wails of terror began rising up from the battered procession. On either side of the crumbling highway, lay the remains of thousands of partially exposed human bones. Earthquakes and more than a century of violent windstorms had unearthed an immense forgotten burial ground. Pieces of bleached skeletons protruded from their graves and skulls rolled across the parched earth as the wind tossed them about like yesterday's trash.

"The Ditchings," someone said and the word spread like a flash fire through the band of migrants. "Ditchings. Ditchings." A mummer from the band of survivors soon turned into sobs and cries. Hannah held on to Bobby's hand and looked into his eyes. He nodded to her without saying a word.

Everyone knew about the Ditchings. Hannah's grandmother had talked about them and schoolchildren had whispered and shivered over the stories of the Ditchings. Within a period of a few years, hundreds of millions, perhaps even billions of people on earth had died and were buried in long shallow ditches, dug in a hurry with no time for sacraments and with no one to grieve. These were the poor souls abandoned by humanity and left to be forgotten. The spirits of the Ditchings, the stories said, were angry and not at peace. They stalked the living and when they found a person alone or vulnerable, the tortured souls of the Ditchings took revenge against the unfortunate victim.

Every child knew that the Ditchings started long ago in another time when the earth was cooler, wetter and green. Billions of people shared the world with many strange and amazing species of animals. At that time, gigantic continents of ice existed on the poles of the planet, and as Hannah remembered her grandmother's stories, soft wet ice sometimes fell from the sky in the winter. This cold, white ice covered the higher mountains, and in summer the soft ice melted and turned into rivers of fresh water that flowed across the land. However, for anyone to repeat these stories was now illegal and dangerous. History was written by the corporate historians. Any other version was heresy. Yet, that very ban made these tales even more exciting as they passed from one person to the next.

"Truth is power," Hannah's grandmother used to say. "Those who keep the truth from others, hold power over those who choose to accept the lies. It was a time of death and fear," Hannah's grandmother, Maddie, told her when they were snuggled together in their attic. She would whisper the stories in a quiet serious voice. "The great glaciers and ice sheets were melting," she always began, "causing the seas to rise and to swallow the land. They melted slowly at first, but as time passed, they began to disappear at a much faster rate."

Maddie also told Hannah of how the glaciers melted and the temperature across the globe began to rise ever higher causing the ice to melt even faster. Since ice glaciers were able to reflect nearly 80% of the sun's heat, when those glaciers began vanishing, earth got warmer at a faster rate. This rise in temperature changed the course of weather patterns and the temperatures of the oceans causing violent climatic reactions.

Storms raged across the continents and tsunami like waves slammed against the coastlines covering cities and lowlands beneath hundreds of feet of ocean. Rivers and lakes overran their boundaries, mixing with the seawater and contaminating the fresh water supplies with salt water, upsetting the balance between fresh and salt water. Ocean life began to disappear.

When the ice melted, poisons trapped in the frozen ice for centuries were released back into the oceans destroying thousands of species of fish, animals and flying creatures. The ozone protections grew weaker and the sun's rays stronger.

Fresh water supplies dried up and droughts spread across West Africa, Central and South America, southern Europe and the southern portion of North America. Forestland and farmlands disappeared at an ever increasing pace, taking with them the food supply for billions of people.

Without the constant flow of water from melting glaciers, the production of electricity stopped in many places around the planet. The world went dark. It was called the Second Age of Darkness. Barbarism governed and plagues stole the lives of both the powerful and the weak. The dead were ditched and abandoned.

However, new communities opened up in the far northern regions of Canada and Siberia where the ice thawed and vegetation started to grow. Decades earlier wealthy investors who knew what was coming, began buying the frozen land and preparing the areas for settlement. Those corporate moguls built forts, stocked them with scarce resources and brought armed militia to protect them. Those people who were chosen to work for and to fight for the corporate kings were offered security in exchange for their loyal services.

This protection came with a price. Absolute obedience to those new kings had to be observed. The past had to be forgotten and a new history was written. No one was to speak of or remember the part humanity played in destroying their own environment and their own lives. Think only of today and the kings will provide for you."

Hannah stumbled, tripping over a piece of broken asphalt. Bobby caught her by the arm. "We're here," he said. "There's shelter. You seemed to be walking in your sleep," Bobby told her. "But there's shade here. We can eat and get some sleep."

The weary group of men, women and children came upon a sprawling concrete structure on the edge of the city. It appeared to be the skeletal remains of a huge open space warehouse. Although most of the roof, which was once supported by widely spaced columns, had fallen and the cement walls had crumbled, there was still enough remaining to give everyone shade and protection from the escalating winds.

The dazed and exhausted survivors entered the building through a gaping hole that had once been an oversized, storefront door. They settled down on the dirt covered concrete floor and beneath the covering of the dilapidated roof. Hannah threw her backpack off and began rummaging through its contents. She smiled as she pulled out a bottle of water and a box of protein paste, a food substitute in the form of a thick, sticky mixture of various nutrients and tastes, often spread on a tortilla or cracker. This particular box contained various flavors of paste pre-rolled in tortillas. Hannah unwrapped one of the rolls and sunk her teeth into the tangy tasting concoction. She rolled the mixture around in her mouth, enjoying the fruit-like flavor, then washed it down with gulps of water. Bobby had already swallowed two of the rolls and was devouring a third.

Blinding sunlight poured through jagged holes in the walls and the wind rumbled as it tore at the frail construction of the old building. Dennis' wife sat with a group of women, helping to feed and hydrate their young children. One couple, perhaps newlyweds, huddled together away from the rest of the group and the pretty blond woman with the injured arm sat alone eating a roll of protein paste. The rest of the survivors, both legal and stowaways, were scattered about the old structure. Zack, Dennis and one of the accountants, a tall black man, stood apart from the others in deep conversation. No one else spoke. Even the children stayed quiet, but the wind kept up a constant wailing. Maybe Hannah slept. She was not sure, but a collection of frightened voices jolted her to her senses.

"Wake up. Hannah, wake up." Someone shook her. "We have to leave. Now."

The sound of the wind was louder. Loose boards torn from the roof of the building, blew through the air like pieces of paper. Parents gathered their children leaving their packs where they lay. In the confusion, Hannah searched the floor for her backpack. Finding it, she tossed it over her shoulder.

"What are you doing?" Bobby said, his voice rushed and frightened. "Leave that thing here. We have to run." He grabbed her arm and pulled her toward the opening. "Look," he said pointing south across the desert. A wall of reddish-brown dirt, hundreds of feet high, rolled toward the crumbling shelter. The dark monster stretched across the wide horizon, ripped at the sky with angry talons, blocking the sun behind a cloud of furry. Static electricity crackled and flashed.

Hannah choked on heavy dirt that washed over her like a tidal wave.

"Run, Hannah. Run."

CHAPTER TEN
The Mission
Oakbourgh

The mission had started. Gage and Rebecca left the confines of the greenhouses and returned to the Montoya mansion to collect their belongings. Except for his weapons, all Gage needed was a single duffle bag. The original assault rifle had changed little over the past centuries. If anything, it had become smaller and lighter making it easier to carry, more deadly and more accurate. Gage checked the weapon before packing it in his bag. It would not be needed for a while.

Gage buckled himself into a chest rig holster and adjusted the straps for comfort. The night was going to be long. He holstered two handguns concealed beneath his long sleeved, light-green shirt. Civilian clothes tonight – his uniform would stay packed for use later.

After placing a double-edged fighting knife into a holster strapped inside his boot, Gage arraigned his black, loose-fitting pant leg over the weapon. A knife, Gage reasoned, is a weapon of last resort. Using a knife requires close contact and that means he would be dealing with a serious threat. It is always better to maintain a distance with a longer range weapon. However, if he found himself in a close quarter situation, a knife would be effective if he could get to it and if he could hold on to it. At that close range, Gage knew, he would be covered in his attacker's blood. In the heat of battle and with his adrenaline raging, an attacker could be stabbed or slashed with a knife and not even feel it. On the other hand, getting hit with a blunt object could take an attacker down in an instant. A good shot with a stick to the hand, knee or shin could break bones and render the assailant vulnerable.

Gage was ready. Clean shaven, hair barbered, clothes pressed, weapons secure he picked up his duffle bag and slung it over his shoulder. Leaving his bedroom, which was next to Rebecca's, he walked down the hall toward an office on the left. The house appeared to be empty. Rebecca's room was on the opposite side of the house from her husband's quarters and from where Montoya's second wife had a suite. This wing of the house was often deserted.

Gage entered a small office and walked to a set of French doors that opened to a balcony facing the back of the house. Moonlight, like a spotlight, shown down on two figures standing next to a small electric car. He hurried down a set of spiraling, wooden steps connecting the balcony with the ground and approached the two figures both dressed in full burkas.

Rebecca lifted her veil and smiled at him. "You're going to drive," she said. "I'll tell you where to go. Get in. The engine is running." She turned and climbed into the backseat of the small vehicle. Patricia followed her.

After placing his bag in the trunk with the women's luggage, Gage folded himself into the driver's seat. His long legs bent into an uncomfortable position.

"The trunk of this vehicle is bigger than the passenger area," he said as he guided the car away from the house and onto the road.

They passed down well-kept residential streets and through a shopping area filled with clothing stores, restaurants and a collection of shops containing, it seemed, nearly all the luxuries of life. Glittering lights and an array of shrubs lined immaculate sidewalks, but the streets were empty. A little further down the road the wall came into view, a massive stone and concrete edifice topped with razor wire and gun towers. That was the third wall, encircling the region inhabited by the ruling classes: the senators; high-ranking government officials; the corporate royalty and their families.

Walls within walls within walls, Gage thought, as they approached the enormous iron gates separating the elite from the workers. A sentry stepped out from a small guardhouse and Gage stopped the car. When he rolled down the window, a hot breeze brushed across his face and the stench of garbage filled the air. The young guard leaned over and perused the occupants of the vehicle, but when Gage showed him his papers, the corporal saluted and waved him through the gates.

Now, they were in the middle section of the city sandwiched between the second and third walls. Whereas the third wall protected the corporate elite, the second wall encircled the working section of the city. Broken and rutted, dirt or asphalt roads and alleyways crisscrossed between factories, company stores, hospitals and warehouses. Rows of well-built, as well as substandard employee housing sat adjacent to factories, railroad tracks and a small airport.

Rebecca guided him along 17th Avenue or The Avenue of the March as the road was unofficially called. That road wound its way from the gates of the third wall, through the heart of the town, to the gates of the second wall. Beyond those gates lay flourishing including grain, tobacco and marijuana. That agricultural area operated as the town's first line of defense.

An outer, or first wall, encircled the entire settlement as well as the agricultural fields. Each of the three encirclements of walls were topped with gun towers and pacing militia.

The first stop for Gage and his companions was The Edmond Hotel, an eight-story structure encompassing an entire city block in the industrial portion of Oakbourgh. Although it was almost ten o'clock at night, late business deals over dinner and couples returning from evening movies kept the streets in that section of town buzzing with pedestrians and cabs. Once the factory night shifts let out, the streets would also be filled with workers scurrying home or to the bars for a few drinks before the two o'clock curfew.

Gage pulled over and stopped next to the curb in front of The Edmond. It was an old hotel with no loading area and the front door of the building opened onto the sidewalk. The three passengers got out of the car. Gage removed the luggage from the trunk and threw his duffle bag, containing his weapons, in the back seat of the car. He placed the women's bags on the pavement by the hotel entrance where a door attendant stood ready to call a porter. Patricia and Rebecca stayed with their bags while Gage parked the car in a dark alleyway a few blocks away.

With his duffle bag slung over his shoulder, Gage walked down the well-lit main street to the Edmond, keeping close vigil on his surroundings. He entered the seedy, yet spacious hotel lobby with worn and faded furnishings. A once luxurious green carpet, now soiled and patched, covered the floor. Rebecca and Patricia were waiting for him by the front counter, their bags encircling their feet.

"We're meeting some people here," he told the bushy-haired clerk behind the check-in counter. "The name's Turner."

Without saying a word, the young man entered something on a computer, gave a terse smile and a slight nod of approval.

"Yes, sir," he said. Two gentlemen are waiting for you in room three sixteen. Sir, you will be joining them in room three sixteen and the ladies are in room three eighteen. Enjoy your stay." As an afterthought, he added, "Ah, do you need help with your luggage?"

Gage shook his head, no. The ladies picked up their bags, holding one suitcase in each hand while Gage carried his duffle bag with the assault weapon inside. The elevator took them to the third floor where they followed a long corridor covered with a threadbare green carpet. They stopped at room 316. Gage gave two rapid knocks on the door and stood aside. As he waited for a response, he placed his hand on his holstered gun.

"Who's there?" a familiar voice called through the door.

"It's me. Gage."

A bolt clanged and the door opened a crack.

"Diego. It's me. Open up," Gage said.

The door was pulled open and in the doorway stood a clean-shaven man with a short, stocky build and close-cropped dark hair. A broad smile spread across his face. He grabbed Gage's hand, slapped him on the shoulder with the other hand and pulled him into the room.

The two women followed and placed their luggage beside one of two double beds with dull orange coverings. A small television was the only decoration hanging on a soiled, bare wall. Another man shut the door and threw the bolt.

"Johnson," Gage said taking the man's hand. "It's been a while. Good to see you old buddy."

"So, what's going on?" Johnson said. He was speaking to Gage, but looking at the women. Johnson, like Diego and Gage, was clean-shaven and dressed as a traveling executive, yet his steel blue eyes revealed there were less innocent talents buried beneath his respectable exterior.

"Man, I never saw anything like it." Diego's words spit out like a machine gun. "I was in Russia. They called me up to the commander's office and I was handed orders. Bam. Just like that. I was on a plane, World Tech plane. I'm tellen ya." He rubbed his hands over his short hair. "And I'm tellen ya. There was no one on that plane 'cept me, the pilot and the goon who met me at the tarmac. The goon escorted me onto the plane and then he just sat there during the flight. Wouldn't say a word. Then, that pilot and that goon switched me to another plane. Wow. This plane was something. Wasn't it the same with you, Johnson? "

Johnson nodded. "Yea. Except I was in the Andes." He took a cigarette from his pocket, placed it between his lips and lit it.

"And that second plane," Diego said. "Well, let me tell ya. Well. . .these people. I sure don't know what you call these people, but they told me to wash up. So I did. Then they gave me a shave and a haircut and these new clothes. Said my orders were to be a clean-cut businessman. Come to this hotel, give the name Turner and wait in this room for further orders. Next thing you know Johnson's here and now you. Still don't have further orders."

"You do, now." Rebecca said. She and Patricia had taken off their veils and thrown them on the bed. "Let's sit at that table over there." She motioned toward the window and a small round table with four chairs. Closed drapes darkened the room, but two bedside lamps with dirty shades supplied the room with a veiled light.

"I guess I haven't introduced you to our boss," Gage said. "Rebecca Montoya and her. . .ah. . .assistant, Patricia"

Rebecca nodded and walked to the table. The two men looked from the women to Gage. This was, Gage knew, an unfamiliar and curious situation for these hardened mercenaries. They were on edge and their quick minds were in tune with their survival instincts. However, they followed Rebecca to the table and took seats. Patricia joined them in the fourth chair and Gage sat on the edge of one of the beds.

"Your mission was supposed to be very simple," Rebecca began. "You were supposed to go to an address here in the factory section and pick up a young girl. She has something we need and you were supposed to get her to give it to you. It's a book. And no, she would not have come with you willingly nor would she have given you the book willingly. Your job would have been to convince her."

Diego lit a cigarette, inhaled and leaned back in his chair. "Yeah, simple," he said.

"So, when you say we, who is we?" Johnson said, his eyes focused on Rebecca's face. Rebecca glanced at him and continued without answering. "The problem is. . .the girl Hannah disappeared two nights ago. We have to find her. The information she has is absolutely necessary to our mission. In time you will understand how important this is, but for now you have to be patient."

Gage's two friends studied Rebecca's face, but remained quiet.

"There was another attempt by World Tech to pick up the girl." Patricia spoke with authority. "Militiamen, dressed as migrants, attacked the city a couple of nights ago. They came into the city and actually went through people's houses, robbed some, but in other homes took nothing. In reality, they were looking for Hannah. They never found her. She was gone when they got to her house."

Patricia took a deep breath and wet her lips. Her dark eyes surveyed the room. "Now, Hannah could be hiding somewhere in the city. Last week, her father signed papers giving Hannah in marriage to an older man. The marriage was only on paper but a ceremony was forthcoming. Not something

Hannah wanted or could ever accept. My guess is that she has left Oakbourgh. Our people are searching the city for her. As you know, it is difficult to hide behind these walls. If she is here, we will know and we will find her."

The men listened to this story with interest.

"A boy, a close friend of Hannah's, also disappeared on the same night," Patricia said. "We believe she is with him and we are pretty sure they both left the city together. They think they have a place to go in Canada. Bobby, the girl's friend, has a cousin living in Canada. However, there is no indication that Hannah or Bobby have been in contact with this cousin, nor any indication that they know what has happened to Bobby's cousin."

"What do you mean, what has happened to the cousin?" Johnson said.

Rebecca drummed her fingers on the table and said, "Annie Miller, Bobby's cousin, has been arrested and sentenced to death for treason. She is scheduled to die."

Diego gave a long, slow whistle and looked at Johnson who blew smoke from his cigarette.

"That means that even if Hannah and Bobby make it to Canada, there will be no one to go to. No one to help them."

The men were quiet.

"One avenue we will explore is the fact that if Hannah and Bobby left the city, they would need help," Rebecca said. "If they decided to cross the desert alone, they would never make it. They would absolutely need help. As you know, there is a thriving smuggling business operating around the globe and there are factions here in Oakbourgh. People are smuggled into Canada, Siberia, Ireland wherever workers are needed. We think Hannah and Bobby are with the smugglers."

Rebecca paused and took a deep breath.

"Bobby's employer reported that on the night Bobby left, a large sum of money also disappeared from their premises.

How that boy got his hands on this money is anyone's guess, but a lot of money is needed to pay smugglers. A lot of money is missing including marijuana and some heroin."

"It would not have been hard for Bobby to find these mobsters," Rebecca said. "Even the smallest of the cartels operate like a business operation. There's recruiters everywhere involved in voluntary human-smuggling and they almost never take people against their will anymore."

"They don't have to do that," Gage said "Crossing borders illegally is the only way average people can move from one city to the next these days. Our corporate government insists that everyone have papers to explain who they are and where they belong and you need these papers before you ask permission to travel,"

Diego ran his hand through his hair. "Yeah, and as you know, movement is heavily restricted and permission is almost never given unless you are on assignment with World Tech or an affiliate."

"Okay," Johnson said. "So you think the smuggles have her. What do you want us to do?"

"We need to find out where they took her and we need you to get her back," Rebecca said in a matter of fact voice. "We have a complicated relationship between the smugglers and the legitimate business world. The government knows these operations exist, but even though illegal, the corporations often use these operations to acquire their workers. World Tech works closely with the smugglers to find and recruit workers; especially now."

"We know," Gage said. "There's so much unrest these days, if those workers are under the thumb of the cartels they're less likely to cause trouble."

Johnson finished his cigarette and pushed the butt into an ashtray. "Look," he said. "We know all about smugglers. I try to keep away from them. These smuggling networks control their workers through violence, blackmail, debt, threats to relatives and other low-life means. I've seen it."

Rebecca nodded and said "These workers, on whom the smugglers prey, come mainly from desperate backgrounds, like Hannah and Bobby, making the workers susceptible to the recruiter's lies. They're fed a mixture of romantic immigrant success stories and hope."

"They're tricked into believing they will get decent jobs and a better life," Patricia said. "Instead, the workers are made to work off huge debts that are impossible to repay. Sometimes the smugglers just take their money and leave them in the desert, but most of the time; of course, the workers are delivered to destinations."

"So, you see," Rebecca said. "We're going to find out where that destination is. Gentlemen, tonight we are going to meet some smugglers and get them to talk."

Part IV

September 1
One hundred years in the
future

CHAPTER ELEVEN
The Coliseum
Tent City, Canada

Annie was brought to the place of killing. It was her time to die. She waited with the other condemned prisoners in holding cells beneath the coliseum where sports were played and executions were carried out on a regular basis. The executions gave the unruly population of Tent City, Canada time to think about their own mortality. They encouraged the workers to choose humility and compliance with the governing employers, rather than to engage in criminal activity. Annie huddled in her cell, her mind alive with memories.

She had never been to any of the games at the coliseum, nor had she witnessed an execution. This great sports arena was under construction when Annie and Robert arrived in Canada as teenaged newlyweds so many years ago. At that time, Tent City, Canada was a work camp consisting of thousands of tents stretching across a cold, bleak landscape. Immigrant laborers, like her and Robert, were brought to that northern region to plant vegetation on land that had once been covered by ice and snow. Together, Annie and Robert were assigned a canvas shelter and put to work clearing the hardpan earth for cultivation. The work was grueling, but their dreams of a rich future were happy.

Their children were born, first Alex then the twins, Gilbert and Greta, and life became more difficult and less hopeful. Shanties replaced tents. New construction was everywhere. Cities sprang up on the tundra, but those cities were surrounded by walls. Annie, Robert and their three children continued to live and work outside those walls in a ghetto of mud streets, crime and with little law and order. Since her family did not possess legal citizenship papers, they remained outsiders – migrants.

A decision for Robert to join the corporate militia would put him and his family on the path to citizenship. That would mean education for their children, a corporate house inside the walls and benefits. Fighting for the corporate kings would mean earning the protection and security that came with citizenship. What had been a plan to ensure their citizenship and their salvation, however, now brought Annie to this place of death.

And what about Robert and her children? Will they survive? Everything, every person dies she told herself, but it is what I leave my descendants that will become my legacy. I fought for life, for my children and for a future I knew I would never see. Life will continue after I am gone, but I have to believe that my children will survive.

Annie spoke out loud, "They will not just survive; they will flourish. There will be justice."

Cleated boots against a concrete floor and the rattling of cell doors echoed against stonewalls. Muffled sighs of resignation and whimpers of fear sounded as prisoners were removed from their cells and led down the corroder toward the hangman's noose. Annie waited in solitude in her caged chamber. Her door opened and a burley executioner stood towering over her frail, crouching body.

Strong arms lifted her to a standing position. Hands cuffed, her arms in chains behind her back, Annie coughed and took a deep breath when a black hood was placed over her head.

Large muscular hands shoved her forward and then held her arms to guide her down a narrow corridor where the coldness of a concrete floor stung her bare feet. A sudden gust of wind struck her body and tousled her yellow prison shift as the smooth, cold floor became gravel that stabbed her feet with each step. Annie realized she was in the arena. Her body tightened and her breathing quickened as she heard a loud murmur arise from a crowd.

"Do you ask God for forgiveness for your crimes?" The voice of the chaplain spoke close to her ear. He had the duty to provide spiritual care to prisoners condemned to death.

"It is better you ask for your own forgiveness," Annie spoke into the blindness of her black hood.

She heard a sigh and felt a hand on her shoulder. "Do you admit to your crimes?" A stern voice said. Annie remained silent.

A loud speaker crackled and a solemn voice filled the arena.

"I was appointed to attend the prisoners here and accordingly I began to visit them." The disembodied voice addressed a hushed audience. "I prayed with them and implored them to repent. I asked them to admit their crimes and to relieve their souls from their miserable bounds of sin. I begged them to accept the consequences of their sins and to understand the necessity of repentance. Three of these condemned prisoners standing before us today have shed tears and confessed. Only one still denies her treason."

Annie heard a murmur fill the air around her.

"Our Lords and employers have granted pardons to the following condemned: John Hiltin, condemned for robbery and assault. He has confessed that he has been a most notorious offender; William Hildebrand, condemned for felony, assault and burglary, admits to having been a great sinner; Jacquas Fee, condemned for bank robbery, acknowledges that he has committed many sins. Our gracious Lords and employers have granted clemency to these three truly repentant offenders."

Thunderous cheers emanated from the spectators drowning out the sound of the shackles being detached from the liberated prisoners.

"Annie," someone called from the applauding crowd. "Annie, Annie," voices started to chant. Although she could not see, Annie heard the shouts of the crowd growing louder. The fingers of her jailers, who were standing on each side of her, dug deeper into the flesh of her arms and their breathing became agitated.

A deafening explosion shook the ground causing Annie to stumble against the men who held her. Screams and gun blasts filled the air. Bullets whizzed past her head. More explosions and gunfire erupted as she felt herself being jerked backwards. Heavy bodies fell on top of her, crushing her against the gravel on the arena floor.

Still hooded and with her hands chained behind her back, Annie remained trapped beneath the unmoving bodies that had fallen across her legs and torso. A stampede of feet and panicked voices mingled with the continued sound of gunfire, but Annie was unable to move. Someone grabbed her arms and began dragging her out from under the fallen bodies. She was powerless to fight.

"We're The Eight," a voice told her and the hood was ripped from her head. A sheet was thrown over her body covering her prison clothes.

Annie felt herself lifted into the air and cradled like a child in the arms of an unknown rescuer. Beneath the cover of gunfire, Annie felt herself carried across the arena filled with screaming people firing weapons and shouting an ancient war whoop. The sheet fell away from her face and Annie saw mobs swarm upon the startled guards and topple the gallows. Amidst a throng of terrified people shoving and pushing their way toward the exits, Annie was carried out of the arena

Outside, Annie saw a sea of former spectators scattering in all directions. She was carried to a three-wheeled cycle with a wooden utility trailer attached behind. The waiting driver lifted the lid and Annie was placed inside the box.

"Be patient," a man said and closed the lid over her head.

CHAPTER TWELVE
The Smugglers
Oakbourgh

Curfew was at 2:00 in the morning, which meant the nightclub was starting to close, but the crowds would not leave until the last minute. Gage and Diego sat at a small, square table near the back of the room each nursing a tall beer. Since they needed to keep their senses clear, one drink was all they would allow themselves tonight.

After Johnson escorted Rebecca and Patricia to the plane, he would meet up with Gage and Diego later. Patricia was a curious woman, Gage thought, who moved between two worlds, the elite as well as the underworld. She was the one who made the necessary connections to meet with the smugglers. Gage and Diego were to wait for a contact.

The music blared, cigarette smoke swallowed the air and inebriated patrons either stumbled or were carried to the door. Gage and Diego, dressed as representatives of the corporations, clean-shaven and in expensive Tyson business suits, were not searched at the door for weapons which had been hidden in their body holsters. From the table in the back of the room, Gage took a sip from his beer, leaned back in his chair and observed his surroundings.

Oakbourgh had sixty-six saloons similar to this one and seven brothels in the Theater District adjacent to the factories. Both workers and the elite frequented these sites. For the rich, these escapades served as an entertaining diversion to an idle existence. Employees, however, were held to strict moral and religious rules covering their work and domestic lives. Although the corporate lords observed no religious preference, the corporate employees were required to promise allegiance not only to the corporation, but also to the designated religion specified by the corporate board. Religious attendance was a requirement for any employee and their family. Employees' behavior was watched and controlled. Their clothing, speech and demeanor were monitored. Yet, this sleazy underworld was tolerated by the officials, even encouraged. Law enforcement, in many cases, turned their eyes away.

There were many reasons for this hypocrisy and Gage was wise to them all. These establishments were tentacles of the big corporations. Wages earned in the factories were funneled back to the companies through these establishments and they were extremely profitable. Furthermore, these moral lapses gave society the sense they were bucking the system, even though of course, they were not. The average worker was much more compliant and easy to control if they were allowed a window of opportunity to break the rules in the Bordello District. Although given the nod of approval, these breaches also left the worker vulnerable to blackmail by the employers if the employers chose to tighten their control.

Diego leaned toward Gage and said, "Check out those women over there. I'd say they're wives of senators. Big shots. What d'ya think?" Diego shook his head and took a drink.

Gage looked at Angie and Michelle dancing and drinking with their company workers. He noticed the women dismissing their bodyguards.

"They're World Tech," Gage said. "And it's better they're not here right now."

Diego nodded, leaned back in his chair and waited.

As Gage watched Angie and Michelle leaving the club with chosen companions, he realized that even wives of the corporate kings found it necessary, at times, to break moral rules. Those corporate women were powerless decorations in their husband's ruling world, yet here among the truly powerless, these women believed they were in control. Were these wives really disrespecting their husbands and themselves? Maybe, Gage thought, but in realty those women were above disrespect from anyone. They were queens and the world belonged to them. As long as their husbands were willing to turn their heads, their privileged position in that seedy world gave them responsibility to no one but themselves. "Slumming," as they called their activities in this walled section of town, was to them a stimulating game.

The bawdy and risqué antics performed live on stage this night and every night were well received by the male after-work public. Those lively skits were too coarse for wives and children to attend, but not for men and women who enjoyed the rough and sometimes erotic entertainment. Worries about putting food on the table and a life of drudgery faded with the laughter, a few drinks and tranquilizing drugs.

The taste of trouble caught in Gage's throat like a bitter seed and sent a cold tingle creeping up the back of his neck. Diego, seeming to also sense a problem, sat up straight in his chair, his eyes revealed an alert mind. A dark, thickset man dressed in simple, factory clothes approached their table. He stopped a few feet from them and said, "Mr. Turner?"

"Yes, I'm Turner," Gage said. The man pulled a chair over to the table and sat down. His eyes, small and callous, scrutinized Gage and Diego. "So you're businessmen." It was a statement more than a question. "Let me see your papers."

Gage and Diego produced the false identification Patricia provided them. The man examined the papers and handed them back. "So, you need workers," he said. "What kind?"

"We run factories in Alaska," Diego began. "We've been hit hard with influenza up there and lost a lot of workers."

The smuggler nodded almost, it seemed, disinterested.

"We need to replace them," Diego continued. "We know that Oakbourgh has a large population wanting to relocate."

"We're looking for workers who'll not give us trouble. Workers who are easily controlled," Gage said." We understand your workers are ah. . .accommodating."

Gage leaned forward, scrutinizing the man across the table. This guy is cunning, he thought. Maybe street tough, but not too intelligent. He's only a front man, Gage reasoned, a screener. In addition, he knew there were others in the club watching this interaction. "You know," Gage said. "There's a lot of rebellion in the factories these days. We want our workers kept loyal."

The man nodded in agreement. "We absolutely keep our workers loyal."

Diego sighed and tapped his finger on his beer glass. "We're looking for mostly teenagers," he said. "Maybe fourteen, fifteen years old. And we would like them delivered as soon as possible."

The smuggler kept his hands folded on the table. "Well, it might take some time to find exactly what you're looking for."

Gage gave a slight smile. "We know you already have shipments going out of here," he said. "We were hoping you could divert some of those shipments to us. We'd, of course, pay you double. . .maybe more. We know this is done. It's not a new idea." Gage spread his hands open on the tabletop.

The smuggler rubbed his nose and shifted in his seat. "We did have a shipment go out a few days ago. Mostly young men. Some teenagers. Some old people. Some children."

"Any girls?" Gage asked.

"No. No teenage girls."

"Are you sure?" Gage pressured.

The man rubbed his chin appearing to be nervous. "Well, there might have been one in that last shipment a few days ago. The day the migrants attacked. Hard to tell. The girls a lot of times dress like boys. Thinking they'll be safer that way. I think, maybe, one was a girl." He paused and wet his lips. "So, how many do you want?"

"Why did you think this one was a girl?" Diego asked.

"Two boys came late to the meeting place. Maybe, 'bout age fourteen the both of 'em. One acting all protective. I'm sure the one was a girl and the other one a boyfriend. So, how many girls do you want?

"Look," Gage said. "We'll take that shipment for a start and order some other shipments later. Where did you say this shipment was headed? Where can we meet the workers?"

"The train. . ." The man started to speak but stopped.

"Everybody knows the rails are used to transport these workers." Gage told him. "We just need to know where to pick 'em up."

"Okay," the man said, his breathing getting heavy. "I don't make no decisions on this. I just take the request to my boss. Someone will contact you again. You guys are at the hotel, right?"

Gage and Diego nodded.

The smuggler stood up. "We'll be in contact." He turned and disappeared into the thinning crowd leaving the club.

Gage and Diego finished their beer in silence before leaving the building. Curfew was in less than ten minutes and Gage, dressed in civilian clothes, did not want the hassle of being stopped. Of course, his World Tech militia ID would grant him immunity, but attention is not what he wanted. He knew the smugglers would be watching, so Gage and Diego planned to lead their pursuers back to the hotel room.

Since Rebecca and Patricia were at the airport waiting aboard the plane, the hotel room was empty. Gage and Diego were to stay in the room a couple of hours, rest up if possible, and then meet Johnson who would be waiting with a car. This time frame would keep the smugglers off guard and make it easier to get to the airport without being followed. Maybe.

Time passed. Gage watched television for a while, but grew bored with it. Corporate controlled television blared into everyone's homes and businesses keeping people appraised of the proper ideology.

"Propaganda for the masses," Gage said and shut off the machine.

Gage and Diego changed back into their militia uniforms and packed their business suits in their duffle bags. Gage opened the window and stepped out onto the fire escape. Followed by Diego, Gage descended the metal steps from the third story to the deserted, dimly-lit alley below. The night was sweltering. Coming from an air conditioned room into heat made it, at first, difficult to breath. Sweat formed wet streaks down his uniform, which helped to cool his body.

The two men separated, each following a designated route. Gage walked at an easy pace through the empty streets. He made no effort to hide from the patrols, but instead, when spotted, Gage slowed allowing his uniform to be recognized. The militia saluted and continued on their way. However, the smugglers were not so easy to fool. Someone was behind him. Gage stopped, spun around while positioning his hand to remove his gun from its holster.

Two men, standing in the shadows of a tall building, stepped forward. "So where the hell do ya think you're going, Mr. Businessman?" One of them said his voice a snarl.

All Gage's senses were instantly alert and focused. The click of a weapon sounded behind his head causing him to pause with his hand still on his holstered gun.

"You have some explaining to do," a voice behind him said.

The men in front of Gage were moving toward him, each holding revolvers. He was trapped, but not for long.

Aware of his surroundings, Gage realized he was faced with more than one attacker – maybe others were concealed nearby. However, the man behind him was close enough for him to disarm. These gangsters Gage reasoned, would use their weapons, but firing weapons would alert the patrols. No one here wanted that.

From the corner of his eye, Gage saw both Diego and Johnson coming out from a narrow side street. Without saying a word, his buddies began to apply swift, forceful kicks and punches to the surprised smugglers.

For a moment, the hand holding the gun at Gage's head faltered giving Gage the opportunity to grab the smuggler's gun hand. Pulling the wrist inward with as much force as he could, Gage heard the wrist break causing the man to drop his weapon. In a single swift motion, Gage kicked the gun away and at the same time rendered a powerful punch to the smuggler's jaw knocking the man to the ground. As the assailant struggled to get up, Gage planted a boot in the side of his head and the man went limp.

Picking up the discarded gun, Gage noticed that Johnson and Diego had disabled the other two smugglers. All three lay sprawled, unmoving upon the pavement. Gage nodded at his two allies.

"Got a car around the corner." Johnson said in a hushed voice. "Let's go."

Gage and his two partners walked away from the dying and injured men and climbed into a small vehicle parked in the shadows of an alleyway. No one said a word as Johnson guided the car through the deserted streets to the airport on the edge of the city.

Rebecca and Patricia waited inside the private aircraft that stood ablaze with the World Tech symbol and the Montoya personal insignia. Johnson took the pilot's seat and Diego sat next to him in the cockpit. In the cabin, Gage sank down in a white leather seat facing Rebecca. She brought her seat to an upright position. He noticed she looked sleepy.

Patricia appeared to be sleeping in a fold-down seat across the aisle.

"So, how did it go?" Rebecca said as the engines began to rev up. "Are we right in our assumption that Hannah is on that train?"

Gage nodded, yes.

Rebecca smiled and heaved a slight sigh.

"We know the route of the train," Rebecca said, "and since the train is headed back toward Canada, we'll be there to meet it when it arrives with Hannah aboard."

Gage did not answer. The plane was in the air now. The hum of the engines lulled his exhausted body. His mind drifted to a time when there was no killing – a time of innocence.

Dusk was upon Gage and his father as they hunted crocodiles in the swamp. The smell of the ocean filled his memories and he felt the tide slap against his ankles. He was safe and unafraid. At eight-years-old, he was experiencing his first hunt and he was proud and excited.

His family and friends were relaxing after a day of hard work. Young children played in their tents and their parents relaxed around campfires. Gage heard music mingled with laughter drift up toward a hot night sky. He lived in a migrant camp, but to Gage, he was just a boy with a father, a mother and a baby sister. He had friends and the world was his playground.

Each day Gage received lessons from his mother. He learned to read, to write and to compute numbers. His mother taught him about the stars, the moon and the history of the planet Earth. Coastal towns and cities disappeared beneath rising seas, Gage was taught, and rising temperatures turned gardens into deserts. Nature's devastation and relentless assaults on the towns and cities of the old democracies was overwhelming, making it impossible for established governments to secure safety for its citizens.

"Democracies flourish with reason and compromise," Gage's mother said "But fear annihilates reason. Without reason there is no compromise. When reason fails and when compromise is impossible, the cunning take power. Our democracies disappeared into chaos."

Gage listened to his mother and tried to understand. She talked about a past that was so different from his world with his family and with the migrants.

Gage was taught that democracies are complicated and very fragile. The corporate kings had the wealth, power and organization to offer security when the ice melted. The vanishing democracies lost their authority to the new rulers.

Citizens were forced into two groups: those who found employment and security within the corporate communities and those who could not. Gage's family found itself among the later, abandoned by the corporations and outside the protection of the corporate walls. They were migrants struggling to survive in a hostile and deadly environment. For Gage however, he was a child living in the warmth of the campfires and under his parent's protection.

Gage slept as the plane glided through the air. His dreams took him back to the happiest, and yet the most devastating day of his life. His first hunt with his father and the day his innocence disappeared – the day the pirates came.

A violent jolt from the airplane, a loud banging noise and cursing coming from the cockpit brought Gage out of his sleep. A sudden dipping and rising of the plane threw him into the air and back into his seat. Through the window, Gage could see daylight, but thick red and black dirt slammed against the aircraft causing it to roll from side to side. The plane was out of control and going down.

CHAPTER THIRTEEN
The Underground
Canada

Streaks of light poured through the slats of the wooden box where Annie was hiding. The pace of the bicycle peddler quickened and pain tore through her wounded body as the wheels on the box bounced and thumped against the pavement. Outside, the sound of excited chatter and occasional gunfire faded into the distance. She was not safe yet, but she was free from the hangman's noose – at least for now.

Annie closed her eyes and trusted her fate to her rescuers. She felt no regrets in joining The Eight. It was the most liberating decision she had ever made. At the time she joined, The Eight had been a loose knit brotherhood, not organized at all. Decades ago The Eight had been a vibrant resistance to those in power, but had since degraded to whispers, superstitions and finally anonymity. This changed, however, with El Espiritu, the spirit man, the ghost.

Only a handful of people knew who he was, or what he was although mummers and hushed gossip about his identity prevailed. The corporate kings, of course, wanted to know who he was and where they could capture him. Some said he was the leader of the Ditchings and he had come back to take revenge against the corporate kings. Annie knew, or was it only a belief that Robert was with Espiritu somewhere in the Rocky Mountains. Was Robert alive and part of Espiritu's inner circle?

Before Espiritu, resistance to the tyranny of the kings consisted of small groups committing uncoordinated, individual acts of sabotage. Out of frustration, ordinary workers committed acts of vandalism against factories and transportation convoys. Illegal, underground groups worked without much success at standing up to their corporate rulers. Many young men joined gangs of pirates and criminals who existed independently on the peripheral of civilization.

Still others formed resistance organizations, which were no match against the powerful, ubiquitous corporations. Espiritu, however, convinced most of the independent resistance groups and migrants to unite into one central organization. Whereas World Tech had united most of the corporations into a system of governance, Espiritu united the workers and migrants. Although Espiritu remained in the shadows appearing in disguise when in public, he was able to convince leaders of those nefarious networks to agree with his plan of unification.

His next step for this resistance network was to form an army and fight the corporate kings in open combat. But, the resistance needed guns and Annie was able to accomplish this.

Getting a night job at the gun factory as a scrubwoman gave Annie access to offices and files containing useful information. She learned where the guns were to be delivered and how they would be shipped. This information passed through an intricate, clandestine communication network that Annie helped to establish. That network, a spider web of operatives, contained cells or groups of ten members each. None of the operatives knew the identities of the other cell members. A dozen individuals formed the nucleus of that web, Annie being at the center. Within a year after getting this secretive method started, four-hundred communication cells had developed around the world.

Annie appeared to be an average working woman going about her daily life, but she was an active leader at the center of a brewing revolution. Besides guns, the revolution needed an army. Word went out through the network that the movement needed soldiers. With Espiritu as the invisible commander, resistance fighters were organized, trained and smuggled to the Rocky Mountains. Annie led the undertaking by arranging shelter, transportation and safe hiding for those fighters. Beneath the noses of the kings, she arranged liaisons, transmitted vital messages and took on the dangerous role of courier laden with documents, arms and the ammunition required for sabotage operations. The ruling elite underestimated the power and abilities of their subjects.

Yet, this phase of her dangerous work ended when she was arrested. Annie had been at the wrong place at the wrong time, but she knew that arrest was the risk of involvement in this dangerous game. Annie was picked up in a sweep of union agitators although she was not participating in their activities that night.

As usual, Annie stayed late while visiting her children at the school. A bright moon shown that night in a sky filtered by a light haze. Her walk through the quiet streets was confident, brisk and without fear. She felt light-hearted and believed the time was close when she and her children would live together once again. Gunfire, shouts and sirens caused her to freeze in her tracks. There were always agitators in the city, Annie knew, but coming upon them all of a sudden in that area on that night was a shock. She had no place to hide. An armed militiaman stopped his vehicle and shouted that she was under arrest. Annie locked her eyes on his uniform and his weapons. She had no choice but to submit.

As a simple woman visiting her children, Annie believed she would be released, but someone was curious about her. Some official thought she was more than just a working mother. The kings were desperate to stop the growing resistance to their power and were compelled to obtain information anywhere they could.

Annie had been tortured every day. With the threat of death hanging over her head at every moment, she confessed to lies. She told her tormentors what they wanted to hear and then recanted her stories later. Never once did she tell the truth. Never once did they break her determination to protect her colleagues and the resistance. The secrets of The Eight were safe.

The ruling elite never understood Annie's importance. Most of her judges and tormentors, with reluctance, agreed she was only a simple peasant caught up, out of ignorance, into a web of crime. Although the corporate officials accomplished nothing useful from Annie's brutal questioning, there were other ways to benefit from this arrest. Annie's public execution would serve as a deterrent to others who wished to follow this misguided philosophy. Annie Miller was condemned to death.

Annie shifted her position in the box. Her body trembled with pain and she groaned. The bicycle jolted to a stop. She heard footsteps outside. Then the box lid opened. Suddenly, bright light flooded her hiding place. The sheet covering her body was pulled over her head and she felt someone lift her out of the box. Sun rays warmed her body, a door opened and Annie was carried inside a building.

She was placed in a straight-backed chair and someone removed the sheet covering her head. Annie blinked from the light and choked back a sick feeling in her stomach. Her hands still chained behind her back caused pain to shoot through her bones and muscles with each movement she made.

Annie found herself in a cluttered storeroom. A table scattered with men's and women's fine clothing made from Tyson cloth, stood against the left wall. Boxes were stacked in a corner and numerous racks of clothing were pushed together. Closed doors stood on opposite walls. Annie thought that one door must lead to the outside and the other to a clothing shop. A teenage boy with a bad complexion and a muscular build, stood beside her. No one else was in the room.

The shop door opened and a middle-aged man entered the room wearing wrinkled cotton overalls. A mass of white-blond curls framed his face and his blue eyes looked serious behind wire-rimmed glasses. The man closed the door behind him and with his face muscles drawn tight, nodded at the teenage boy who stood beside Annie. The boy disappeared out the door leading to the outside.

Without saying a word, the man knelt down on one knee and freed Annie's hands from her chains by using a sharp lock-pick. She rubbed her hands together and felt the blood start to circulate again.

"Are my children safe?" Annie asked.

The shop door opened and a plump woman with curly, steel-gray hair partially covered by a scarf tied beneath her chin, entered the room and shut the door behind her. "Don't worry," she said with a cheerful lilt to her delivery. "We have your children. They're safe and on their way to the mountains. You'll be with them soon. Now, come dear. We need to find you some new clothes. Those you're wearing need to be destroyed."

"I think she'll look great in blue." A woman, perhaps in her forties, her skin a light shade of brown and her black braids tied in swirls on top of her head came into the room carrying a light-blue dress. Annie noticed large diamond rings on her fingers and her ankle-length pink dress was made of Tyson cloth. Her demeanor was calm and alert. A younger woman with a long, yellow braid followed her carrying a pair of shoes.

"We'll try these," the younger woman said.

All of a sudden, the storeroom was alive with intense energy. From a dungeon cell to this small room filled with beauty and life. The dichotomy startled Annie. She was entering the underground. Although Annie had never met these people, she knew them well.

On one level, they were respected members of society, workers and managers, housewives and government officials. On another level, they ran the underground. Guns, supplies, information and human beings passed through this network of operatives. They lived dual lives and in constant danger. Annie was not just part of that network; she had been a major organizer. Now, her life was in their hands.

The three women hustled the locksmith out the back door and helped Annie to stand. They striped her of her prison clothes, helped her into the new dress and tied her hair into braids on top of her head. When Annie was dressed, the dark-skinned woman and the young blond covered Annie and themselves with full burkas and led her out onto the floor of the dress shop filled with colorful Tyson designs. Sparkling beads and accessories hung on hooks. One section was devoted to women's shoes.

Most clothing stores in the factory districts sold the typical worker's uniform of blue shirts and tan slacks for the men, white blouses and long black skirts for the women. Simple, coarse cotton attire was worn when not at work, and since dyes were expensive, those clothes were usually white.

However, Annie now stood in a shop called by the public a copy-boutique. These copy-boutiques imitated the high-fashion boutiques abundant behind the third wall. Workers purchased a lower grade of Tyson fashions at a cheaper price from these copy-boutiques scattered throughout the factory districts. Prices were set to allow most workers to afford a special outfit for private gatherings and special occasions. Since fashion rules served to add an additional layer of control over the employees and their families, releasing the restraints of the conservative dress code was like allowing steam to escape from a boiling teapot.

Working women covered their heads in scarves. Some women, not all however, believed burkas offered protection and chose to wear the full coverings when on public streets. Although dress styles were not mentioned in any government law, strict, conservative dress codes were preached from the pulpit with a blessing from the corporate kings.

Wealthy wives from the third walls often ventured into the working districts for shopping excursions, bargain hunting and lunch parties. They came in chauffer driven vehicles and dressed in burkas over stylish Tyson designs.

Four women wearing burkas, designer shoes and diamond rings huddled together near the accessories. Annie overheard them discussing the escape of a dangerous criminal.

"The streets are full of police," one woman said. "They're stopping everyone." The four women, after animated discussion, decided to abandon their shopping excursion and hurried from the shop.

Annie pretended to peruse the racks of clothing as she waited for instructions. The plump woman with the steel-gray hair, stood behind the counter where three women, covered in veils, waited to purchase armloads of colorful dresses and sparkling accessories. The women turned toward Annie and nodded.

When the women's transactions were finished, the three shoppers surrounded Annie and led her outside where a limousine sat waiting. A chauffeur opened the car door and the women climbed into the passenger area of the vehicle. The young blond girl and the dark-skinned woman were waiting inside the vehicle where two soft bench seats faced each other. A glass window separated the passenger area from the driver. All six women remained quiet as the limousine pulled away from the curb and began moving through the streets of Tent City.

Annie leaned back and inhaled the pleasant aroma of perfume which filled the vehicle. She knew she had been passed along to the next curriers who included the dark-skinned lady and the young blond who had helped her out of her prison clothes. These operatives were her guides and protectors.

The two woman who dressed her had manicured polished nails and smooth, soft skin. Gold and precious stones decorated their fingers. The other three women in the car seemed to be servants. Their nails were broken, their hands calloused. No one removed their veils, but Annie could see their eyes, confident and unafraid.

Annie knew these brave women were the wives, daughters and sisters of the wealthy elite who chose to fill their time working outside the walls. They volunteered in hospitals, orphanages, work houses, and in prisons. Many of these women took a step further by supporting illegal unions and The Eight. They supplied food to picket lines, observed trials and paid bails. Some joined The Eight.

The limousine moved through the streets of Tent City where militia was everywhere and blockades slowed the traffic to a crawl. Through the closed windows of the car, the women watched bicycle peddlers and pedestrians being stopped, questioned and sometimes searched.

When their limousine came to a full stop at a blockade, a gun-toting Militiaman peered into the car. Annie kept her head down. The women remained calm. Annie sensed each slow steady breath keeping rhythm with the beat of the women's hearts. When the chauffeur lowered the window, a stone-faced officer peered into the car and surveyed the veiled women. His eyes scanned the women's hands.

"You women need to get home right away," he told them, keeping his eyes on their jewelry. "Go on. Get out of here." He waived them through the blockade. Raising the windows, the limo driver passed through the heavily guarded barriers.

The women looked at each other with assurance, but not a word was spoken. How lucky, Annie thought, that no one questioned wealthy, veiled women and their servants.

The car continued away from Tent City and out into the countryside toward the city of New Town. The women remained silent. A long, well maintained road stretched before them. In the distance loomed the walls and gun towers of New Town,

Canada, through which Annie had been taken yesterday on her
way to her execution in Tent City.

The limo was stopped again at the outer wall of New
Town and then again at the gates of the second wall. The
automobile, filled with wealthy passengers and their servants,
was allowed to pass into New Town without suspicion.

Annie stared out the window as they traveled through
the heart of New Town, past factories, corporate shopping areas
and apartments. They passed the building where Annie had
worked, and the school where her children had lived.

My children are no longer there, Annie's mind told her.
My children are on their way to Robert. They are safe and
Tanika's son Michael is with them. This was something Annie
had to believe. She sighed and her shoulders slumped.
Information that Tanika had been killed the day Annie was
arrested had flowed through the prison where Annie had been
held. Promises were made between Annie and Tanika to protect
each other's children, and those promises would be kept. Annie
turned her body to look back toward the school and to keep it in
her eyesight as long as possible. The car turned a corner and the
school was gone.

When the courthouse and jail came into view, Annie
held her breath. A shudder passed through her body. The dark-
skinned lady sitting next to her placed a soft, bejeweled hand on
her wrist and gave her a gentle pat. Annie looked at the women
and their eyes met.

"I'm okay," Annie said and settled back in her seat. Her
body relaxed. Yes, she told herself. I am okay.

A wide boulevard led them to another set of guarded
gates. Behind this wall was the private world of the corporate
kings. A uniformed militiaman stood straight, saluted and
waved the limo through the gates. Annie watched with curiosity
as this securely guarded world of golf courses, fountains and
walled mansions drifted by her window. Soon they moved

down a narrow, winding street with spacious homes on each side. At the end of the street, a set of iron gates swung open. The limo driver followed a long driveway that ended in front of a sprawling home made of stone and bricks. A thick carpet of lawn decorated with colorful flowers and graceful trees surrounded the home.

The chauffeur opened the door and the women, their arms filled with packages, stepped out of the vehicle. Annie noticed a sweet fragrance floating on the chilly air and she noticed the scent of pine trees. She was escorted through the front door of the mansion into an enormous entryway with polished wood floors. A sparkling chandelier hung some fifteen feet above their heads and several finely furnished rooms lead off from the entryway. Once inside the house, the women removed their burkas. Servants collected them and the packages, and disappeared into one of the adjacent rooms.

Annie was exhausted and felt sick to her stomach.

"We're going to take her upstairs." A slender woman in a long, black skirt spoke as she hurried down a wide staircase. She wore a long-sleeved white blouse with a broach fastened at the throat. Soft white curls framed her face, and her clear complexion and green eyes reminded Annie of the young girl who traveled with her from the dress shop to this splendid house.

The woman threw her arms around the young girl.

"Mom. I'm okay," the girl said. "I told you I could do this."

"She did fine," the dark-skinned lady said and gave the older woman a hug. "We're safe."

The young girl's mother turned to Annie took her hands and looked into her face. "We'll help you," she said. "Can you make it up the stairs?"

Annie nodded and started to walk, but pain overwhelmed her. After all she had been through, Annie was not able to go any further.

"Please. Just wait a moment," she said. "Just let me rest a minute. I'll be alright if you give me a moment." Annie sank to her knees and struggled against losing consciousness.

She felt someone, a man she thought, pick her up and carry her up the stairs. Annie could smell his cologne and she felt his muscular arms holding her. He placed her on a bed and she felt the women remove her clothes.

"We have a doctor for you, dear," someone said.

"Oh, yes, and a dentist. Your poor teeth are broken," another voice said.

"Are my children safe?" Annie said to the voices. "Is Tanika's son safe?"

"Don't worry, Annie," someone said. "Your children are safe. Sleep now. We'll wake you in the morning."

Peace, safety and darkness overtook Annie. She slept.

CHAPTER FOURTEEN
The Storm
The Desert

Someone said run. Just run. Bobby and Zack were beside Hannah.

"We have to climb," Zack yelled. "We have to get as high as we can. The higher the better. The higher we go, the thinner the dust. If we stay here, we'll be buried."

Zack picked up a small child and grabbed Hannah's arm. Bobby pulled her outside while Zack shouted for the others to follow. People awaking from sleep, stumbled to their feet. Most were barefooted. They grappled for children and some for packs. No one understood what was happening until they stepped outside. A huge cloud of dust roared toward them like a great, black tidal wave. Six whirling columns of dust, drifting upward like swirling cigar smoke, preceded the wave.

Hannah fled with the others toward the city as the storm chased them. Hot wind and swirling dirt swallowed the atmosphere as Hannah ran. With Bobby close beside her, Hannah followed Zack and the other survivors into one of the buildings and climbed up through an enclosed stairwell. She heard voices and footsteps of the survivors hurrying up the steps. Up, up she went with the wind screaming through the holes in the broken walls of the building.

The storm raged and blackness covered their world.

Exhausted, sunburned and terrified Hannah and Bobby took shelter in a small windowless room within the tall building. Maybe it had once been a closet, Hannah thought. She and Bobby huddled together in a corner and wrapped their arms around each other. The dark confines of the room calmed them and made the storm outside less terrifying. The other survivors had scattered throughout the tall building and found protection wherever they could.

"We need to sleep," Bobby said. "We need our strength. We're safe for now and the storm will be gone in the morning."

Hannah smiled and rested her head against his chest; her backpack safely beside her with the special secret tucked inside.

"When we are old, we will talk about this," she reminded Bobby. Hannah's mind drifted and she slipped into the world of peaceful dreams. The sound of the wind became the sound of the factories humming outside her Oakbourgh home. She was now snuggling against her grandmother in the small attic of her father's house; the house safe behind the walls of Oakbourgh. Bobby was there smiling at her. They were playing factory workers and chasing lizards. Now it was before the march and she could hear her mother humming as she cleaned the house.

"We can't keep the dust and dirt out of the house," her mother kept saying. "But we can mop it up after it gets in."

Hannah laughed in her dream world. As she slept in that hidden place high above the ancient city, the laughter became a peaceful smile.

Morning. Open your eyes. Hannah took a deep breath, raised her hands over her head and stretched her entire body. She was lying on a bare wooden floor looking upward into blackness. Thin streaks of bright light threaded through the darkness, hurting her eyes and causing her to close them again. A slight thump followed by scraping sounds jolted Hannah out of her dreams, almost to her senses.

"Wake up, Hannah. I want to show you something." Bobby's voice filled her head. She felt his strong hands gently shake her body and his warm breath on her face. She reopened her eyes and rose to a sitting position.

"What is it?" she mumbled while rubbing her eyes.

"The storm's over," Bobby told her. "Most people are awake, but not everyone. You have to see what's out here. Look."

Hannah and Bobby had taken shelter in a closet within an abandoned conference room. The door to the room was ajar leaving a narrow slit between the wall and the door through which a stream of light filtered. Pale morning sunlight filtered through the crack bringing with it a slight breeze. Riding on the breeze were tiny particles of dust, dipping and swirling, dancing about like tiny, magical fairies.

Hannah tasted grit in her mouth and felt it between her teeth. The dirt clung to her clothes, stuck in her throat and coated her lungs. Rolling over on her side, she coughed and gagged as the thick dirt stuck in her throat.

"My backpack," she said, starting to panic as her eyes darted around the dark, windowless room.

"It's over there in the corner," Bobby said. "Take it easy."

As her eyes adjusted to the dim light, Hannah spotted her backpack and relaxed.

"I know what you're looking for." Bobby told her. "You and that backpack. You seem to think it's more important than your life." He retrieved the backpack, carried it over to Hannah, knelt down and opened the pack.

"I guess it's lucky you have this thing right now," he said as he took a small bottle of water out of the pack, opened it and handed the water to Hannah. "Here, wash the dust out of your throat."

Hannah took a drink and swallowed. The taste of dirt did not disappear. A second, longer drink cleared her throat of the grit, but not of the taste.

"Here, Bobby. You drink." She handed the bottle to him and he took a long drink. When he finished, he placed the half-empty bottle back in the pack.

"Come over here. You have to see this," he said as he helped Hannah to stand. She rose to her feet, picked up her backpack, slipped it over her shoulder and followed Bobby into an adjacent room. Zack stood on the opposite side of an empty room leaning out of a large, oblong opening in the far wall. The hole looked as though the opening had, some time ago, been a huge window. The glass was gone, blown out by years of storms and vandalism.

Hannah and Bobby walked across the empty room toward Zack; their bare feet making footprints as they moved through the thin layer of brown and gray dirt. They stepped over broken glass, pieces of wallboard and unrecognizable debris strewn everywhere.

Scorching sunlight poured through a broken-out window where Zack stood looking out over an abandoned and decaying city sprawling for miles across an arid desert. The majestic Rocky Mountains beneath a yellow haze stood toward the west.

The building in which they found refuge rose twenty floors above the earth. Below sprawled thousands of forlorn and deserted buildings arranged between ribbons of empty streets now filled with dust. They stood like massive stone structures, broken and ravaged by nature's fury, reaching upward toward a yellow sky. Each building stood as though it was a monument to a once powerful and wealthy civilization. Hannah stood beside Zack and looked in amazement and wonder. In the distance she noticed plumes of black smoke billowing upward, creating dark clouds that floated above the vulnerable landscape.

"Static electricity from the storm set fires," Zack said. "Parts of the city are on fire. We're safe for now, but we're going to have to leave here soon. We'll have to get with the others and head north."

"Nothing in Oakbourgh was ever like this," Hannah said her voice a reverent whisper. "There must have been millions of people living here." Her throat, still parched from the desert storm, stung as she spoke.

"There were," Zack told her without taking his eyes from the scene below. "Hundreds of millions of people lived all over this land. Billions lived on the planet."

Hannah slipped her hand into Bobby's and gave it a comforting squeeze. "Where did they all go?" she asked.

"They died," Zack spoke, his voice void of emotion.

"But not all of them died. They must have gone somewhere," Hannah said. "It looks as though they just left."

"And very quickly," Bobby said.

"Most of them died," Zack answered them. "But some went north and found employment with the corporations. Others were not so lucky."

"The Ditchings," Hannah said. She turned away from the window and sat down with her back against the wall. Bobby joined her. Zack heaved a deep sigh and sat down facing them crossing his long legs over each other.

"So, where's everyone else from the train?" Hannah asked.

"Most are sleeping in the other rooms up here. After the storm let up, some of the men went back to get the supplies."

"Would you tell us about the Ditchings?" Hannah said.

Zack nodded and took a deep breath. "I remember the stories my grandfather use to tell me," Zack began as though repeating a story he had told many times before. He spoke in a hushed voice. His blue eyes appeared to be seeing the past as though the picture was right before him.

"My grandfather told me about how the storms came all over the earth, year after year. Each year was worse than the last. No one believed what was really happening though, and even if they did, there was nothing anyone could do about it. Everyone went about their lives living like they did in the years before. Changing nothing.

Then the floods came, washing away the topsoil and making it impossible to plant. Food became more and more scarce and expensive." Zack paused a moment, wiped the sweat from his forehead with the back of his hand and coughed.

The morning temperatures were rising. Bobby took the bottle of water from Hannah's pack and offered Zack a drink. The old man took a mouthful of water, swallowed and handed the near empty container back to Bobby.

"Old men love to tell stories to the young," Zack continued. "Some think it's the best way to remember and appreciate history." He smiled. Talking about the past seemed to excite him and at the same time to calm him.

Hannah and Bobby had heard those stories from Hannah's grandmother, but they were each eager to hear them again. In this quiet moment and in this strange and fearful place, a sense of peace settled over Hannah as though someone had placed a soft warm blanket over her. She felt safe.

"I know it is forbidden to be talking about these things, but it has to be done," Zack said. "You children will go on into the future where I cannot go, but you need to tell your children and grandchildren what I tell you." Zack paused and moistened his dry lips. "The corporate kings always approve the history for people to hear and the history of the kings has always been different from the legends of the people." A faint smile crossed his lips. "Some people call them myths, but these stories are in fact the truth."

"I know the stories of Blue Eden," Hannah said without thinking. Her face froze in terror. These were secret stories and never to be shared with strangers.

"Yes," Zack told her with a slight nod and a smile. "Blue Eden is part of the story of our earth, but the story I will tell you is only about our planet Earth. According to the corporate text books," he continued, "the earth had always been a great desert and the powerful corporations have always been the keepers of the land. The corporate kings knew where to find the water and how to drill for the water. They also understood how to make sure the water was used in a way that would ensure a safe and prosperous livelihood for all those loyal to the corporations. Those who went against the corporations and against corporate truth not only doomed themselves, but the rest of the world."

Hannah sat quiet as Zack spoke. She liked how his beard moved when he spoke and how the light sparkled in his eyes. The story Zack was telling was the history Hannah and Bobby were taught in school, but the forbidden stories told by Hannah's grandmother were always the children's favorite. Those were the stories about Blue Eden and about the creation of a lush garden planet that could support human life.

Zack cleared his throat and continued. His pale, blue eyes looked sad and carried a faraway expression. "Bobby and Hannah," he said. "That prominent city out there was once filled with millions of people. Most were good people, some were not, but all of them closed their minds to the horror that was before them. The people looked inward and not outward." Zack sighed and shrugged. "Maybe not facing the truth was the only way they could continue to live. You see." He heaved a deep sigh.

"Africa and the Middle East were hit first by the temperature changes. Those countries had depended on food imports because political unrest and famine were already common there, but as the warming increased, famines and drought began to spread to once prosperous communities around the world. Less and less food was produced and governments began to save their food and water supplies for their own people.

Millions across the world began to starve. Those who lived in the areas of plenty began to build walls to keep out those who were desperate. Soon, people all over the world began to migrate to areas of the planet where they could find food and fresh water."

"And then the oceans rose over large parts of the land," Bobby said. "And that made more migrants because their homes were under water."

"Except for Canada," Hannah said. She smiled and gave a slight giggle as if she was hearing the happy ending to a fairytale. "Bobby's cousin is in Canada."

"Many parts of Canada and the far north also disappeared beneath the rising sea," Zack said. "Unfortunately, many places in the far north were lowlands. When the glaciers and ice sheets melted, ocean water washed across those lowlands like a tidal wave. But the north also became warm and there was enough new land for the corporations to organize settlements there."

"Wait. I hear something." Bobby said. "Listen." He cocked his head and looked toward the door that led into the hallway.

Hannah heard scuffling as though people were walking in the building. "Someone is here," she said.

"It sounds like the others are waking up," Zack said.

"Is everyone safe?" Hannah asked.

Zack shook his head. "We lost two." A defeated look passed across his face. "We handed the children to the young men because they're strong and can run faster. We got all the children to safety, but," he shook his head. "One of the women, the medic, had trouble running. Her feet were badly swollen and her husband tried to help her but they disappeared in the storm. We tried to find them, but we couldn't. I just hope they managed to survive. Otherwise, there are now two children without parents."

Sadness and fear settled in Hannah's stomach.

"The storm's over, now." Hannah said. "The wind's still blowing a little, though."

"I've seen these things last for days," Zack said. "But I think this one is calming down. We can't rest here for long. We'll have to gather our supplies and go into the mountains and then we can head north. The mountains have rough terrain, but it'll be safer to travel on high ground. The dust storms aren't as bad in the hills and there's more places to find shelter there."

"Why were you going to Canada?" Bobby said, and then looked embarrassed for asking such a personal question.

Zack stood up and walked to the window. "My wife and I were going to Canada to be with our children." Zack looked out over the city. "We were too old to get passes to enter Canada so we were forced to enter illegally. There was nothing in Oakbourgh for us anymore. Our children were gone and we knew the mines were drying up. We also knew it wouldn't be long before the corporations abandoned the city.

"I have to tell you," Zack turned away from the window and looked down at Hannah and Bobby. "We were so grateful our three children were able to get to Canada. That's where the future is. Our children were young and the corporations needed young people to build new communities in the wilderness. My wife, Linda, and I were old and coming to our time of uselessness. Linda and I hoped to get to Canada to be with our children though. They wanted us there. They have good jobs and were able to support us." Zack smiled and his eyes gleamed. "One's a teacher. The other two are doctors." He paused." But now Linda is dead." His hands trembled and his jaw tightened.

"Me and Hannah's goen to Canada to be with my cousin," Bobby said.

Zack smiled. "Linda and I grew up in California – at Lake Tahoe." Zack said. "There was good water in Lake Tahoe then and our families were comfortable. We were citizens and allowed a good life." Zack shrugged and sat down beside Hannah.

"We were lucky. I was allowed an education and I became a mechanical engineer. Most of the time I worked in aircraft maintenance."

"Wow." Bobby said, his face glowing with awe and respect. "I'm going to be an auto mechanic someday. Have you ever flown an airplane? Someday I'm going to fly, too."

Hannah listened to the joy in Bobby's voice and she giggled with happiness. They were discussing the future and their past as though they were in a comfortable living room. There was no danger, no fear. Hannah felt safe.

Zack laughed. "Yes, I have flown, but it has been a long time. They say you never forget, though. Speaking of flying, we are going to have to get with the others and get ready to leave. I will tell you, there's more of those dust storms coming. I've seen them too many times."

Muffled cries bounced against the bare walls of the hallway breaking the serenity of their few moments of safety.

"Well, look what we have here. Some fancy travelers." Three of the foulest men Hannah had ever seen walked into the room. They smelled as bad as they looked. Each carried weapons – clubs and spears made of poles with broken glass attached to one end. Their skin was burned dark and scared from the sun, and their clothes, mere rags, covered their emaciated bodies. For shoes, they had wrapped rags around their feet. Filthy hair and whiskers, matted in knots and tangles, framed their faces. They had woven bones into their hair and beards.

"Migrants," Hannah gasped. There was no place to hide. Zack placed his hand on a thick piece of metal lying beside him. Before he could use it as a sword, one of the migrants slammed his foot over the potential weapon and attempted to smash Zack's face with a club. In a single fluid movement, Zack rose up, kneed the man in the groin and wrenched the club from the surprised migrant now rendered helpless with agony. As Zack knocked his assailant to the ground with a punch to the stomach, one of the other intruders grabbed Hannah's backpack.

"This is all they've got," he yelled. "Let's get out of here."

"No," Hannah screamed. She jumped to her feet and chased after the thief. Zack's attacker knocked her to the floor then scrambled to his feet. Hannah rebounded and dashed after the migrant.

"Let 'em go," Bobby yelled as he grabbed Hannah's arms.

"I can't," she screamed back at him. "I need my book. You don't understand." Hannah broke away from Bobby and ran out into the hallway. The three migrants had joined several of their companions who were coming out of a room opening into the hallway.

Strong hands grabbed Hannah from behind as she ran, lifting her into the air. Twisting and kicking, she dug her nails into her assailant's hands trying to force him to let her go.

"Stop it, Hannah, It's me, Zack. Forget the backpack." He sat her on the ground and whirled her around to face him. "Leave it, Hannah. Leave it."

Several young men, armed with clubs and broken glass, survivors from the train wreck, approached the migrants. "Leave us alone," one of them said. "We've got nothing."

"Give me the pack you stole," Bobby yelled at the attackers. He picked up a long, sharp piece of wood and held it in front of him as he ran at the migrant who had taken Hannah's bag. Zack pulled Hannah backward as a violent clash erupted between the men.

Clubs cracked against clubs, clubs against bodies. Shuffling feet – running feet. Men running – men on the ground. Two migrants gasped in pain. Someone was on the ground not moving. Bobby was lying on the floor, pale and bleeding. He had been stabbed. Blood covered his torso.

Stunned and in shock, Hannah sat down beside Bobby and with gentle hands, touched his cheek. He moaned. She felt her body shake. Tears poured from her eyes. Hannah wanted to scream, but she had only enough breath for short gasps.

Hannah leaned over and whispered into Bobby's ear, "When we are old, we will talk about this."

Bobby turned his head toward her, exhaled and breathed no more.

CHAPTER FIFTEEN
The Army
The Desert

Gage awoke to darkness, his adrenalin surging as the plane shook and buckled. Outside, lightning flashed through a thick blanket of red and black dirt clouds that slammed against the fuselage. Besides the sound of crackling electrical charges, the plane creaked and groaned. Overhead bins banged open against the walls of the plane and luggage flew about the cabin. The engines were silent.

The plane was in the midst of a dust storm. Those storms could be sudden and almost always disastrous for anyone unfortunate enough to encounter them. The fury of the storm was tossing the plane out of control. With good pilots, and Gage knew Diego and Johnson were good pilots, an aircraft could glide for quite a distance without engines, but Gage also knew that their fate was not in the hands of the crew. Instead, they were at the mercy of a raging dust storm.

The pitch and roll gyrations of the aircraft became more extreme. Gage felt the seat belt dig into his flesh as he was tossed about in all directions. The plane was tumbling out of control. They were going to crash.

Gage had no time for fear. His training and experience kept his mind focused on survival, but now there was nothing he could do but ride the plane down. He caught Rebecca's eyes and held them. Fear clouded her expression, then calmness. They said nothing and waited.

The fuselage shook and rattled as Johnson maneuvered the plane into an attitude of least harm. Gage followed in his mind the procedures Johnson was using to minimize the forward motion and to pick the nose up. The plane needed to fall on its tail in order to minimize the crash damage. Gage also knew the pilots would empty the fuel tanks in order to avoid a fiery collision with the earth.

When the plane hit the ground, tail first, metal screeched as the fuselage twisted and tore upon impact. A massive gash ripped across the tail section. Wind screamed through the jagged tear blowing choking dust into the cabin of the broken plane. The killing dirt invaded Gage's eyes, nose and lungs. Although he covered his face with pieces of clothing, Gage could not get away from the invasive dirt. The dust storm enveloped the downed plane.

Gage snapped his seat belt open and jumped to his feet as Johnson and Diego entered the cabin from the cockpit.

"Is everyone okay?" Diego shouted and choked on dust.

Johnson motioned toward the cockpit. "Come on," he said. "We can seal off the cockpit from the dirt." He signaled for everyone to follow him.

Gage pulled Rebecca and Patricia out of their seats and gave them each a shove toward the cockpit. The women stumbled to the pilot's compartment and once they were all inside, Gage closed the door. Since the cockpit was not damaged it could be sealed tight, preventing the dust from entering.

The men stood, allowing the women to take the two seats. No one spoke as the plane rocked and groaned from the force of the wind beating against the downed aircraft.

After a few moments of silence, Patricia spoke. "Is anyone hurt?"

"It'll take a year to get the dirt out of my lungs," Diego said.

"Bumps and bruises," Rebecca added.

"So far, so good." Gage made a long, slow whistling sound as he exhaled.

Johnson took a pack of cigarettes from his pocket and when he put one in his mouth, Patricia said, her dark eyes flashing, "I wouldn't do that if I were you. We need to breathe in here."

Johnson nodded and returned the cigarettes to his pocket.

"I was flying low," Johnson said and took a deep breath. "Flying low is what saved us. We were just plain lucky." He paused and heaved a sigh. "The wind was out of the south, blowing steady, but it picked up speed. When that damn dust cloud hit, I couldn't climb fast enough to get above it, but you gotta know why I was flying so low."

Gage's interest peaked. "Why," he asked.

"I was flying low following the train tracks. That train we've been looking for has been splattered all across the desert."

"What do you mean?" Rebecca's body tightened, her eyes opened wide with an expression of disbelief.

"It looks like someone blew up a bridge, or maybe it just collapsed. I was buzzing the wreckage when the storm hit. I didn't see anyone moving down there. Um. . .most of the train fell into a gorge, but some of the cars seemed to have broken off and stayed on top of the ravine. Looks like a big dust storm came through afterwards and covered a lot of the wreck. You know, those dust storms blow dirt over everything, then blow the dirt away again."

"We're going to have to get out of here and investigate the wreckage," Rebecca said. "We have a land rover in the hold and hopefully it wasn't damaged in the crash. We'll use the rover for transportation."

"We don't have a choice but to use the land rover," Gage said. "This plane isn't going anywhere." He looked at Rebecca. "It looks like this little girl we're chasing could be dead."

Rebecca gave him a look of anger, but not one of desperation. Gage could tell her mind was working, but on what, he wondered. This woman was a total mystery to him.

"As soon as this wind starts to die down, we'll have to get out of this cockpit," Gage said. "All systems are off and if we stay in here, we'll cook."

With no energy systems running, the temperature in the airplane was rising. Mid-morning, hazy light filtered through the cockpit window.

"We can't stay in here," Gage said. "Looks like the dust is thinning outside, but the heat is getting worse in here. Let's go see what we can salvage from the hold. We'll get the land rover out and get it running."

Gage noticed the long dresses and soft, slip-on shoes the women were wearing.

"I know you weren't expecting a hike in the wilderness today, but. . .you'll have to change your clothes and I hope you have different shoes. Not much lives on the desert, but there are some nasty insects that will attach themselves to. . ."

"Never mind," Rebecca interrupted. "We have other luggage and shoes packed in the hold. These will have to do for now, though. Let's get the land rover out. "

"Let's go," Gage said. He left the cockpit and entered the cabin. The others followed him. Dust still swirled throughout the cabin, so Gage covered his nose and mouth with pieces of clothing he found scattered through the cabin. He first attempted to open the exterior cabin door, but it was too damaged to open.

"Over here," Diego said pointing toward the back of the plane.

Warm Wind blew through a wide crack in the tail section, bringing flying sand into the passenger area.

"This big opening appears to be the easiest way out." Diego said.

Gage found his duffle bag and retrieved his weapons. He checked his assault rifle and threw it over his shoulder. Johnson and Diego did the same.

Gage examined the jagged opening in the rear of the plane, wide enough for one person at a time to pass through. Being careful not to rip their skin on the sharp edges, Gage led the way as the passengers slid through the opening one by one. Outside, the wind pelted them with dirt as they emerged from the fuselage.

Although sitting upright, the tail section, broken and leaning to one side rose high above the mounds of dirt displaying the World Tech logo and the Montoya family crest.

The women covered their faces with veils and the men wrapped bandanas around their noses and mouths.

"I think the worst of the storm is over," Diego said.

"I know from experience," Gage said, "another storm could be following close behind, or it could be days before another one comes through. Either way, we need to unload that land rover from the hold and get it supplied with water and food. Maybe, if the girl is dead, we can find her body and retrieve whatever it is you want." Gage looked at Rebecca. "Let's get to work."

Everyone, using their hands and pieces of debris, worked to clear the dirt away from the door of the hold. Gage and Johnson released the cargo hatch and climbed inside. The land rover was secured in place and undamaged.

Rebecca and Patricia changed into sturdy boots but chose to wear their long skirts and long-sleeved blouses. Each woman placed a few pieces of luggage aboard the rover, which contained two bench seats, front and back and could hold six passengers. Rather than repair an expensive, broken highway system, rovers were invented to hover a few feet over rutted terrain, ditches, broken roads, roadless wasteland and water.

After loading food, water and medical supplies into a small storage trunk in the rear of the vehicle, Gage took the driver's seat and started the engine. Rebecca climbed in the rover beside Gage. The others took the back seat. The rover rose and Gage guided it out of the hold into the desert.

"Head due north," Johnson said. "You'll run right into the train wreck."

The rover moved northward. Inside, the air conditioner blasted causing Gage's sweat-drenched clothes to chill his body. Outside, the wind had settled down and the dirt, although still flying, was not as thick. It was not yet noon, and in the distance, the barren Rocky Mountains were visible overshadowing a sprawling, decaying city.

Gage followed the train tracks glittering in the sun as the land rover floated over them. No one spoke.

The train wreck appeared before them like a neglected graveyard. Gage maneuvered the rover around the overturned boxcars and through the field of debris. Crates of merchandise were scattered everywhere, some empty, some buried beneath mounds of dirt. Empty water barrels had been picked up by the wind and slammed into the railcars.

Gage stopped the rover at the edge of the gorge, turned off the engine and got out of the vehicle. While Diego, Johnson and Patricia investigated the field of damage, Gage and Rebecca walked to the edge of the ravine and looked down at the wreckage. The storm was gone. Now, only a slight breeze brushed against the desert.

"If she's down there, we can stop looking for her," Gage said, his voice matter-of-fact as he stared down at the fallen train and bridge.

Rebecca bit her bottom lip, a look of deep concentration on her face. "She's not down there," Rebecca said. "Let's keep looking up here." Her dark eyes carried a troubled expression.

"Hey, I found something," Diego called out.

Gage glanced back toward the overturned boxcars where Diego was kneeling beside what looked like a human body.

Gage and Rebecca joined Diego who had found the body of a middle-aged man dressed in expensive business attire.

"This guy's dead," Diego said. "But it looks like he might have survived the crash. He was left here, but someone tried to make him comfortable."

"Other's survived the crash, too," Patricia called from several feet away. "There's a mass grave over there," She motioned with her hand in the direction of the site where the survivors had buried some of the victims.

"And look at this." Rebecca picked up a piece of a broken barrel. "There was never any water in this barrel," she said. "This must be where they hid the migrants." Rebecca threw the piece of barrel to the ground. "I've heard that's one way migrants are smuggled."

"You're right," Johnson said. "They must have hid them in the barrels. Look, I just found evidence they used drugs, probably to sedate them. I guess the next questions are, how many survived and where did they go?"

Gage cast his eyes on the distant city. "The storm destroyed their tracks, but the only place they could go is that city out there."

From out of nowhere, the shadow of a corporate gunship passed over the train wreck, flew over the gorge and turned to make another pass. Gage understood that anyone traveling through the desert unescorted by corporate officials was considered a migrant and shot on sight. Gage, Johnson and Diego were wearing the corporate uniform, but Gage doubted a pilot could see that from the air. If bullets started to rain, there was no place to find shelter except maybe against the sand dunes and the scattered debris.

Again, the plane passed over them. The group fell to the ground trying to make themselves as small as possible.

This time, the plane slowed and hovered over them. A voice from the gunship spoke through a loudspeaker mounted under the craft. "Standup and put your hands in the air. Throw your weapons to the ground."

Gage realized the militia did not intend to kill them, at least not now. They would have done so already. Gage instructed the others to do as ordered, guns down, hands in the air. The aircraft settled on the ground. The engines stopped.

A pilot jumped from the plane brandishing a weapon and glanced at the three uniformed militiamen. The officer's eyes rested on the insignia Gage wore, signifying him to be a corporate bodyguard of the corporate kings. The officer saluted Gage and told everyone to lower their hands. The young officer, his face covered in a full black beard and mustache, bowed to Rebecca.

"Your ladyship," he said. "I'm Officer Bryant. I've been looking for you. I noticed your plane half buried in the sand and I saw your insignia on the tail. I realized you were caught in one of those damn dirt storms. Normally, our mission is to search for migrants and pirates out here on the desert, but when I saw your plane, I called in a search and rescue operation. I'm glad I found you. This desert and those mountains over there are a battlefield right now. It gets more dangerous every day."

"Yes. I'm very glad you found us as well," Rebecca said, stepping forward. "We were on our way to Canada when we crashed."

"Of course." Bryant said. "Unfortunately, I can't take you to Canada, but I will take you to our military camp. It's a few miles north of here, right at the base of those mountains. I assure you, your stay at the camp will only be temporary. From there, someone will take you to Canada."

Rebecca nodded in agreement. "At this point, we have little choice," she said. "The problem is I don't see how we are all going to fit into that small aircraft."

"You're not," the officer said. "I can take you two ladies and that's all."

Rebecca sighed. "Patricia, I'm taking Gage with me. Get my bag and put it in the plane." She turned toward Officer Bryant. "I need to have a talk with my men. Please excuse me for a moment."

Bryant bowed in compliance.

While Bryant helped Patricia put the small bag into the aircraft, Gage walked with Rebecca, Johnson and Diego just out of hearing range from the rescue pilot.

"I need to take Gage," Rebecca said. She looked at Johnson and Diego. "Patricia is staying here with you. Take the land rover and find the girl. If she is still alive, she is close by. If she is dead, find the survivors and question them. Gage and I will find you. Stay with Patricia. She knows this desert and she knows where to go." Rebecca paused and rubbed her forefinger over her lips. "Also, it's best if you dress as civilians. Change out of your uniforms. We know you're out here, but the migrants out here don't like to see militia."

Gage's body tightened. He felt uneasy about leaving his buddies behind in the desert, but he understood the situation and the mission. He would return for them as soon as he could.

"Won't be long," Gage told them. "I've got your back." The two men nodded and gave an okay signal. Gage was the last to climb into the warship. He crowded together with Rebecca on the flight deck behind the pilot. Rebecca insisted on taking the small bag with her which she held on her lap. The plane rose into the air and headed northwest.

The hum of the engines filled the cockpit and everyone remained silent until Bryant announced, "Hold on a moment." Bryant changed course, dove and circled a cluster of tents. After pulling the plane up and making a final circle, Bryant radioed his position. "There appeared to be no humans or livestock anywhere," he said into the radio.

"Normally, we would have destroyed that migrant camp," Bryant explained to Rebecca. "But, since we have you aboard, we're going to have to leave that job to others. We need to get you to safety."

"Yes, I appreciate that you not engage in battle right now," Rebecca said.

"We've been looking for evidence of a large army of migrants out here, but so far we haven't found anything of significance. Oh, there's something going on out there, for sure. We've found some scattered primitive tent camps like that one you just saw. You must know that thousands of people have been migrating out into those mountains over there," Bryant nodded toward the Rockies. "Where those migrants are hiding is a mystery. We can't find 'em. The migrants attack our camp and then disappear. There's a million hiding places across this wasteland, filled with deserted towns and cities as well as old military bases. But, how those people are surviving and where they are going is anyone's guess."

"It has always been the opinion of our corporate leaders that the migrants and workers are too ignorant and simple to ever organize themselves," Rebecca said. "Our leaders have really paid them little attention."

"Well, I think they're starting to pay attention to them now," Bryant said.

Down below, Gage could see an army camp with thousands of solders clustered around hundreds of campsites, stretching across the landscape. Corporate warships sat idle, waiting for action. Gage leaned back and relaxed as the plane glided to the ground.

When the plane stopped, Gage alighted from the aircraft and found himself in the familiar surroundings of a corporate military camp. Most camps were laid out in the same standard grid pattern with officers' quarters in the center surrounded by the enlisted men's camps. Mess tents, medical cabins and supply tents filled every vacant space. From Gage's experience, those camps were wretched places harboring boredom, malfeasance, fear, disease and death.

Bryant led Gage and Rebecca through the camp toward the quarters of General Mullans, Rebecca's cousin. Since most of the men were either sleeping or resting, the camp was quiet. Gage could hear an occasional clang of cooking utensils or the sound of muffled voices behind tent walls as they walked through the camp.

An army camp at high noon in that desert inferno would mean that most of the men were sleeping. Gage knew the average soldier's day in this desert environment was spent sleeping during the hottest time of day and drilling in the morning and evenings. During this drill time, men would practice using their weapons and perform various maneuvers. When not at drill, militiamen cleaned the camp, dug trenches for latrines and prepared food.

There was always plenty of protein paste in various flavors; easy to ship and to store, but fresh water was always a problem. Gage ran his hand over the stumbles appearing on his face. A clean-shaven face represented the high-ranking officers and the elite, although many military officers wore full beards in an attempt to show solidarity with their men.

"Stop," Gage took Rebecca's arm.

"What's that I hear?" he said.

Loud sobbing and the voices of children were coming from one of the tents. Gage stopped before the entrance to a canvas shelter where two armed militiamen stood guard. The flap of the tent was pulled back and Gage was surprised to see four young children huddled together on pallets placed on the dirt floor. The tent was stifling and the children's clothes were drenched with sweat.

Gage dropped Rebecca's arm and walked to one of the guards.

"Why are those children here? Who are they?"

A curious expression crossed the guard's face and he glanced at Bryant for instructions.

"Look, I've been out on maneuvers all morning," Bryant said. "Those kids weren't here when I left this morning. What do you know, corporal?"

"Nobody tells me nothin'." The guard shrugged. "Rumors say they were brought here as hostages for ransom. I heard they belong to some important criminal, some woman who escaped from prison. I heard the higher-ups think Espiritu will be interested in getting them." The guard shrugged again.

CHAPTER SIXTEEN
The Gathering
The Desert

Annie Miller was free. The walls of Canada were behind her as was the prison and the brave people who helped her. Before her stretched the great American desert, and somewhere amidst the sand dunes and mountains was her husband, Robert. The sun sank in the western sky as Annie looked south. An endless parched, flatland reached into the distance and a yellow sky curved down to meet the torn and lifeless land. In the west, the Rocky Mountains rose out of this barren desert and somewhere in those mountains was Robert. She would soon be with him and her children, but for now she was alone.

Annie adjusted the broad brimmed, straw hat she wore, placed her backpack on the ground and sat down on a flat brown stone covered in gray dust and protruding out of the earth like an ancient grave marker. She placed her automatic weapon across her knees. A lightweight Tyson fabric covered her body from her neck to her ankles and beneath the coat she wore a simple white blouse and white cotton pantaloons. On her feet were tall boots that covered her calves. A net covered her straw hat and fell over her face and neck. Yes. She was prepared for the desert, a blast furnace of killing heat. But, for how long?

This day was almost finished. It had started early in the morning with the sound of blinds opening and bright light invading the blackness of her slumber. A voice spoke to her.

"Wake up, dear," the voice said.

Annie, in that state between sleep and reality, held her breath and a shudder passed through her body.

"We need to get you started on to your next location," the voice said.

Annie opened her eyes. The young woman with the long blond braid and the bejeweled fingers stood next to her bed with a glass of orange juice on a tray.

"Oh, be careful," the girl said when Annie attempted to sit up, but winced in pain.

"Your ribs are broken, but the doctor has given us some medication for you and some instructions." The young woman held her hand out toward Annie. "I have two pills for you. One is for pain and the other is an antibiotic."

Annie, with pain pulsing throughout her body, pulled herself up in bed, took the two pills and placed them in her mouth. She washed them down with a drink from the glass of orange juice. The girl who served her looked no more than eighteen. She was average height and slender. Her clothes, although simple, looked expensive.

"What is the date?" Annie asked.

"It's September first. Finish your drink." the girl urged. "You need your strength. It's real orange juice."

Annie drained the glass then closed her eyes. She had never tasted anything so sweet or delicious.

"We need to get you up and dressed," the girl said.

The brown-skinned lady with well-manicured hands and large brown eyes entered the room with the girl's mother, but no one introduced themselves. Names in this business were never mentioned. In most cases, aliases were used.

"We'll bring your breakfast up here later," the mother said. "We've had you on pain medication all night to help you sleep. You have a busy day ahead."

Annie was not yet wide awake, but her mind was alert. The pain pills were working. She sat in a soft bed, leaning her head against a pile of pillows. For a moment, Annie thought that perhaps she had died in that arena. Perhaps this was some sort of afterlife.

Sweet fragrances filled her senses. Pale yellow curtains framed a window with an outside view of green lawns and flower gardens. Framed pictures hung on the walls and a thick carpet covered the floor. A vanity stood against one wall and when Annie's eyes caught her reflection, she gasped in horror. Dark bruises covered her nose and both eyes were almost swollen shut.

"Don't worry about that now." The mother sat down on the bed and put her arm around Annie's shoulder. "They broke your nose and some of your teeth as well as some of your ribs," she said. "It will take a while, but the bruises will fade. Your nose will heal." The mother smoothed Annie's hair "We had a doctor and a dentist in to see you while you were sleeping. Your wounds will mend. No vital organs were damaged, but you lost some teeth, two on the left side. Don't worry. You're strong."

"I saw you at the courthouse," Annie said. "You were both at the courthouse." Annie looked at the dark-skinned woman and the mother. "Not at the trial, but at the sentencing. I remember you."

"We were, indeed," the dark eyed lady responded as she stood gazing out the window. "If my husband knew what I was up to, he would have me executed. On the other hand, my friend's husband," she gestured toward the fair skinned mother. "He's with us one hundred percent. He's going to fly you to your next rendezvous in his private plane. His wife and I are going with you."

"I'm going, too," the teenage girl responded.

"My sister lives in Montana." The mother shook her head and spoke without looking at her daughter. "My sister lives close to the border and this will be the excuse we need. We will drop you off close to the town and you will be picked up and taken into the desert from there."

Annie knew that the Montana territory, now belonging to Canada, was a wild, uncivilized region where Tyson cotton crops flourished in the dry, desolate terrain. Well-guarded, walled estates sat adjacent to migrant camps and militia outposts.

"Mom, you know how important it is for all of us to go." The blond girl bit her bottom lip, but showed no other emotion.

The mother sighed. "Yes, my daughter is going with us. It will be like a family visit to the country. No one will question us."

"Why are you doing this?" Annie asked. "Why did you join The Eight? You have everything."

"Maybe we joined for selfish reasons." A sandy-haired man walked into the room wearing expensive casual clothes and dark-rimmed glasses. His brown eyes rested on Annie's face and he shook his head. A look of disgust crossed his face. "Those bastards," he said. "I'm so sorry."

Annie recognized this man, Senator Durand, a powerful corporate senator. Government positions, like Durand's, commanded tremendous power and respect. Duran had close associations, both business and personal, with the Montoya and Sato families. This association assured Duran an even more lucrative and respected position.

Although Duran and all senate leaders maintained prestige and authority, real control belonged to the wealthiest chairman of the most powerful corporation. Oversight of government had passed with little incidence – sometimes with stunned silence – to tyrants who promised protection within the walls. Elections by the people became a nuisance and were outlawed decades in the past. The power of decision was handed to corporate boards.

However, no government official could obtain an office without passing a series of exams designed to ensure who was allowed to move into the next level of education, graduate, or establish a career. Those with the most money and most power were ensured their children would pass.

Government positions, selected by corporate boards, were expensive to buy, but proved to be profitable investments. The job of the senators was to keep money and resources flowing in the right direction and into the correct pockets. Much of the time, those pockets belonged to the senators.

Although The Eight was grateful to have such wealthy and influential collaborators on their side, those corporate spies were looked upon with suspicion. Annie knew, however, that The Eight could never have come this far without the support of those powerful insiders.

"What did you mean when you said you joined The Eight for selfish reasons?" Annie said.

Sometimes Annie wondered if her own reasons for joining The Eight were selfish. The Eight brought her closer to her husband, but it also gave her a strange sense of worth that work in the factories never gave her. It was true she wanted to be with Robert and her children more than anything. Annie dreamed of finding Robert and bringing him home. There were times she still wanted a normal life, but other times she needed more than just a normal life. There were times she needed freedom from being normal. Sometimes, Annie needed The Eight.

Duran came closer to the bed and looked down at Annie. His eyes revealed a deep intelligence and a kindness she had not seen for a long while. "There's a revolution getting ready to explode, Annie, and you know that. I want to be on the right side of this revolution when it comes. You're on the right side and you're going to win. I'm going to be there with you. That's my selfish reason."

The blond mother, Duran's wife, sat on the edge of the bed and gave a short laugh.

"My husband has the third eye and so do you, Annie. So do I, my daughter and my dear friend over there." Duran's wife glanced at the dark-skinned lady standing by the window.

"I don't understand," Annie said.

"The third eye is a curse," the blond woman said. "We see and feel things others can't, Annie."

"Or won't" her husband said.

"Yes, or won't." The woman looked up at her husband and smiled. "The third eye isn't about money or power because the third eye is power."

"The third eye is the power to connect with other people," she continued. "We feel their happiness and their suffering." She took Annie's hand and leaned close to her. "Annie, we understand what the future can be. We believe we have the power to change the future, to make it better not just for us, but for others. Unfortunately for us, because we feel what others feel, life is not always about us. Annie, if you or I turn our backs on the suffering of others, that pain will be transferred to us and it will stay with us forever. In that way, the third eye is truly a curse."

"We disagree with our colleges in power," Duran said. "There's a better way and you are the one who is leading the way, Annie."

"You have saved my life." Annie said. "Thank you."

"They're going crazy looking for you," Duran said. "We need to get you out of the city as quick as possible. You've been sleeping long enough. The plane is ready and you need to reach your next rendezvous point."

Duran walked to the door, stopped and turned back toward Annie. "You can rest on the plane. You've got a long journey ahead."

Duran's family took Annie by plane from New Town, Canada to Billings in the Montana territory. From there, she was handed to couriers who took her by rover to a migrant work camp on the edge of the desert. Annie waited, huddled in a stifling tent for her next contact.

No one questioned Annie's temporary presence in that harsh, primitive camp. Migrants came and went with secrets, and each secret was a tragedy no one cared to share. Dignity and respect was given by never asking. "Live and let live," was the migrants' code.

Few of these camp dwellers had ever traveled or even left the corporate lands on which they lived and worked. Information was provided to them through corporate televisions situated in every village. It was illegal for a migrant to own a phone, rover or computer. The migrants cultivated the Tyson cotton crop, genetically engineered to survive in the near waterless deserts of Montana, North and South Dakota and Idaho.

A small aircraft transported Annie from the Canadian border to her present destination in the American desert. Her courageous guides who had led her from the hangman's noose and through the safe houses, evaporated like disinterested spirits once they brought her safely through the dragnet, over the borders of civilization and to this place in the wilderness.

The sun was descending in the west, and Anne waited alone in the desert for her next currier. Colorful auras, created by the sun's rays piercing the thick hazy atmosphere, danced on the horizon. Not even a hint of a breeze appeared to cool the sweat pooling on her body. The dry heat took on an odor of death and decay.

I never thought heat could smell like anything, Annie told herself. But it does. She gave a sigh as she remembered the pungent aroma of the pine trees she and Robert were employed to plant on the northern Canadian tundra. The smells of life, she thought. The sweet smell of rebirth.

Annie opened her backpack, took out a plastic bottle filled with water, opened the lid and held the bottle beneath her nose. She smiled at the scent of fresh, clean water. Annie took a sip of the precious liquid, placed a pain pill in her mouth and washed it down with another swallow of water. After replacing the water bottle in her backpack, Annie stood up, slung her weapon over her shoulder, pushed her dark glasses up on her bruised and broken nose and peered out across the silent desert.

There is movement, she thought, or is it a mirage? Far in the distance, she could see the figures of several men moving in her direction. Could it be the militia? Annie readied her weapon for firing. There was no place to hide. The figures came closer. Five men riding camels came to a halt about 75 feet from her. Annie held her weapon against her hip ready to fire.

Each of the five men banished weapons and each wore a bandolier crisscrossing their chest. They were dressed in loose-fitting white trousers and shirt and a broad-brimmed straw hat with netting covering their faces. Their camels snorted and stomped seeming unhappy about stopping.

"So," the man in the center spoke, leaning over the head of his camel and looking at Annie. "You must be what we have come to rescue." He gave a deep laugh and reached up to remove the netting from his face.

"Don't," Annie yelled and pointed her weapon at him.

"Hold on a minute," he said. "I'm here to take you south. I'm Ivan. You've been sending me weapons and information for a long time. I came here myself to personally escort you across the desert. You are a very important package." He laughed, loud and deep from his belly. "A small package, but important."

Annie stepped back and motioned for him to remove his netting.

Slowly the man raised the netting from his face and folded it back over his hat revealing a face covered in a thick red beard. Woven into his beard and his long braided hair was sparkling glass beads and small mirrors. Tattoos covered his muscular hands.

"So, you're Ivan," Annie said, lowering her weapon. "Okay. Let's go." She looked at the camel and sighed.

"I'm sorry," Ivan said while maneuvering his camel to a sitting position. "We need to ride for about an hour. We'll transfer to a land rover later and then we'll go the rest of the way in the rover." Ivan dismounted, took her backpack and threw it to one of his men.

"Camels are slow," he said, "but they make for a more difficult target from the air. Our group will split up and that will make it harder for the militia to spot us. It's easier for the pilots to lock onto the land rovers."

Ivan took Annie in his arms and hoisted her onto the back of the camel. He mounted the animal, straddling the saddle with Annie behind him.

"We're going around that city over there," he said, pointing toward the ruins. "And into those mountains. Hang on."

The procession began to move. The motion of the camel as it plodded across the desert caused pain to shoot through Annie's body, but fortunately her pain medication made it bearable. Annie felt calm and confident. As they moved southwest, their traveling companions began to disappear into the desert. Soon, Annie and Ivan were traveling alone. Ahead stretched the parched American wasteland and beyond that the Rocky Mountains. Somewhere in those scorched and barren mountains was her husband, and in those mountains she would be reunited with her children. What else would she find, Annie wondered?

No, she told herself. This is no time for fear. Now, there is only time for action and purpose. Annie straightened her shoulders and a smile settled on her lips.

Light was fading when they reached a camp consisting of five small tents pitched in the shadow of the foothills. At first glance, the camp seemed to Annie to be deserted although on a second look, it was a camp in the midst of packing-up. At least a dozen armed men appeared from behind tents, small hills and nearby boulders. The other camel riders, who had started out with Annie and Ivan, began to arrive. The camp came alive with action. Men gathered equipment and began to take down the tents.

Ivan dismounted and helped Annie from the camel. He led her to a large bolder toward the center of the camp where she sat, her weapon across her lap. She closed her eyes and heaved a sigh of relief. The camel ride was over. Annie removed her hat and ran her fingers through her tangled hair then looked down at the rock-littered dirt and noticed a trail of ants crawling across the ground. She moved her feet, careful not to step on them.

Annie remembered learning about ants when she was a little girl. Insects adapted to most ecological conditions they encountered. She was taught that most desert insects do not drink water because they get the needed moisture from the food they eat. Those insects, under survival conditions, had turned to cannibalism. They not only devoured each other, but they consumed any other living thing they could disable. Were they any different from us, Annie wondered?

Something stirred close to her and Annie looked up to notice a young boy watching her from a distance. His blue shirt and tan trousers were tattered and ripped, his bare feet bandaged. The boy's skin was badly sunburned. Annie sensed an oppressive sadness emanating from the child. He stood so still, just looking at her. Annie smiled and nodded at him.

"Are you in pain?" Ivan asked.

Annie turned her eyes away from the boy and looked up at Ivan.

"I have pills when I need them. Who's that child over there?"

"What child?"

"The boy over there?" Annie looked back to where the child was standing, but he was gone. She sighed and looked at Ivan.

"Have you seen my husband?" she asked.

Ivan nodded. "I've talked to Robert."

"Is he well?"

Ivan looked into Annie's face. For a moment, a question formed on his lips, but he paused and changed his mind. "Robert is a man with an old and powerful soul," he told Annie. "Robert is a man of ideas, a man of principles and a man of peace. But there's a war coming and Robert works closely with Espiritu. We," Ivan paused. "I, you, Robert, Espiritu are all together at the heart of this revolution. It's going to explode very soon."

Ivan's jaw tightened. "Robert is also a man to be feared." He raised his eyebrow and cocked his head. "Even I fear Robert and I rarely fear anyone."

Without saying another word, Annie stood up, her weapon slung over her shoulder. She walked to the edge of camp and stopped to stand alone atop a mound of dirt and rocks. Annie had been told that several violent dust storms had passed through that area within the past few days and more were coming. Ivan was taking her high into the mountains where, she was told, they would avoid most of the storms. Yet, Annie knew that all of the dangers that lay ahead could not be avoided. Many people would die. Millions were dying now. More than five billion had died over the many decades since the ice melted. Everything dies. It matters not that you die, Annie reminded herself, but how you live your life.

A hot breeze tossed her loose hanging hair. Annie still wore the same white blouse and cotton pantaloons and she was grateful for the pair of comfortable, leather boots.

Twilight arrived, but the camp was fully awake. Most of the tents were down and folded into small bundles to be carried on the backs of camels. The smell of coffee mingled with the hot, acid air.

"I have coffee for you," Ivan's voice startled her.

Annie turned and looked up into Ivan's cold blue eyes that seemed to show no life at all. His red hair was decorated with pieces of glass woven into multiple braids and his bushy beard covered the lower half of his broad face.

"We'll have to eat while we're moving," Ivan told her. "Protein paste rolled in a tortilla. We're lucky we have it." His lips moved little as he spoke. His dark, broken teeth explained his sour breath.

Annie took the tin cup from him and sipped the cold, black liquid. He stood beside her, a revolver holstered at his side. He wore filthy, white cotton pantaloons tucked inside combat boots and his loose, long-sleeved shirt fell to his knees covering his tattooed body. A belt of ammunition encircled his waist.

"When did you see my husband?"

"Six weeks ago. Maybe less."

Her eyes widened. "It's been three years. Three years for me and my children. Tell me," she said, holding the cup of coffee in both hands. "Who is my husband now? What has he become? I know what I've become." Annie turned her face toward the desert as her mind filled with images of her young, laughing husband. She felt his strong arms encircle her body and she tasted his kisses. Their dreams were simple yet exciting – a home, a life in Canada, a future.

"Your husband, Mrs. Miller, is with the leader of The Eight." Ivan's voice brought Annie back to the present. She took a long drink of her coffee and wiped her lips with the back of her hand.

"And who are you, Mr. Ivan?" Annie said. "How do you fit into his world?"

Ivan shifted his stance, resting his hand on his holstered gun. "I am a man of opportunity," he said. "I have been called a pirate, a terrorist, a criminal. I may be all of those things, but I am also a businessman."

Annie gave him a questioning look.

"Yes, a businessman," he answered her silent question. "A businessman with little difference from those corporate kings who live in luxury behind walls. They have tremendous power and wealth. But power and wealth is theirs only until someone else takes it from them. Espiritu and your husband are going to take that power and I am going to be with them when they do."

"Unless they kill us all," Annie said.

"Look," Ivan said, pointing toward the desert.

Annie turned and saw a scattered band of people walking toward them. There were men, women and children. Migrants, she thought. A sorry looking group dressed in civilian clothes, or as it seemed to Annie, civilian rags. Most had backpacks and all carried weapons.

"They've come here to see you," Ivan told her.

"Me?" Her voice betrayed surprise and confusion.

"You're Robert's wife, Mrs. Miller. People are coming here to fight beside your husband and for him. They know he is the one closest to Espiritu, and they know about the work you have done with The Eight. These groups are scattered across this desert and as you know that is dangerous. The militia is flying daily reconnaissance and destroying any person they encounter. The bigger the concentration of people, the easier it is for the militia to see us from the air."

"But they keep coming."

"Yes. Espiritu is a great leader, and when his plans are complete, our world will be changed. Those people's lives will be better, or at least that is what they believe. Espiritu gives them hope. Robert found a huge piece of Blue Eden and he knew what to do with it. He started organizing, beginning with the underground scientists."

"The Eight," Annie said.

Ivan nodded. "Through The Eight, word spread that Blue Eden was now a reality." Ivan shifted his stance again and looked out over the desert. "Most people just wait for the future to happen, or they wait for someone else to tell them what to do about the future. Espiritu doesn't wait. He knows how to make the future happen the way he wants it to happen. He makes people trust him. These people . . ." Ivan gestured toward the approaching crowd, "are ready to follow Espiritu into his future. They trust him to make their lives better. But you already know all of this, Annie Miller."

Annie took a last drink of her coffee and tossed the remaining liquid to the ground. "I know my husband," she said. "And I know the times we live in."

Annie stood beside Ivan and watched the approaching partisans grow to about 50 people. Most of them were in their twenties, but there were also some with graying hair. Women and children intermingled with the men and everyone seemed to hold some type of weapon.

"This is dangerous," Annie said to Ivan while keeping her eyes on the crowd. "We're making a large target for the militia."

"They don't care," Ivan told her. "They want to see you. They need to know you are real. They need to feel your power; the power of The Eight. The power of your El Espiritu."

The group stopped about 40 yards from where Annie and Ivan stood. A pulsing energy emanated from those migrants; an energy of determination and defiance.

Everyone remained silent for a moment and then, almost in unison, the migrants raised their weapons over their heads. Great cheers exploded into the air. Annie dropped her coffee cup to the ground and slipped her rifle from her shoulder. Holding the weapon with both hands, she lifted it high above her head. Standing like a stone statue, she raised her chin in the air, but kept her eyes leveled on the cheering people. The cheers erupted even louder. Children clapped and danced while the adults swayed and stomped their feet.

"We have to go." Ivan told her in a hushed voice. He gently took her by the elbow and turned her away from the crowd. Annie lowered her gun and walked with Ivan back to the camp, now packed and ready to move.

CHAPTER SEVENTEEN
The Cannibals
The Ruins

"Someone help him." Hannah's voice was half scream half sob. "Please. He's hurt. Do something."

Hannah sat beside Bobby, her hands smeared with his blood. Tears poured from her eyes. She rocked back and forth and gasped for breath. Nausea overwhelmed her and she held her stomach to keep from vomiting.

Hannah looked up at the people standing in the hallway their faces drawn and stricken with horror. They turned their eyes away from her to the eyes of the others and back to Hannah again. No one moved to help Bobby.

Zack knelt beside Hannah and put his arm around her shoulder.

"Hannah. It's over now," she thought he said, but that didn't make sense.

Dennis leaned over, picked something up that was lying on the floor next to Bobby, and his face turned pale. He knelt beside Zack and showed him what he had just retrieved from the ground.

"Cannibals," Hannah thought Dennis said. "I've heard about this, but I've never seen it. I've heard they wear human bones tied to their clothes. These bones must have been torn off those men's clothes in the scuffle." Dennis shook his head. His face looked pale beneath the sunburn. "Now things are starting to make sense. Those thugs that attacked us were scouts coming up here to check us out. They wanted to see who was here." Hannah saw fear cross Dennis' face. "They're hunting," he said.

Dennis and Zack stood up. "Yes," Zack, said. "And they'll be back. We've all heard about these gangs of cannibals but. . ." His voice trailed away to an inaudible utterance." It makes sense about the bridge," he said. "The corporation wouldn't have blown the bridge. The migrants wouldn't have either. But the cannibals would have. It's possible they blew the bridge just to kill as many people as they could. They aren't interested in the cargo, only the human cargo."

The woman with the auburn hair, wife of one of the accountants, took off her burka and covered Bobby's body. Blood soaked into the white material. "Did I hear you say cannibals?" the woman asked as she knelt on the floor beside Hannah, her green eyes betrayed near panic.

Hannah looked up at Dennis and Zack standing beside her. They were talking, but for some reason she could not understand what they were saying. Their words were muffled and far away.

"Well, we know which way they went," Zack said, ignoring the woman's obvious sense of terror. "And we're going in the opposite direction from them. Two of those savages were injured and they left a blood trail going that way." He gestured toward a stairwell.

"They're using sticks and spears," one of the accountants said. "They don't have guns. At least these guys didn't."

"My husband went this morning with some men to see about our supplies," the green-eyed woman said. "Are they in danger?"

No one answered her question.

More survivors entered the hallway chattering in hushed voices about cannibals and escape.

"We gotta get out of here," the train porter said. "If we find the militia patrols out there, they'll help us for sure. I've got papers. Most of us do. We can speak for those who don't."

"Me too," someone yelled. "I've got papers."

Agitated voices filled the air. Hannah sat on the ground unable to move or to understand the conversation going on around her.

"We sent nine men out to collect our supplies," Dennis said. "We're to meet up with them back at the building on the edge of the city. Look. Evidence points to those thugs being cannibals, but we can't be sure."

"They're savages," someone called out.

"They're human beings," Dennis said. "They're desperate and trying to stay alive out there. So are we. That levels the field. We're going to survive." The volume of Dennis' voice was rising. "We're going to make it to Canada, but we have to think. We have to use our heads and we have to stay together."

Hannah heard Dennis sigh. She watched him look around the hallway at the group of survivors, most of them women and children.

"Everyone, start collecting anything you can find that will work for a weapon, "Dennis said. "And find anything that will burn. We're going to set this place on fire and at the same time have a funeral. The fire will be our escape cover and keep those savages disoriented. They'll be more worried about the fire than about us. If those thugs are still in the building, the fire will drive them out and give us a chance to escape."

"You, boy," Zack said as he pointed at one of the teenage boys. "Take her out of here." Zack gestured toward Hannah and then turned toward the woman with the green eyes. "And, mam, take those children down the hall. There's another stairwell at the end of this hallway. The rest of you, get weapons and make a bonfire."

"Come on, girl," a voice said. Hannah felt herself being lifted up. She kept her eyes on the covered body as she felt hands grasp her arm and pull her away from Bobby. She lacked the strength to resist. Frightened voices, shuffling feet, blistering air and a thin veil of floating dust touched her senses and then drifted away.

Hannah felt hands around her arm and shoulder and someone pushed her forward. Her feet moved away from

Bobby, but her heart still lay with him. Someone guided her back to the room with the broken-out window overlooking the city. A voice said, "Stay put."

Excited voices, muffled voices, sounds of shuffling feet filled the room from the hallway, but outside the building stretched a lifeless world. Hannah moved as though in a trance to the large, broken-out window and stared out over the silent metropolis below. The city's heart stopped beating just like Bobby's heart and just like mine, Hannah told herself. The fire in the distance, started by the storm was growing. She could see the red flames consuming the neglected city and sending black smoke and ash into the atmosphere covering the city like a shroud.

"Things that were once alive turn to ashes," Hannah spoke out loud. Tears that once flooded her eyes and spilled down her cheeks had stopped flowing. Her emotions became trapped within a sheath of disillusionment and confusion.

"I lost my best friend. I lost my book," Hannah spoke out loud. Maybe there was someone in the room with her, maybe she was alone. Hannah spoke to the wind. "I don't know how to go to Canada. I can't go if Bobby doesn't go with me."

Why had Bobby abandoned her? Hope disappeared with Bobby's death.

"Once hope is gone, your life slowly slips away from you," Hannah's grandmother had said.

Hannah leaned out the wide opening. A hot wind blew ash from the distant fire into her hair. She took a deep breath and inhaled the smoky air.

"Bobby would not fail me," she told herself. "I climbed down the drain pipe and met him in the darkness." She leaned further over the edge of the window. "How can I have hope if you're not here with me?" Hannah spoke out loud.

"Did you say something, girl?" A voice spoke from somewhere nearby.

"I said, once hope is gone, your life slowly slips away from you." Hannah stared down at the dead city beneath her.

The voice spoke to her again. "Yeah, so what else did your grandmother say? I had a grandmother a long time ago. She used to say a lot of things."

Hannah turned away from the window and looked toward the voice. Bobby was standing before her, smiling and happy. No, it was not Bobby. It was someone else. The boy in the desert. The boy with the brown eyes who called her girl. "You ain't no boy," he had said.

Hannah's memory took her back again to her attic room and to her grandmother.

"She told me that I must never give up hope. It is not just the dream of hope that keeps you alive. You have to pursue those dreams, no matter the cost. To do nothing, bankrupts your soul. Grandma always said that. But I don't know what to do. My dream is a nightmare now. I don't want to be here anymore, but I don't know where to go."

"So, you think any of the rest of us want to be here," the boy said. "We're all in the same boat. I sure don't know where I'm going to end up, but it's sure as hell away from here. I'm still alive right now and I'm going to make the best of it. Go ahead and stay here if you want to. Burn with the building," the boy said.

A heavy smell of smoke followed by a white cloud drifted into the room. Frightened voices in the hallway shouted in unison. "They're comin' back move fast have to leave carry the kids move fast."

"Are you comin', girl?" The boy took her arm, gave it a tug and then let her go. He hurried to the door, turned and waved for her to follow. Smoke was now pouring into the room and she could hear the crackling sound of a healthy fire.

"You're going to get me in trouble, girl," the boy said. "Zack told me to look after you. Hurry." He waved for her to follow, his face held a determined look.

Hannah followed the boy into the smoke filled corridor. A wall of flames stretched across the hallway and was crawling up the walls. Adults carrying wailing children were running away from the fire. Older children scurried behind.

Someone shoved a small child into Hannah's arms and yelled for her to hurry. The toddler wrapped himself around her body and pressed his face against her shoulder. Hannah held the child tight and moved with the flow of men, women and children. She looked back over her shoulder and saw several figures standing behind the barrier of flames stretching across the hall. The ominous figures stood watching the band of survivors flee down the corridor and enter the steep stairwell. Down Hannah went, into the narrow, windowless passage.

Darkness closed around her. The exit door behind her slammed shut and a steel bolt clanged preventing anyone else from entering the escape route. Smoke, however, rolled through cracks and chased the fleeing prey.

The child Hannah carried was a cumbersome burden. She shifted him in her arms and the boy squeezed her neck even tighter. His short, steady breaths were warm against her neck, and the rhythm of his heart beating against her chest calmed the rhythm of her own heart. At each floor, the procession stopped and someone made sure the stairwell door was locked. Hannah realized that this ensured no one else in the building could enter the stairwell. On two occasions as they descended, Zack and two others entered a floor at a landing and set the abandoned offices on fire. The ancient, decaying wood particles erupted easily with the touch of a match, and the desert breeze whipping through the building, fanned the flames into an unstoppable inferno.

The fire was above them, pushing them downward. An explosion caused by the encroaching fire, erupted somewhere in the building, shaking the walls of their dark tunnel. A child screamed and her cries of fear and frustration pierced the nerves of even the most stoic survivor. Down the group continued away from the smoke and into darkness. Whatever was waiting for them outside the tunnel and in the city was not on Hannah's mind. She simply proceeded at the pace of the others into the unknown.

The procession came to a halt at the bottom of the stairs, and with caution, Dennis opened the door. Light filtered into the dark stairwell. The men, carrying makeshift clubs and spears, exited first. A nervous accountant held the door while the women and children filed out into what was once a small alcove lined on both sides by now lifeless elevators.

Hannah followed the others into a two-story rotunda with a wide staircase leading to a balcony which circled above the first floor. On the opposite wall was the exit to the outside, a gaping hole that at one time must have been an expansive glass door. Ash floated on the air and the smell of smoke filled the building.

Hannah slid the child to the ground and held his hand as she walked with him across the dusty, marble floor of the rotunda. She searched the empty room as she moved with the procession toward their escape.

Was someone on the balcony? The group stopped and herded closer together. Hannah felt human bodies press against her as the group tightened. Someone cried out in fear. Others gasped. Standing above on the circular balcony were about twenty savages surrounding Hannah and the group. Several of the savages carried automatic weapons, but most carried spears. Human bones were tied to their clothes as well as to their matted hair and beards. A growing blanket of smoke and black ash floated down from an expanding dark area on the ceiling, but the savages stood stoically watching their prey below.

Two ragged, barefooted men, each brandishing rifles, appeared before the front exit blocking the way out. Hannah searched the faces of those barbaric men, looking for the thugs who murdered Bobby and stole her book. Those exact culprits were not to be found, but Bobby was dead and Hannah realized these people surrounding her were the cause of his death. Those savages were to blame.

Acknowledgement of Bobby's fate became hate and hate became rage. Hannah picked up the child and shoved him into the arms of a person standing next to her. She pushed her way through the crowd and charged at the armed man standing before the exit. Running with all the force that was in her small body, Hannah threw herself against his bulky frame. Like a tiny bullet slamming against its target, Hannah made contact and sent the startled warrior flying backwards. She kicked, bit his flesh and tore at his face with her fingers. Hannah felt the man's hands grasp her flaying arms as he regained his balance. He stood up with her in his hands and threw her against a wall.

The anger boiling in her mind was not cooling. Hannah started to stand in order to run at him again, but the room erupted into a ball of flames. The ceiling above the balcony gave way, sending burning timbers and debris crashing against the mezzanine railings and down onto the first floor. Bodies fell with the timbers and fire rained from the ceiling. The sounds of gunfire and stampeding feet blended with the sounds of terrifying screams.

People were running toward the exit, but Hannah noticed other people running into the burning building. Those coming in carried guns and were shooting up at the balcony.

"Hurry," they yelled. "Get those kids out of here. Get out of here, boy,"

A man with a well-manicured beard glared at her from a distance. Hannah struggled to her feet and coughed when hot smoke entered her lungs. She searched the stampeding crowd for the child she had carried through the stairwell and noticed a woman taking the boy out the door. Hannah joined the last of the panicked group as they rushed toward the exit and out into the street. Fresh air hit her in the face and she took deep breaths in an attempt to clear her lungs.

Hannah stood barefoot on the rocky pavement. The sound of gunfire stopped. She noticed a small platoon of armed men helping women and children into two rovers parked a short distance from the burning building. They were not uniformed, but instead wore an array of civilian clothing, floppy hats and bandanas. All of the men held their weapons in ready mode and kept focused eyes on the environment. Hannah also noticed that the group of men who had returned to the sleds for the abandoned supplies were also with these armed men. She wondered what happened to the savages. They seemed to have disappeared. Maybe they escaped, she thought. Maybe they were killed.

Two men and a woman caught Hannah's attention. They stood apart from the group and seemed to be watching her. The men were dressed in expensive business suits, and the woman wore a burka. When they noticed Hannah looking in their direction, the woman nodded at her. The two men smiled.

Hannah shivered. She could not take her eyes off of them. The woman whispered something to the men and they nodded in agreement. Hannah watched the woman climb aboard one of the rovers as the two men blended into the group of male train survivors.

Hannah remained standing with the men and boys as the rovers with the women and children crowded on board started to move.

"Start moving," a young civilian trooper yelled to the group. "We've come here to rescue you, for God's sake." Hannah, along with the men, began following the armed procession.

"Who are those two men in business suits who were with that woman in the burka?" Hannah asked one of the armed rescuers walking beside her.

"We've been patrolling this area picking up immigrants. We don't ask who they are when we pick them up. That gets sorted out later." The young man slowed his pace when he noticed Hannah shoeless and stumbling on the sharp rocky ground.

"These cannibals are out here hunting for prey," he continued. "And there's a corporate army about five miles north of here. This ain't no place to be."

"So who are you?" The train porter asked. "Where are you taking us?"

The soldier gave a slight sigh. "We're the good guys. There's a corporate army about five miles from here that's moving up into those mountains and it's looking for us. We've got strongholds up there." He gestured toward the mountains. "This desert is full of immigrants coming here to join us. The army is killing the immigrants when they can find them and the cannibals are capturing them when they can find them. The cannibals are also taking our soldiers and the army patrols. This is where you are right now. You have a choice. You can try to make it back to the corporate army and join them, or you can come with us."

As Hannah walked, she looked back over her shoulder at the burning building. Red flames leaped out of the windows scorching the concrete walls. Thick clumps of ash emanating from the fire that was started by the storm sprinkled down from the smoke filled sky.

"Goodbye, Bobby," Hannah whispered. "Goodbye."

CHAPTER EIGHTEEN
The Children
The Mountains

Gage was accustomed to the reek of camp life, but first-time visitors were often overcome by the appalling stench. He noticed Rebecca holding a cloth over her nose as they were led through the camp by Officer Bryant. Over a thousand men, housed together in the sweltering desert, who had not been afforded the luxury of a bath in weeks or months, produced an odor beyond description. Overflowing latrines added to the offensive stench as did the smell of chemicals used to stave off the constant threat of insect bites.

Most of the men in the camp were resting if that was possible in the desert inferno. Temperatures could reach 150 degrees Fahrenheit. Although many tents were closed canvas, most men slept on pallets in open-air canopies enclosed with netting. Beneath one such shelter, a group of young recruits were racing cockroaches across a strip of canvas. Gage saw a curious expression cross the men's faces when they noticed Rebecca and Gage following Bryant through the camp.

Gage knew that other recruits were engaged in card and dice games, and that prostitutes occupied their own area of the camp. Most commanders made some effort to control vice in camp, but others did little or nothing to rein in the vice. Gambling, drinking and prostitution were always rampant and in some cases encouraged as long as it did not interfere with their duties. Women were usually allowed to accompany the armies when on campaign as long as they kept to their own section of camp.

Bryant led Gage and Rebecca to a well-guarded collection of tents in the center of camp. A small group of officer's tents, with insignia indicating rank, surrounded a larger canvas structure appearing to be about 20 feet in diameter.

"General Mullans knows you're here," Bryant said as they approached a small security tent. "But we may have to wait."

An officer stepped out from the security tent armed for his duties as a sentry, bowed to Rebecca and saluted Gage. He wore a short-trimmed beard and mustache.

"Could you please wait a moment until we hear that the General is ready to see you?" He motioned for Bryant to come inside the tent and for Gage and Rebecca to remain outside.

"You're going to meet my cousin, Buzz Mullans," Rebecca said. "But, don't call him Buzz. He hates it. "

"I wouldn't think of it." Gage said with as much respect in his voice as he could find in order to camouflage his contempt. "I know of General Mullans and I know for a fact he's been called a lot of things, but how did he get the name Buzz?"

"I'll tell you some day, but not now. It's a long story. His name is John Mullans or General Mullans as he prefers everyone to call him. He's from my mother's side of the family. . .the Irish side. For some reason, he's always loved the military, but he has never been a fighter. At least not when we were kids. He always loved being a spectator rather than a participant. I don't know. Maybe that changes when you put on a uniform."

"I don't know what makes people what they are," Gage said to Rebecca as Officer Bryant and the sentry were coming out of the tent.

"I'll catch you later." Bryant said to Gage, saluted and then bowed to Rebecca before hurrying away.

"Follow me," the young sentry told them. "The General will see you now."

Gage and Rebecca followed the sentry through a maze of officer's tents and stopped before the opening of a huge, sand-colored tent in the center of the camp. The smell of barbecued meat and spices drifted on the air overpowering for a moment the stench of the encampment.

When the sentry threw the tent flap open, Gage entered one of the most amazing sights he had ever seen. Although the outside of the tent was simple and unmarked, the inside walls were a patchwork of the most magnificent textiles, specially dyed weavings and embroideries. Much of the work was woven with gold and silver thread. The window openings were elaborate geometric cutouts edged with gold. The ceiling had similar panels of different textiles and woven art. Large solar-powered fans stirred and cooled the stifling air.

A set of curtains divided the canvas room in half and in front of the curtain stood a table with six cushioned chairs. The table, sitting on the bare desert floor, was set with a white linen cloth and three fine china place settings.

The center curtain was pulled aside and General Mullans strode into the dining area. He was about six feet tall, broad-shouldered, yet slender. A bushy black beard covered his chin and blended into a mustache and sideburns. He returned Gage's salute then his dark eyes came to rest on his cousin, Rebecca.

"Well, well Becca," he said. "What a miracle you were found out there. I was told your plane crashed. You're not injured, are you?"

"No. Not really. Just shook up a bit. This is my body guard, Officer Gage. We left two of his men and my assistant in the desert."

"And, we need to go back for them," Gage said.

"If my patrols find them, they'll get picked up. It's a big desert." Mullans sighed. "Sit down, Becca, and you too, Officer Gage. You both will join me for dinner." Mullans looked at Gage. "I see by your insignia that you're a pilot?"

"Yes, sir. And so are my two men we left in the desert."

"Then you are all needed," Mullans said after pulling out a chair and sitting down. "Please sit down." Rebecca sat down across from Mullans. Gage remained standing.

"I need a plane," Gage said.

"We'll start a rescue mission in good time," Mullans said. "For now, sit down."

Gage gave a slight bow and sat next to Rebecca. Patience was necessary he told himself. Inside he was boiling but he needed to play their game for now.

General Mullans picked up a small bell on the table and rang it a few times. Two servants, dressed in corporate uniforms appeared, filled glasses with water and orange juice and set platters of meat and vegetables on the table.

"This is as luxurious as I can get it out here in the field and I'm sorry to say, this may be the last decent meal we have for a while." Mullans shook his head and began filling his plate as he spoke. "I have my personal food and supplies flown in on a daily basis, but. . .the last plane was shot down. Can you believe it? Shot down!" Mullans clenched his fists and hit them on the table, shaking the dishes. "How are those ignorant migrants doing this?"

Gage studied Rebecca's cousin and a sour taste formed in his mouth. This was a man of money and privilege, not one to be fighting battles in the wilderness. Yet, it was typical for the kings to choose family members to administer war plans while the real fighting and dying was left to others.

"Cousin Rebecca," Mullans continued. "I can't offer you much comfort here, and I'm not sure when I can get you transportation to Canada. You see, we're in a bit of a curious mess here." Mullans took a long drink of orange juice closing his eyes as he drank.

"This is not exactly what I expected out here," Mullans said. "This was going to be an easy assignment, an important one yes, but easy. I intend to lay to rest for good those myths about Blue Eden and this El Espiritu. How hard could that be?" Mullans shrugged his shoulders.

"We're dealing with a handful of ignorant peasants. Their heads are filled with superstition rather than work ethics. Fortunately, the majority of the workers stand with the corporations." Mullans smiled and continued.

"Once I stop this nonsense, I've been promised the governorship of Ireland. But. . ." He slammed his fist on the table, rattling the dishes and spilling orange juice over the tablecloth. "We've been losing planes and men every day. Our planes are being targeted and hit by missiles. Not only when they're in the air, but also here in camp as they sit on the ground. We send platoons out and they never return."

As Gage watched Mullans cut a piece of meat and stuff it in his mouth with the end of his knife, Gage's anger boiled toward this shallow man. Mullans spoke while chewing.

"Our drones are destroyed before we can get any information back. Our supply trains are being robbed and those migrants even blew a bridge." Mullans took a drink of water, swallowed and wiped his mouth with a cloth napkin. "Now, blowing that bridge is something I don't understand because those migrants rely on those supply trains as much as we do. They rob them constantly." Mullins lips curled into a dark snarl. "And the desertions."

The word desertion moved through Gage's mind. He took a bite of his steak. The meat was tough and dry. Protein paste would have tasted better today, he thought. He glanced at Rebecca and noticed she had not touched her food. Gage took a drink of water. Maybe it's not the food, but the company that is so distasteful, he thought.

Mullans leaned across the table and looked into Rebecca's eyes. "Maybe this is luck, cousin. Some would say this is God's will that you have come here. Rebecca, remember when we were children? I always chose you to be my partner when we played games and we always won. You and I make a great team."

Mullans picked up his glass of water. "Woman as you are, Rebecca, you are smart and devious. You're stuck here with me in this hell for a while and I think we need to make the best of this." He took a drink and sat the glass down.

"Rebecca, I want you here in the room, listening, when my advisors and officers are speaking. When they leave, you will tell me what you think." Mullans leaned back in his chair and laughed. "I listen to all ideas, but I always make the final decision. If the plan fails, it was their idea. If it is successful, it was my decision." Mullans laughed. "Of course, I never lose."

Gage shifted in his seat. It was all he could do to keep quiet. Patience, Gage told himself, but his patience was wearing thin.

"Officer Gage," Mullans continued. "We're in need of pilots. We have a shortage, so you are now under my command. I need you to fly missions."

"Of course, my officer will fly missions for you. Your mission is my mission." Rebecca smiled, her demeanor calm, but her eyes glowed with a curious energy. "And of course cousin, I will assist you. Family is always important and you are correct. We have always worked well together."

Gage remained quiet but his mind processed his understanding of the situation. Rebecca Montoya is a queen and she is World Tech. There is nothing more. He had allowed himself to think, for a few moments, that there was something else.

"Your excellency." A sentry pulled the tent flap aside. "Someone is here to see you, sir. . .a Mister Grimes, sir."

"Yes, send him in." Mullans appeared excited. He smiled. "Mister Grimes is one of our agents. He's infiltrated this group of migrants."

A man in a broad-brimmed hat, a bushy brown beard, and dirty, shoulder-length hair entered the tent. He was dressed in a white cotton shirt, loose-fitting white cotton trousers and an automatic rifle was slung over his shoulder. Grimes scanned the room, assessing Gage and Rebecca.

"Come in. Come in. Sit down." Mullans waved to him. "Special treat today. Her Ladyship Montoya and her personal militia are here. Her plane crashed in the desert and we have rescued her. She is my cousin so you can speak freely."

Grimes stood quiet with his eyes resting on Gage and Rebecca. Acceptance appeared on his face and the man took a chair next to Gage.

"Me and my agents got picked up by the migrant patrols," Grimes said after taking a breath, "There's ten of us, men and women. The migrants took us to a stronghold in those mountains and we went through a processing center." Grimes shook his head and laughed. "People are coming to those mountains from all over the world. I have to tell you. Those migrants are organized."

Mullans, his face intent, clutched his hands together.

"It's like a city up there," Grimes said. "Well, more like a commune. Everyone is interviewed and given jobs. They don't seem to worry too much about infiltrators."

"How are they attacking us?"

"They've got an army." Grimes said. "Weapons. Some corporate militiamen have defected and are training the migrants."

Mullans slammed his hand on the table. "I want to know about those missiles. Where are they getting them? How are they shooting down our planes?"

"I'm telling you what I've got so far," Grimes said. "They've got communes scattered all over those hills. They're living in tents but there are caves up there, too. . .man made caves. They're storing supplies and weapons in those caves. My agents haven't seen the weapons yet, but we will."

A servant appeared and placed a glass of water in front of Grimes. He took a drink and wiped his mouth with a napkin.

"We also know there is something else up there that only a few people are allowed to see." Grimes continued. "There is some kind of electronic fence around the area and they have sentries posted everywhere. What they have in there I can't imagine, but I aim to find out. As far as their military, well, they have passion, but not much skill. They're training every day. They even have a few pilots and a couple of planes."

Gage watched Mullans lean back in his chair and rub his palms together. The sour taste of disgust welled in Gage's throat.

"Where are they getting their water and food? I know they were robbing our trains, but why did they blow the bridge?"

"First, they didn't blow the bridge." Grimes said. "There's a tribe of savages living out there too and the migrants believe the savages set off the explosions. Or, maybe the bridge just collapsed from disrepair. It doesn't matter because they've found a water source."

"Water." Mullans sat up straight. "You've seen this water?"

"No. I haven't, but it's there, somewhere in those mountains. Also, they're using the water source to grow their own food."

"What about this Espiritu? Have you seen him?" Mullans said

"No one has seen him. The Spirit Man? He is no spirit. He's real, alright. As real as you or me. He'll be found and he'll be killed. We'll make him into a spirit." Grimes' serious expression broke into a smile and then into a loud chuckle. Mullans joined him with a deep belly laugh. Gage noticed Rebecca nod her head.

"What do you know about this Annie Miller," Mullans asked. "She escaped from the coliseum. Do you know where she is?

With a deep sigh, Grimes rested his hands on the table. "The word throughout the communes is that Annie is on her way to the mountains. This woman is, indeed, the passion of the movement. She represents the working mother, the grieving widow."

"Yes," Mullans interrupted. "And we have her children right here in camp. They were captured as peasants were trying to sneak them out of Canada. Unfortunately, those who were with the children were killed when we apprehended them." Mullans sighed. "We could have gotten valuable information from them. Oh, well, I'll use these children to get those migrants to stop launching raids against our army. I need you, Grimes, to get a message to Espiritu."

Grimes smiled and nodded. "Well, I might suggest leaving one of those kids in the desert with a message," He said. "I can suggest a place where the child will be found and picked up," Grimes took a drink of water and held the glass in his hand. "Killing the child and leaving its body will send even a stronger message, don't you think? The migrants will be told that we will kill all the children if they don't stop these assaults." Grimes smiled and tapped the glass with his forefinger. "How will that look if their mother-symbol sacrifices her own children? I'm sure Espiritu will pay attention."

Gage's muscles tightened. He placed his hand on his holstered revolver.

"Killing the child will only enrage them more," Rebecca said. "Leaving the child alive will show we have a sense of decency, compassion."

"My dear Becca," Mullans said, leaning back in his chair, a smirk forming on his lips. "I value your advice, but there is no room for decency or compassion in war. Hell is what war is, and in hell, only the devil survives. Whatever you think you were when the war started, is never what you are in the end. . .even if you win." Mullans turned toward Gage. "I know you understand what I'm talking about, Officer Gage."

Gage leveled an icy glare on Mullans but said nothing. Money had purchased Gage's freedom but his life still belonged to the corporate kings – or did it, he thought. He was not a slave anymore. Bravery and competence on the battlefield had earned him enough rewards from the corporations to buy his freedom, but he still served the kings as a well-paid militia officer. How much longer could he remain a servant? Gage wondered. His body relaxed as the thought came to him again that soon he would no longer be a servant. He needed to wait, but not for long.

"Grimes," Mullans spoke without noticing the heavy silence that chilled the air. "You have done well, but I need more. My army will be moving into those mountains in a few hours. It will be easier for the migrants to set up ambushes in those rugged mountains but we can do the same." Mullans tapped his plate with his fork.

After a pause, Mullans spoke. "Have your agents keep us informed of the locations of the ambushes, and we'll hit them first. I realize they know we're coming, but with the size and strength of our army, we can break them. My men will take those strongholds, one by one, until we have this Espiritu in chains. We will know his secrets." Mullans dismissed Grimes with a wave of his hand.

Grimes rose from his chair, bowed low and left the tent. Mullans did nothing to acknowledge his spy's departure.

"And now cousin," Mullans said, as he addressed Rebecca.

"You will be given a tent here in the officer's garrison. Officer Gage will bunk with the other pilots. In this heat, you need to rest when you can. In a few hours, we will break camp

and start to move into those mountains. For now, finish your
dinner." Mullans waved his hand. "Fill your plates."

Gage stared across the table at Mullans. The fans blew
air against his skin and the aroma of the meal teased his pallet.
Gage lifted his glass of water and his world exploded. A sudden
flash of light, an explosion and Gage was hurled through the air.
Table, dishes, tent poles and bodies tumbled together as the
general's canvas tent floated down to cover them.

CHAPTER NINETEEN
The Secret
The Mountains

Armed guards, dressed in civilian clothes, stepped out from behind boulders and hills and raised their guns in a salute as the land rover moved up through the rugged mountains toward the hidden migrant sanctuary called The Farmhouse. Dawn had yet to come. Neither Ivan nor Annie spoke during their journey. Annie sat in the rover beside Ivan who guided the vehicle through the moonlit night over a roadless wilderness. The higher up the mountain they traveled, the closer they came to the stars, and the closer Annie came to her family.

The rover gave a jolt, then stopped and settled on the ground. Ivan opened the vehicle's door and helped Annie step outside. The air felt cooler and the atmosphere had become thinner. Guards appeared from out of the shadows holding guns and oversized flashlights. This time, Annie thought, the guards are here to protect me.

One of the guards opened a door in the side of a sheer cliff camouflaged by a rock facade. Ivan led Annie through the door and down a passageway of stone steps. He took her through another door that opened into a spacious rectangular room furnished like a comfortable living room. At one end of the room sat an overstuffed sofa and chair and at the opposite end, a kitchen table with six chairs. Plastic cabinets covered the wall next to the table and a translucent flat screen display was mounted on one wall. Multi-colored, cotton throw-rugs brightened the concrete floor and two electric fans with lights hung from the ceiling.

Annie looked around the room. "A strange, civilized home hidden in a savage land, " she said.

"There is more to see," Ivan told her. "Many more surprises."

A door in the center of the far wall opened and a figure entered the room.

"Robert." Annie's voice was more like a cry. She felt her heart stop for a moment. Her knees buckled. He was beside her, his arms cradling her body. She pressed her face against his chest and inhaled the scent of his skin and hair. So much time had passed. Warm tears fell from her eyes leaving wet smudges on his gray cotton shirt. A door closed. Ivan was gone and they were alone.

Robert picked her up, carried her to the sofa and sat down with her in his lap. He brushed Annie's hair away from her face and stared into her eyes.

"Oh, Annie. I am so sorry." His fingers caressed her swollen bruises with a touch so gentle she sighed with pleasure.

Annie cupped his face in her hands and kissed his lips. They held each other, tasted each other's kisses again and again until Annie pushed away from him. She looked at this man she had not seen for three years.

Robert had changed. He was heavier now and no longer looked the innocent young man she had married. His light-brown hair was pulled back from his face and tied into a long braid. The simple, gray shirt and pants he wore looked new as did the high-top boots. He was clean shaven.

Robert's eyes revealed sadness and a maturity much older than his years. Yet, they were still his eyes. His innocence was gone, but Annie sensed that somewhere inside this man, her husband, hope was alive. When she touched him, she felt his energy.

"Where are our children?" Annie said. "They're here, I know. I want to see them." She felt her body warm with excitement and anticipation.

Robert brushed his hand over her hair and gave a nervous sigh. "They're not here, yet. But, they will be soon."

"What are you saying?" Annie rose to her feet and glared down at him. "They should have been here before me. What's happened? Where are they?"

"Annie, listen. They're safe. You'll see them soon. I promise." Robert stood up and placed his hands on her shoulders. "We're all going to be together. Soon."

Annie felt a cold terror crawl through her body. "Oh, Robert." She turned and walked away from him. "Why couldn't you just come home?" She turned and looked into his pinched and colorless face. "Why, Robert? Why couldn't you just come home and be ordinary? Look what we've become. We hide like rodents in the night. We put our children in jeopardy." She felt tears sting her eyes and cursed herself for crying. This was not supposed to be a day to cry.

"Annie." Robert's voice was gentle. "In times like this, no one can be ordinary. You, certainly, have never been ordinary." He laughed. "Not even the first day I met you." Robert smiled and looked at her with tenderness. "You have never been the type of person who goes to work with your head down, pretending not to think about the day you will become useless to the corporations. You have never been content to give your life to the corporate kings and passively allow them to throw you in the streets when you become unprofitable for them. There has always been more to you than that. There's an energy in you, Annie." Robert walked closer to Annie and held his arms out to her. "Your work saved my life, Annie, and the lives of countless others. Our work together is bigger than either one of us. "

Annie sat down on the sofa and buried her face in her hands. She looked up at him and sighed.

"Is this where you've been all this time? Here? In this farmhouse?"

He shook his head and paced the floor.

"I've been on the move, Annie. That's why I couldn't have the children come here. This place needed to be safe before I brought them here. And, I needed you in Canada."

Annie watched his face turn dark and troubled. She watched him walk to the cabinets, open them and take out a bottle of water and two glasses. He set them on the table.

"Come join me, Annie." He opened the bottle and poured the liquid into the glasses. "Come. Sit here. We can talk." He held up a glass and laughed. "We have water and real glasses like civilized people. Come my beautiful wife and sit with me. I will tell you about The Farmhouse, The Eight, Espiritu. And then, Annie, I will show you something. Yes, I can't just tell you. I must show you because you will never believe it unless you see it with your own eyes." Robert pulled a chair out and motioned for her to join him.

Annie rose from her seat on the sofa and sat down in a chair at the table across from Robert.

She watched him lean back in his chair and take a deep breath. "Annie, I am going to tell you how I found Blue Eden and how I became Espiritu."

Annie held her breath for a moment.

"You always knew, didn't you, Annie? You knew the identity of Espiritu."

She nodded in agreement. "I always suspected, but I had to pretend I knew nothing." She gave him a short, curt smile. "If you want to keep a secret, you have to forget the truth. You have to push it so far back into your mind that it becomes lost."

Robert smiled, but sadness enveloped him. "You know why I joined the militia, Annie."

"Yes. Of course, I do." She said, "We wanted citizenship. We wanted something better for ourselves and our children. We wanted to belong."

Robert nodded. "One day my employers came to me. No." He shook his head. "Not the militia commanders, but people from World Tech." He seemed to choose his words as though he wanted to remember exactly what happened.

"World Tech told me that I had been picked to participate in a top secret mission. They would not tell me where I was going or what it was about until the operation was under way. I was to leave immediately."

"I remember, "Annie said. She shifted in her chair. "One day you just did not come home."

Robert took a drink of his water and set the glass down. "There were six of us. They dropped us in these mountains and told us to explore. They would pick us up in a week and we were to report on anything we found that was unusual." Robert laughed.

"They never told us exactly what we were looking for, but we knew. We had all heard Blue Eden rumors; the secret hidden up here. We all thought that was crazy. They gave us two rovers and a month's worth of supplies."

Annie watched her husband's face as he spoke. He appeared relieved to be telling her this story.

"Well, it wasn't long before we were attacked. Migrants. Savages." He shrugged his shoulders. "They still live in that abandoned city. They get their water supply from several shallow pools in caves up here in these mountains. That and of course, robbery and murder." He drummed his fingers on the table.

"We killed the migrants. They were a small group. We were better trained and better armed." Robert sighed. "But, they knew the terrain and fought better than we expected. We were ambushed."

Annie listened as Robert told her his story.

"Four of our guys were killed. Kyle, Tanika's husband, was wounded. During the fight, Kyle and I fell through a shaft that led to a passageway and to this room." Robert spread his arms out. "This is what my employers were looking for, Annie.

This place had been sealed and hidden for more than a century, but nature unwrapped it for us. Earthquakes and storms broke open this hiding place and allowed us to find it." His face glowed with excitement.

Robert drained the last drop of water from his glass and set the glass back on the table.

"Before the savages attacked, our patrol came across the remains of a house. It was really nothing but a broken foundation mostly covered in dirt. Parts of a hearth and chimney were scattered about. People had lived there before the ice melted, Annie, probably a family. Now there was nothing left. Everyone in the platoon tried to imagine who the people were who lived there, what they did and what their house looked like. We called it The Farmhouse."

Robert leaned across the table and placed both his hands over Annie's. "I imagined it to be a place where we would live, Annie. I believe everyone in that patrol was thinking the same thing. I imagined a peaceful place where we and our children could be happy and safe." He shook his head.

"During the attack with the savages, I became engaged in a hand-to-hand struggle. I got slammed up against the side of a cliff and something gave way. I fell through an opening with a savage at my throat. Fortunately, Kyle came behind us and saved my life. He killed the savage." Robert closed his eyes and placed his hand on his forehead.

Annie remained silent. She wanted him to tell his story in his own time and in his own way. She waited.

"When Kyle and I found this room, it was empty," Robert continued. "Later, I tried to make this room look how I thought that farmhouse would have looked. Now, this place is called. . . "

"The Farmhouse," Annie said.

She leaned across the table, caressed his cheek with her fingers but said nothing.

Robert stood up. "Come with me Annie. I'm going to show you the secret that changed my life and is going to change the universe."

Robert took Annie's arm and led her through the door on the back wall. Several closed doors lined a hallway that ran from where they stood to an elevator on the far end of the corridor. Annie followed Robert down the hall and to the elevator where he pushed a button. Gears clanked and machinery whirled.

"By the way, this elevator wasn't working when Kyle and I first came here," Robert said. "We used the stairs." He laughed.

"I thought Kyle was wounded." Annie said. "Wasn't it difficult for him to explore?"

"His wound needed attention, but he wasn't injured that badly," Robert said. Machinery groaned and doors slid open. Robert led Annie into the elevator car. The door shut and the car moved downward.

"I believe, though I have no proof, that World Tech had Kyle killed," Robert continued. "I believe World Tech would have killed all of us who were on that patrol no matter what we found or did not find. World Tech wanted no leaks. They wanted no one to find out that they were looking for Blue Eden. The men in our patrol were, after all, disposable."

Robert pushed a button and the elevator jerked to a stop. Annie lost her balance and grabbed hold of Robert's waist. He steadied her.

"Annie, we flipped a coin. Kyle and I actually flipped a coin. It could have been him standing here and I could be dead. I won that coin toss. He lost."

"I don't understand," Annie said.

Robert rubbed his eyes with the tips of his fingers. "When Kyle and I climbed back out of the passage, the battle was over. Everyone was dead. . .savages and militia. We returned to the passage to find out what exactly this place was. Well, once we discovered the secret, we had a decision to make. Do we give it to the corporate kings, or do we take it to The Eight?"

Robert pulled Annie close and placed his chin against her head. "For Kyle, it was an easy decision. He insisted we go to The Eight. For me. . .well. . .it was more difficult. The corporations were good to us. The future was secure and safe. I had a family."

"So did Kyle," Annie said as she turned her eyes to look up into his face.

Robert pushed her away from him, but continued to hold her wrists by his outstretched arms.

"You know I grew up in Oakbourgh, but what you never knew is that my parents were members of The Eight. Yes, Annie. I grew up with secrets. Not that they told me anything, but children listen. I also knew to keep my silence. I knew I could never tell what I heard, so I forgot the secrets." He sighed. "I was always loyal to my employers."

The elevator groaned, but stayed between floors. Annie saw a veil of tears form in his eyes and disappear. "But, now I had to decide what to do with this information."

Robert wet his lips and continued. "Annie, you know we were in Canada when our families died in the march. Maybe that had something to do with my decision. Maybe it had everything to do with it. Our families died because they were tired of the rest of humanity sacrificing themselves for a handful of corporate kings. They were not going to give their lives to the corporate kings anymore. If our families had to die, they would die as human beings, not chattel."

Robert held Annie close to him. "Everyone dies, Annie, but it is what you do with your life that matters. My family stood up to the kings even if it meant their deaths. Each of those deaths on that day of the march was a voice saying that life belongs to all of us, not just to the kings. There is going to be a fight for Blue Eden, Annie, and we're going to win. We have to win." Robert reached his hand toward the elevator button.

"Wait. Stop." Annie put her hand on his arm. "You said that you flipped a coin. What do you mean?"

Robert nodded and drew his hand back. He explained that one of them would have to go back to World Tech and report on what happened. One of them would have to tell World Tech that they were attacked and that they found nothing."

Robert's voice became soft. "That was Kyle. We put my uniform on one of the dead migrants. Our dead platoon officer had an extra uniform, so I put that on. I kept his insignia for later use. We hid one of the land rovers and I took the other. Kyle was to report that the battle was bigger than it was. He told our employers that the savages took the rovers." Robert shook his head and stood silent for a moment.

"I took the rover to Oakbourgh." He continued. "It was easy to get through the gates with the officer's uniform and insignia. Once inside the walls, I went to see a lady named Maddie. She was a person I knew could be trusted. Maddie had been a friend of my mother and they both worked together with The Eight. Maddie's ancestors had been some of the original scientists who worked on the Blue Eden Project and Maddie's daughter was the one who uncovered the first piece of lost information concerning Blue Eden. That information had been hidden in the museum where she worked."

"That is what the girl has in the book." Annie said.

"Yes." Robert looked into Annie's face. "And I gave Maddie two additional pieces of information in order to prove I was telling the truth. When Maddie saw what I had, she knew exactly what to do. She contacted other members of The Eight and the society was reborn. But Annie, there are three pieces of information that need to be brought back here. Those pieces are now in the hands of three different people. We need all those pieces." Robert turned and pushed the elevator button. The car bounced and continued its descent.

When it stopped and the doors opened, Annie froze in astonishment. An aircraft with a fuselage nearly 60' high, 20' wide and 250' long stood in the center of a maintenance hangar. Robert took her arm and guided her out of the elevator to within a few feet of the massive airship.

"It's got a wingspan of over two-hundred feet, Annie, and it will carry one hundred passengers and ten crew members. It's designed to take us to Blue Eden."

"There are five of these ships. Five hangars were built against the mountain and camouflaged to blend into the mountain. There's a small village beneath us with a good water supply. Annie, all this was abandoned when the ice melted and the age of darkness fell. And there's so much more. I will show it all to you. We're bringing all of this back to life." Robert took Annie's hand. She looked up into his face. His eyes glowed with excitement.

Scores of men and women employed at various tasks within the building, stopped their work and looked in Annie's direction. A low murmur passed among the workers and grew louder as more people came into the hangar. Several workers stood on top of the massive wings of the aircraft and others crawled out from underneath its belly. Groups of people left their workstations and others stepped outside rooms adjoining the hangar. Someone started to clap and others joined the applause. The sound of hands coming together filled the windowless hangar.

Annie cocked her head in her husband's direction.

"It's for you, Annie," he said.

She turned her head toward the people honoring her, bowed her head and gave a curtsy. The applause became stronger.

Annie felt Robert place his hand on her shoulder. He whispered in her ear.

"Ivan needs to talk to us. There's a problem. Ivan is with Colonel Chang, a military advisor."

Annie walked with Robert to a far corner of the hangar where Ivan stood talking with a gray-haired, bearded man with dark skin. Ivan looked up as they approached. Dark shadows veiled his face.

"We've been shelling Mullans' army, as you know, and yesterday we destroyed most of their planes," Ivan said. "But we've got bad news."

"Go on," Robert said, his manner calm.

Ivan turned his eyes toward Chang and nodded.

"After the last shelling which was pretty bad," Chang said "the corporate army regrouped, as expected, and moved up into the mountains. A little after midnight they attacked our first stronghold, an outpost, really. Fortunately, the children and elderly had been moved to safety at other communities, but the attack was brutal. The corporate army took some prisoners and killed everyone else in sight."

Annie stood listening to this conversation. She heard concern, but no fear in their voices.

"Our fighters are not as well trained as the corporate militias," Chang said. "But our people are accustomed to hardships. Word about the battle is moving through the communities and so is anger. Our people are ready to fight. We have already used our missiles against the army. Now, we need to wipe them out completely."

Robert rubbed his chin between his fingers. "In good time," he said. "Mullans' army is isolated. There are no replacement troops on the way. We are certain we can overwhelm them."

"Yes," they all agreed.

Robert wet his lips. "Most of Mullans' men have given their services to the corporate oligarch for a variety of reasons. We all know this but if we are to win, we must not forget why these people fight." Robert seemed to study the faces of each man.

"Keep in mind that some men believe the corporate government should continue; others believe the corporations will protect them and their families. Still, others serve as soldiers of fortune under any command which they believe will be successful."

Robert paused a moment and shook his head. "And there has always been that small number of people who are influenced by a base desire to rob and plunder. However, if they knew the scope and power of our weapons, only the most foolish would continue to fight." Robert sighed and continued. "When we destroy Mullans' army, and we will, another army will come for us. The next army will be bigger and will come better prepared to annihilate us."

Part V

September 2
One hundred years in the
future

CHAPTER TWENTY
The Book
The Mountains

Hannah sat crossed legged on a cot where she was told to rest, but rest was not possible. Although her body ached from head to foot and fatigue imprisoned her mind, sleep would not come. The moment she closed her eyes, a sense of apprehension took control and she awoke in sheer panic. In her nightmare, Bobby was dead and she was lost.

Her cot sat inside a long rectangular tent with rows of cots, each holding an injured person. Many of the patients, Hannah noticed, were survivors from the train wreck. Across the aisle from Hannah, Dennis' wife sat beside a sleeping child. The blond woman, whose arm was injured in the train wreck, slept on another cot.

At one end of the long tent, a dark-skinned woman wearing a white, cotton outfit sat behind a metal desk concentrating on a computer screen. On the opposite end, two open tent flaps allowed morning sunlight to infiltrate the canvas clinic. Two solar fans circulated hot, stale air.

Although a plate of protein paste rolls sat on a tray in front of her, the sight of them made Hannah ill.

Instead of masculine work clothes, Hannah now wore a simple, blue nightgown. Her feet were bandaged.

A young woman with green eyes and blond hair pulled back into a tight bun sat on a small stool beside Hannah's bed.

"Don't be afraid dear," the woman said. "You're safe now. I'm your nurse and I'm here to tend to your sunburn."

Hannah pulled away from the woman. "Where is safe?" She asked.

The nurse smiled and began to wash Hannah's body with cool water and lotion. With each touch of the cloth, Hannah's raw, blistered skin stung causing her to recoil.

The nurse ignored Hannah's discomfort and continued her work." You're in one of our strongholds," she said. "We call it stronghold number two." The nurse spoke with a slight lilt to her voice. "Our patrols picked up you and your companions in the abandoned city. You're lucky they found you. That city is not a place to be and neither is the desert."

The soothing lotion began to alleviate the pain from Hannah's sunburned skin and she began to relax.

"I understand you're quite the hero," the nurse said. "They say you attacked those savages with all your might." She gave a short sigh. "Oh, your feet are a mess with blisters, but they'll heal. I've seen worse though, believe me. We'll keep the bandages on for a little while longer." The nurse stopped her work and gathered up her medical equipment into a shallow tray.

"Oh, I mustn't forget," she said. "We have a pair of soft shoes here that will fit you nicely when your feet are better." She picked up a pair of shoes from the floor by Hannah's bed, waved them in front of Hannah's face and dropped them to the floor. The nurse stood up and looked at Hannah.

"You don't remember how you got here do you dear?"

Hannah heard the words the woman spoke but she did not acknowledge them. Pain, fear and loneliness blurred together in her mind.

"Now eat and drink lots of water," the nurse said as she looked down at Hannah. "We need to get you better and out of here." She placed a hand under Hannah's chin. "Don't worry, dear. You're safe. When I return, I'll take those bandages off your feet."

The nurse smiled and walked out of the tent leaving Hannah to sort through her fractured memories. It was easy to forget the past trauma, Hannah thought. Memories brought pain. Yet, there were things she wanted to remember.

Hannah put the tray of food on the floor, covered herself with a sheet and rolled into a fetal position. She closed her eyes and tried to shut out the present. Her walking with the others away from the burning city, the cannibals and walking toward the mountains was not a dream. Hannah could still feel the rocks as they stabbed her feet. She could feel Zack beside her and that teenage boy. He was with her in the room with the broken-out window. He called her girl and kept talking to her. What the boy said was not important to her. Maybe he was just scared like everyone else.

Hannah remembered the three strangers, two businessmen and a dark-skinned woman, who appeared out of the desert and joined the group. The strangers kept looking at Hannah in a curious way and whispering together. The woman said her name was Patricia, and she wanted to know Hannah's name and where she came from. Hannah turned away from her. She knew those three strangers were not at the train wreck, but where did they come from? Why were they so interested in her?

"Maybe I was only imaging those curious looks and the whispers." Hannah thought. "Those three people are migrants, like me. They are alone, just like I am."

At some point on their trek toward the mountains, Zack picked Hannah up and carried her in his arms. He placed her on a land rover and she remembered being taken to a camp filled with armed men and women who gave her water and wanted her to eat. But, her body rejected all nourishment. She was given a pallet beneath a lean-to and told to rest until she could be moved to a stronghold. Strangers spoke to her. There were faces and voices, but Hannah ignored them all until she heard the name Annie.

"Annie Miller. Annie is here." The name Annie rippled through the hillside camp. "The lady Annie escaped from prison in Canada," people said to one another. "And Annie Miller is here in camp. They're taking her to Espiritu."

A shot of energy surged through Hannah's veins when she heard the name, Annie. Could this be Bobby's cousin?

"No. Not possible." This Annie Miller was one of the important leaders of the revolution. People walked past the lean-to where Hannah sat and she heard them talking about the brave leader, Annie, from Canada.

Stars appeared in the dusky sky and light from a faded moon shown down upon the camp. Until now, Hannah had taken no notice of her surroundings. She and the other survivors had been brought to a haphazard migrant camp site, pitched in the shadow of the foothills. As Hannah sat beneath the lean-to, her feet bandaged, the rest of the camp hummed with action. While heavily armed men and women stationed behind small hills and nearby boulders kept watch for approaching danger, others took down tents and packed them on camels and in rovers.

Hannah crawled out from beneath the lean-to and managed to stand on her bandaged feet. Although her feet throbbed, the thick bandage offered protection from the rocky ground.

"Where is Annie? I want to talk to her," Hannah asked a passing armed soldier.

"She's right over there on the other side of that hill." The young man paused and pointed toward the center of camp. "But you won't get close enough to talk to her. There's a big crazy looking man with her. You can't get near her."

If she could not talk to Annie, maybe she could at least see her. Hannah hobbled to the other side of the small hill and as she rounded the hill, a woman with loose-hanging, reddish-brown hair came into view. Dressed in white cotton pantaloons and a white blouse, the woman sat on a large bolder looking as though she was deep in thought. She wore leather boots and held an automatic weapon on her lap. Her wide-brimmed hat was on the ground beside her and Hannah noticed the wire-rimmed glasses on her bruised, swollen face.

A strong energy emanated from this woman causing Hannah to take a few steps back. She took a deep breath, inhaled the powerful energy that felt like a wind she could almost see. As Hannah watched her, Annie turned her head and rested her eyes on Hannah. A questioning expression crossed Annie's face, a slight smile touched her lips and she nodded in acknowledgement.

Hannah stood unmoving as she observed the scene before her. A muscular man covered in tattoos and with cold, blue eyes stood beside Annie. His red hair was decorated with pieces of glass woven into multiple braids and his beard filled the lower half of his broad face. He wore filthy-white cotton pantaloons tucked inside combat boots. His loose, long-sleeved shirt fell to his knees. A belt of ammunition encircled his waist.

"Are you in pain?" the man asked, causing Annie to turn her eyes away from Hannah and to look at him. At that moment, Hannah slipped away behind the hill and sat down in the dirt. Her swollen feet throbbed too much to stand any longer.

"So what do you think, girl?" The tall, brown-eyed boy, who always called her girl, sat down beside her. "I heard you asking about Annie. Is that the Annie you're looking for?"

Hannah looked at this boy with no name. She saw his work-worn hands, his bone-thin body and his tattered clothes.

"I don't know," Hannah said. "But she is like magic, isn't she? Were you close enough to feel it. . .that power. . .that energy." Hannah's body tingled from the sensation of the woman's power.

"Yes. I felt it. Everybody does. It's like some force inside her. Hey, look over there."

Hannah looked in the direction the boy was pointing. Through the twilight, Hannah could see a scattered band of people walking toward the camp. There were men, women and a few children. Migrants, she thought. They were a sorry looking group dressed in civilian clothes, or as it seemed to Hannah, civilian rags. Most had backpacks and each carried weapons of some kind.

"They keep coming," the boy said. "They're coming here to see Annie and to fight in the revolution."

The rising moon and setting sun provided enough light for Hannah to see Annie walk away from the bolder toward the approaching group. With the rifle slung over her shoulder, Annie walked to a small mound at the edge of camp, stopped and looked eastward across the desert. Beside her, a revolver holstered at his side, stood her ferocious-looking companion. They stood together talking and drinking coffee. A slight breeze lifted and tossed her hair.

"She is magnificent." The words came from Hannah in a whisper as she watched the approaching migrants grow in number. They stopped a short distance away from where Annie stood. Rays of moonlight filtered through the twilight illuminating the scene.

Everyone remained silent for a moment and then, almost in unison, the migrants raised their weapons over their heads. Great cheers exploded from the group. Hannah watched Annie drop her coffee cup to the ground and slip her rifle from her shoulder. Holding the weapon with both hands, Annie lifted the rifle high above her head. Standing like a stone statue, Annie raised her chin in the air, keeping her eyes leveled on the cheering people. The cheers erupted even louder. Children clapped and danced while the adults swayed and stomped their feet.

Hannah felt the excitement. She wanted to join the crowd, but instead she remained a silent observer in the shadow of the hill.

Transfixed, Hannah watched as Annie lowered her gun and the crowd dispersed. Annie and her body guard walked back toward the center of camp and boarded a land rover that disappeared into the night, leaving Hannah alone with questions about this amazing woman. Yet, Hannah was not entirely alone for the camp was full of armed migrants using flashlights to move about. Darkness had fallen.

"There are some rovers over there," a man's voice spoke to Hannah from the dark. "You need to get on one of them." A flashlight beam moved from her face to her bloody and swollen feet. "I guess I'm going to have to carry you," the man said.

"I can walk," Hannah said with defiance. She heard a sigh. "You don't want to get left behind, boy. They have a place for you on the rover. Come on. Don't waste time."

A man's muscular arms lifted her up and placed her aboard a rover filled with other migrants. Hannah recognized some of them as survivors from the train. Others were strangers to her. The rover traveled through the night for hours, moving upward and deeper into the mountains. Most of the travelers in the rover were quiet. Sometimes a child would whimper. Hannah felt like a prisoner with no choice but to go where ordered. She wondered if the others felt the same. At dawn they arrived at a stronghold. Hannah felt a surge of anticipation ripple through the group of migrants.

As the land rover moved through the stronghold, Hannah noticed a community of tents and half-built structures spread over a dry, mountainous landscape. There were no walls, but armed soldiers, men and women, patrolled the settlement. People walked about in simple, cotton clothing and no one wore a militia uniform. Children laughed and romped in the dust.

When the rover stopped, the driver told his passengers to join a group of about fifty people sitting on a dirt floor beneath a large, free-standing canopy. Hannah was the last to disembark from the rover. Someone took her arm and led her to a place beneath the canopy where she sat down among a group of unwashed ragged, men, women and children, many speaking in regional accents, dialects and languages. Some of the train wreck survivors were among them looking stunned and frightened. Hannah scanned the waiting people for Zack, but she could not find him.

Five metal desks sat in a row beneath the canopy and a worker sat behind each desk. A balding man with brown teeth and thick glasses beckoned Hannah to sit at his desk.

"What is your name?" he asked.

"Hannah."

He looked at her, sighed and tapped his pen with his forefinger. "Do you have a last name?

"Merrick," Hannah said. The man wrote her name in a book then asked her where she came from and why she came to the stronghold.

"A train wreck," Hannah said.

The interviewer squinted through his glasses. He looked down at her name and tapped his pen on the table. "You're in need of medical care," he said. "I'll get someone to take you to the clinic."

Someone carried Hannah to the clinic where another person changed her clothes. Kind voices, caring voices spoke to her. Hannah answered their questions and then turned her face away from them.

"So, girl. How are ya feeling?" The brown-eyed boy, who kept calling her girl, sat down on the stool next to Hannah's cot in the hospital tent.

Hannah curled up on her cot and pulled the sheet over her head.

"Everyone's saying you're a hero. The way you charged at that cannibal." The teenager threw his head back and laughed. "That took courage. Especially coming from a little girl like you. Now all you do is lie over here, not talking to anybody, acting like you're afraid of your own shadow."

Hannah tossed the sheet from her head and looked at him. "You keep calling me girl. I have a name."

"I know. It's Hannah. I heard Zack and your friend call you that."

"You mean my friend Bobby."

"Yeah." The boy nodded as he spoke.

Hannah pushed herself up on one elbow. "Where is Zack? Have you seen him?"

"He's here. I suppose you'll be seeing him soon enough."

Hope of seeing Zack warmed Hannah's heart for a moment.

"Everyone is choosing jobs," the boy continued. "I've been working in the kitchen. Best job I've ever had. I'm a dishwasher." The boy grinned from ear to ear. "In Oakbourgh, I mostly worked in the fields, but sometimes I worked in the mines. Say Hannah, do you know who our rescuers are? Do you know where we are? I mean, you've been stuck in this hospital tent. Do you really know what's going on?"

Hannah looked at this teenage boy whose eyes were those of a grown man. "I don't suppose they're cannibals here and I don't suppose they work for the corporate kings. Does it matter who they are?"

The boy laughed and his brown eyes sparkled. "They're migrants, Hannah, fighting the corporate army and yes it does matter." A thoughtful look crossed his face. "I'm thinking about joining them. I mean, I'm thinking about joining their army."

Hannah sat up straight, her legs stretched out beneath the cover. "We're prisoners here," she said. "If you don't join them, they'll leave you in the desert. Maybe even kill you."

"People are coming from all over to join them, Hannah. There's a revolution coming. Don't you pay attention?" He shook his head and waved his arms in the air.

Hannah gave a slight shrug of her shoulder. "We were going to Canada to be with Bobby's cousin, Annie Miller. We were happy. Now, everything's changed." A sickness welled up in Hannah's stomach.

The boy sighed. A look of disgust crossed his face. "Quit feeling sorry for yourself, girl. Get better and see what's going on out there. This camp is huge and they're making permanent buildings out of stone and concrete. The migrants found a water source here and it doesn't belong to World Tech. Girl, they're taking anyone who wants to come here. No one is turned away."

Hannah could not help but feel his excitement.

"What is your name," she asked.

"Griff," he said.

"Only Griff?" Hannah gave a soft laugh. "No last name?"

"I don't need a last name. If I ever find a name I like, I guess I'll use that one. I did the same with my birthday since I don't really know exactly how old I am. One day I just picked a birthday for myself."

Hannah frowned. "What about your parents? Didn't they tell you your birthday? Didn't you say you had a grandmother?"

"My parents died when I was about four. . .I'm not really sure about my exact age, though. I grew up behind the first wall in Oakbourgh, but I got passed around a lot." He looked down at his hands and his cheeks flushed. "I had a grandmother, once. She died." Griff looked up. "I guess that's more than you needed to know, isn't it? I know I talk too much, but I really haven't had a chance to talk to anyone in a long time."

Hannah looked at Griff's face – the square jaw and high cheekbones. He needed to talk to someone, Hannah thought. Listening to Griff speak started to lift her out of her own darkness. "I like listening to you," she said. "I guess we're both alone, aren't we?"

Griff sighed. "There are a lot of people who've been asking about you. There are people waiting to visit you, too."

"Who wants to visit me? I don't know anyone." Hannah curled her knees up and hugged them.

"Everyone knows you. I told you that," Griff said. "You're famous and I have a special surprise for you. Dennis' wife told me to give you something she borrowed from you."

"I didn't loan her anything," Hannah said. "I don't understand." Hannah glanced across the aisle at Dennis' wife sitting in silence beside her sleeping child.

"She said to thank you for carrying her little boy down the stairwell and taking care of him." Griff leaned closer to Hannah. "I'm to tell you that before the dirt storm hit, she borrowed this book from your knapsack when you fell asleep. Her kids wanted to hear the story, but when the storm came, she shoved the book in her pocket and ran with everyone else." Griff pulled a leather-bound book out from beneath his shirt and held it out to Hannah. "I think she's a bit embarrassed about taking it from you without saying anything. That's why she doesn't want to face you."

Horror and rage formed a scream that emptied the breath from Hannah's lungs.

"She killed Bobby. Why didn't she tell me she had the book? He's dead because of her. . .because of this book." Hannah gasped for air through tears that flooded her throat and drenched her face.

Griff's eyes opened wide in astonishment. He leaned away from Hannah and held the book against his chest.

A shadow moved across Hannah's bed. "If you don't want that book, I'll take a look at it. How yaw doing, Hannah? I'm Diego. This here is Patricia. Remember us? We came by here to see how you're feeling."

Hannah rubbed her face and looked at the two strangers through her tear-filled eyes. The third member of their group stood by the tent entrance, a cigarette between his lips. Hannah recognized the three strangers who had whispered about her. Hannah's grandmother's warning came back to her.

"There will be many people who will come to you and try to take this book, but you must only give it to the person who will use it correctly. When that person comes, give it to them, but give it to no one else. It is not something I can explain to you, Hannah, but when the time comes, you will know who is to have the book. It is the secret hidden inside this book that people want and nothing else."

Diego held his hands out to take the book.

CHAPTER TWENTY-ONE
The Battle
The Mountains

Explosions, flashes of light and darkness. Pain consumed Gage's body. The roar of waves and the salty smell of the ocean assuaged voices that filled Gage's mind and took him away from the Army camp to the time the pirates came. He was eight-years-old. It was dusk and blistering heat scorched the air. Joe Gage and his father were hunting alligators, an ancient beast that survived by praying on fish, garbage, humans and each other. A crescent moon sprinkled a faint light over the swamp which contained debris washed ashore from monsoons and floods.

The pirates came in boats from the south. At first, Joe and his father thought they were militia patrolling for the corporations. It was illegal to hunt without permits and punishment was harsh. Joe's father instructed Joe to hide behind the rotting logs, broken slabs of concrete and rusting metal that littered the shoreline.

From their hiding place in the semidarkness, Joe and his father watched groups of armed men come ashore. The dress of those men and the way they spoke made it apparent they were pirates from the South. Young Joe knew that there were many such gangs of thugs and thieves living outside the corporate walls and many of those gangs survived as organized syndicates of crime working with established corporations.

"I want you to run," Joe's father whispered. "Run quickly and alert the sentries guarding our camp. Have them prepare for a fight. Hurry now."

Joe, excitement and pride running through his veins, left his father and ran back through the swamp toward the camp. As he approached his campground, Joe began to scream, "Pirates. Pirates coming."

As his warning pierced the serenity of the evening, multiple shots rang out from the direction of the shore. Joe froze in horror. His young mind realized that he was told to run to safety while his father fired shots to warn the tent village. The screams of a child would not be enough to activate the village. Those shots, Joe knew, would also alert the pirates to his father's position.

The camp erupted into a frenzy of movement. Men readied their weapons, women ran for their children, but the pirates were a better armed and a stronger force than the people of this placid tent village. Those battle-hardened invaders entered the campsite and overpowered the migrant's most skilled defenders.

Within the mayhem of battle, Joe found his mother holding his baby sister beneath her arm. With his sister under one arm, Joe's mother took his hand and ran toward the swamp. Stumbling and sometimes falling, Joe's small legs could barely keep up with her. They were not to escape this day.

At the edge of camp, a massive man grabbed Joe's mother and threw her to the ground. Joe's sister, screaming in terror, tumbled from her mother's embrace and rolled across the dirt and rocks. Joe's mother attempted to struggle to her feet only to be hit again with an arm as wide and hard as a club. She fell unmoving, her face a river of blood.

"Run, Mom. Run." Joe pelted the monster warrior, his mother's attacker, with rocks.

Wielding a fish knife he was to use on the hunt, he ran at the attacker with all his might. Joe felt the blade sink into flesh and the taste of blood splatter across his face. The beast was wounded. It whirled around and attempted to catch Joe by the arms, but young Joe was quick. Able to sprint away from the aggressor's bulky frame, Joe turned and charged at him again. Before he could strike, however, strong arms grabbed him from behind and lifted him up into the air. Joe gagged from the stench of his abductor's body that smelled like rotting fish. Still fighting, kicking and flaying his fists, Joe's captor carried him toward the beach. For as long as he was able, Joe kept his eyes on his mother lying silent beside his baby sister whose tiny arms stretched out toward him. Joe called their names but no one answered.

Metal dishes clanged and someone called his name.

"Joe, wake up." Gentle hands touched his face. "Joe. Wake up."

Gage opened his eyes. Bright light blinded him, forcing Gage to close them again. Cool water soothed his skin and Rebecca's voice swirled in his head. He felt her lips close to his ear.

"Joe. We have to leave here. You need to get up. You need to get dressed."

Although pain racked his body, Gage opened his eyes and pushed himself to a sitting position. He leaned his back against a rough adobe wall and adjusted his blurry sight to his surroundings.

He was on a cot in a room with concrete floors, just large enough to hold a double bed. A portable canopy stood over the bed offering shade from sunlight that flooded the roofless chamber. An opening, covered by a canvas curtain, led to the outside. His clothes and holstered sidearm sat stacked beside his assault weapon in a corner. Rebecca, a dirty white scarf draped over her shoulders, sat beside him holding a metal cup filled with water. Her clothes, unchanged since the crash, were soiled and wrinkled.

"Here. Drink the water," Rebecca said as she held the cup close to his lips.

Gage took a drink and wrenched in pain as he handed the cup back to Rebecca.

"I know," Rebecca said. "Our bodies have been through hell. First the plane crash and then the explosions. Lucky for us, nothing was broken. You have a mean cut on your head though. You've been out for hours."

Gage touched the bandage wrapped around his forehead. He was striped to the waist. A cotton sheet covered his shorts and bare legs.

"So, what happened?" His voice was hoarse and his throat felt like he had swallowed sand.

Rebecca, still holding the metal cup, took a drink. "The migrants attacked the army camp with missiles while we were having dinner with Mullans. They targeted every plane in camp destroying them. The shock wave from the explosions hit our tent and sent everything flying, including us. Mullans and I are doing fine, but you got hit pretty hard with something. Maybe the table."

Gage looked around the grimy cell. "Where are we?" he asked.

"Last night, while you were still unconscious, Mullans' army overran a migrant stronghold. It was deserted when the army got there, but a platoon of migrants put up a good fight from positions in the hills. The migrants were all either killed or captured."

"So, they knew you were coming," Gage said. He studied Rebecca's face. She gave him a strange look and nodded.

"Yes, they knew our militia was coming," she said. "And it wasn't that difficult for our army to overrun the small, migrant outpost. Our militiamen are loyal to the kings and highly trained. However. . ." Rebecca took another drink of water.

"The migrants are not well trained, but they have proven to be fierce fighters. And they have weapons World Tech does not have." Rebecca leaned close to Gage. "You know, we may think World Tech has superior weapons. Our militia can use radar to lock onto a target and be pretty accurate in hitting it, but the target has to be close. These migrants, on the other hand, are using missiles that are being launched from so far away our officers can't even pinpoint the area. Planes are being knocked right out of the sky. The migrants are deadly accurate in their attacks." Rebecca took another drink and offered the cup to Gage. He waved the cup away.

"Between the attacks yesterday and the taking of this outpost," Rebecca continued, "Almost two-hundred men have been killed and a hundred eighty-five wounded. Reports say there are ninety-three missing, either captured or. . .they joined the migrants. Besides all of that, supplies are running short. Mullans told me that migrant attacks are escalating on supply convoys."

Gage placed his bare feet on the floor and sat on the edge of the cot. "Ninety-three missing. So much for loyalty to the kings. It's time for me to find my men. I'm taking a plane if there's any left out there, and you're coming with me."

Rebecca put a hand on his arm. "You have a new mission."

"Oh, no." Gage threw her hand away and stood up. The sheet covering his legs slid to the floor. His head throbbed and the room swirled.

"Sit down," Rebecca said. "You can't get up so quickly. You need to take it slow. Your men are safe. Sit down."

Gage returned to the cot and took a drink from the cup Rebecca handed him. "Go on." He said. "Talk. Then we're getting out of here."

Rebecca took a short breath. "In the confusion of the missile attack on the army camp, the children escaped. Mullans sent a patrol out to find them, but it wasn't until morning that they were discovered. They were brought here to this captured

migrant outpost where the army had established its new base
camp. Mullans was furious."

"Get to the point. What is this new mission?"

"Just listen." She drew out her words, her eyes dark and
cold. "My cousin was so angry those kids escaped, he wanted to
kill all the children and send their bodies to the migrants. I
talked him out of it." She shuttered. "I convinced him to allow
you to take the oldest boy to the migrants." Rebecca put her
hand on Gage's arm and leaned so close he could feel her breath
on his face. "I'm coming with you. And. . .so are all the children."

Gage's muscles relaxed and a sense of peace washed
over him. Gage understood the time had come for him to defect.
He would take the children to The Eight and not return to the
militia. Gage had made his decision. He would defect to the
migrants. Those last chains of bondage that had imprisoned his
soul broke open. His spirit was free.

"Get dressed," she said. "Mullans said you're to take the
oldest boy in a land rover. It's just outside."

Gage watched Rebecca walk to the opening leading to
the outside. She put her hand on the curtain covering the door
and hesitated a moment before turning back toward him.

"You were calling a woman's name," she said.

"What are you. . ?" Confused, Gage fumbled his words.

"In your sleep, you called Annie and your mother. Was
Annie your sister?" Rebecca gave Gage a questioning look then
pulled the curtain back and left the room.

Gage got up and started to get dressed. His body ached,
but the pain in his soul was greater. He remembered his baby
sister, Annie, the girl with the outstretched arms. The day the
pirates came was the last day he saw her and the last day of his
innocence. Gage slipped his pants on as memories flooded his
mind. The pirates took his childhood, taught him to be a warrior
and sold him to the corporations.

He buttoned his rumpled militia shirt over his holstered guns, slung his assault weapon over his shoulder and stepped outside. The camp was bustling in the early morning. Breakfast was over and some soldiers were practicing maneuvers while others were cleaning up the destruction made during the assault on the migrant outpost.

Mullans' army had moved its base camp to the conquered out-post which had been established over the ruins of an abandoned village. Scorched building foundations, partially buried, gave evidence of wildfires that once swept through the local arid landscape and around the world. Five migrant bodies hung from gallows in the center of camp. On the other side of the gallows stood an expansive hospital tent which appeared to be overflowing with injured militia. Gage realized that Rebecca must have secured a private room for him to recuperate.

Tension permeated this captured armed camp in the middle of enemy territory. The World Tech army was the aggressor, but the migrant defenders had advantages. This was the migrants' domain. They knew where to hide and they had supplies, including water. Gage had already experienced their fire power.

A World Tech land rover with Rebecca inside sat beside the hospital tent. Rebecca motioned for Gage to join her. He hurried toward her, past the gallows and into the driver's seat.

"Start the rover," Rebecca said. A white scarf streaked with dirt, covered her head, crisscrossed beneath her chin and tied in a knot behind her neck.

"We're lucky," Rebecca said as the engine whirled. "There's only a minimal number of troops left here. The bulk of the army is on the march toward the next stronghold."

Rebecca rolled her eyes toward the sky. "Mullans is hiding out in his quarters surrounded by his aides and body guards. Migrants keep launching sniper attacks on the camp."

The rover rose a few inches above the rocky terrain as gunfire erupted and explosions rippled through the stifling air. "My cousin has locked the children in a metal storage shed behind the hospital," Rebecca said. "He's adamant they won't escape. We'll see about that."

Gage guided the rover to an 8'x10'x12' high storage shed sitting behind the hospital tent with the doors wide open. Officer Bryant stood beside the empty shed, his assault weapon poised for action.

"It's okay," Rebecca said as Gage's hand went to his pistol. "He's with us. I've been making plans while you were sleeping."

Gage felt Rebecca's hand on his arm. His adrenalin slowed, but he remained ready for battle. He threw the rover door open and stepped out. Four children huddled behind Bryant who lowered his weapon, then picked up a blond-haired boy about six-years-old. Gage lifted a little girl in his arms and placed her on Rebecca's lap. Bryant, still holding the boy, hustled the oldest boy and his brother into the back seat of the rover and climbed in after them.

As the sound of gunfire and explosions continued to grow louder, the rover moved away from the outpost and into the mountains.

Annie stood in a room hidden deep inside the mountain. She had been led from the hangar, down another elevator and through long hallways to a room lit by artificial lights attached to the ceiling. Ten people sat working behind strange looking computer monitors sitting on long tables. Large flat panel screens, each depicting different moving scenes, hung on the walls. Annie stood with Robert by the doorway.

"This is what Kyle and I found."

Annie sensed the wonderment in Robert's voice.

"I want you to meet some people who are helping us to understand all of this." Robert nodded toward a slight-built young man with a beard and curly hair. "Annie, Ray is heading a team of people who are reverse engineering what we found here."

Annie's mind strained to contain her excitement and curiosity. "What exactly is reverse engineering?" She asked.

Ray gave a broad smile, left his work station and joined Annie and Robert.

"This is truly amazing stuff," Ray began. "In the simplest terms, reverse engineering is taking something apart to figure out how it works. We can discover the technological principles of a device or system that way. The device or system in question can be mechanical, electronic, biological or chemical." Ray held his hands out and counted the list of words on his fingers.

"Like Sharon over there. Hey, Sharon." Ray waved at a pretty blond women sitting behind a computer. She looked up, smiled and went back to her work. "Sharon is reverse engineering a process that genetically altered plant and animal life in a way that enabled those plants and animals to grow at a faster rate. This process allowed terraforming to be accomplished in a much shorter time." He sighed. "This process can be tricky. If we take something apart, we might break it or not be able to reassemble it. Fortunately, The Eight left instructions and blue prints. But." He rubbed his beard with his finger and thumb. "Even with blue prints, we need to physically take some of these devices apart to understand them."

Annie felt Robert's hand on her shoulder. "Thanks, Ray," he said. "Now Annie, I'd like to show you what Victoria is doing." He led Annie to the back of the room where a dark-haired woman with violet eyes sat studying information on a computer monitor. She smiled and offered her hand to Annie.

"I'm so glad you're safe," she said.

Annie took Victoria's hand. "Thank you."

"The Eight left thousands of chips containing books, movies and a recorded history of the past centuries," Robert said. "Victoria is going through those chips and putting together an educational program for children as well as adults. Look up there, Annie." Robert gestured toward one of the large flat panel displays on the wall.

Annie looked up at the screen. "That looks like the desert outside the mountain," she said.

Robert took a deep breath. "Yes," he said. "That is the desert outside below this mountain. It's all about communication."

"What? I. . .I," Annie stammered.

"Communication. It's the most important thing." Robert said. "The computers the corporations use today are really just empty boxes. They store information, yes, and they can connect with each of the other computers through wires. But, it's highly controlled and no one can own a computer unless they're licensed. The same with phones."

Annie nodded.

"We have learned that before the ice melted," Robert said. "Nearly everyone had a computer and a phone. They were connected in ways other than wires. Sometimes they were connected by satellites, machines put very high in the sky to communicate with other machines here on earth through coded messages."

"But how is that possible?" Annie felt her heart beat quicken.

"We're learning all of that now. People are coming here from all over the world to study and to learn. Members of The Eight are finding them. You know, Annie, you were responsible for contacting many of these people and sending them here through the underground. I know many were picked up and brought here against their will. . .kidnapped. But, once they got here, they discovered this work was fascinating. Few objected to being here."

Annie looked down at the floor and then turned her eyes to Robert's face. "Yes. I would get information about who you wanted or what skills you needed and made sure that person was delivered."

"Annie, most of those satellites are still orbiting the earth. Some have fallen. . .but look." Robert pointed to an image of the desert displayed on the screen. "Right now a satellite is keeping track of Mullans' army. From this room, we can zoom-in and see what he is eating for dinner." Robert laughed and rubbed his hands together.

"We can lock onto Mullans' planes and shoot them right out of the sky. As a matter of fact, we can sit here and watch our men overrunning the outpost Mullans' army took last night. We're taking it back now as we speak." Robert laughed.

"When Kyle and I found this, I had a problem understanding why all of this was abandoned. But Kyle had an explanation. The corporate kings just didn't need it right then, so they sealed it up and forgot about it."

"But they wanted power and control," Annie said. "This is power." She looked around the room.

"Yes," Robert said. "But, the power of nature was greater, both in a physical and a psychological way. The forgotten history is all recorded here. Annie, according to these records, when the ice melted, temperatures rose and the civilized world changed. Entire modern cities disappeared beneath hundreds of feet of ocean as did low-lying islands and coastal areas. The food, water and energy sources disappeared. Diseases spread. It was pure panic. When there is panic, things of importance get left behind. Annie, when people run for a life boat, they trample anyone who falters." A sadness shadowed Robert's face.

"After Blue Eden got left behind, all of this was forgotten when the ice melted and the darkness came. But, we are bringing in a renaissance, Annie. This knowledge was put here for us to find and to use. It was not meant for a few kings, but for all humanity. This is not the end but a new beginning. Annie, this knowledge can mean the rebirth of our planet."

Robert's eyes were shinning. Annie placed her hands on each side of his face and felt the warmth of his skin.

These really are not times for people to be ordinary, Annie thought as she saw the passion in her husband's face.

"We need to talk to Ivan and Chang," Robert said as he glanced over Annie's shoulder toward the door where the two military advisors were standing.

Annie looked behind her and sighed. "Robert. Why do you stay so close to Ivan? He's a monster."

"Sometimes, Annie, we need a monster on our side." Robert said.

"He's not on our side, Robert. He's not on anyone's side but his own. I don't trust him."

Robert brushed Annie's chin with his fingertip. "Well, that makes two of us, but he's with us for now. We need him. He's helped me organize the migrants and pirates in areas of the world I can't get to. Come on. I need to talk to him. "

Annie watched Robert walk away and then followed him to join Ivan and Chang. They were looking up at one of the flat screens mounted on the wall.

"Mullans only left two-hundred men at the outpost," Chang was saying as Annie approached. "Mullans is still at the outpost he captured last night, but he sent the rest of his army on a march further into the mountains. We have five hundred migrants surrounding the outpost and they are constantly sniping at Mullans' militia. We can easily take that outpost back and capture Mullans, to boot."

"Our real concern is Mullans' fourteen hundred men heading for our safe house number two," Ivan said and sat down at a computer. "We have a plan. Watch the screen up there." He pointed to the flat screen with images of Mullans' army.

"You can see the corporate militia moving west," Ivan said. "We have a thousand migrants scattered in those hills. We can perform multiple hit and run ambushes on the militia as they approach our stronghold number two and drive Mullans' forces northward. Do you see that mountain there?" The picture zoomed to a closer view. "We can keep hitting at them with gunfire and keep them moving in the direction we want them to go and that direction is up that mountain."

"Any good militia leader, and Mullans' militia has the best, will head for high ground," Chang said. "There's a small plateau overlooking a sharp ravine." Using a hand-held laser light, Chang placed a red pointer dot on the screen. "You can see a ridge about six-hundred yards long on top of that plateau. There's a gradual drop off on one side with steep drops on the other three sides."

Ivan laughed, deep and loud. "Mullans and the rest of those corporate kings can't believe a bunch of ignorant migrants could ever outsmart them, but we will." He leaned back in his chair. "So, Chang. Explain what you came up with."

Chang nodded. "The plan of attack is to lure Mullans' army up onto that mountain plateau. Our migrants will surround the plateau and trap Mullans' army in a storm of fire from above and all sides. Our militia will be divided into four parts, each part responsible for one side of the bluff. The bulk will be where the land gradually slopes downward because that is the only avenue of escape for Mullans' men. The other three sides of that plateau are steep drop-offs."

Annie listened to Chang explain his plans knowing full well that the migrant army lacked experience on a regular field of battle.

"Once Mullans' army is in place on the mountain, we will hit them with missiles. That will greatly diminish their numbers and may even panic them. Meanwhile, our militia will scale the three steep slopes while the bulk of the army will approach from the sloping side."

"And what if you can't drive them up the mountain?" Robert asked.

"We're already sending orders to evacuate stronghold number two. If we can't put them on the plateau, we will confront the corporate army at the stronghold."

Diego stood poised to take the book from Hannah, his arms outstretched, his expression soft and seductive.

Prepare to evacuate. A loud speaker crackled. Hospital staff, children and noncombatant women are to move to evacuation points at once.

Hannah rose from her bed and lunged at Diego. "No," she screamed. "No."

Griff leaned backwards and tightened his grip on the book.

"Go away. Go away," Hannah stood between Griff and Diego screaming the words until her throat hurt.

"Hey. Hey. Hey. What's going on here?" Two hospital workers, both men about forty – one with arms and a chest like barrels, the other man thin and wiry – grabbed Diego.

"What's going on here? Why are you bothering this girl?" The barrel-chested man spoke with authority.

"We're sorry." Patricia stepped forward. "Sir, we didn't mean to upset anyone. We didn't realize she was so ill. We'll leave. Come on Diego. We'll come back later."

The hospital workers released Diego, but kept their eyes on him and Patricia as they walked toward the entrance of the hospital tent which was bustling with action. Patients were being lifted onto stretchers and carried out of the tent. The loud speaker continued to crackle and issue orders for evacuation.

Hannah sat down on her bed and looked at Griff, who held her book. She leaned over, picked up the pair of soft canvas shoes sitting on the floor and stuffed her bandaged feet into them.

"Can you drive, Griff? Can you drive a rover?" she asked.

"What? Sure. Not hard."

"Then come with me," Hannah said. "If you want to, that is. If not, give me the book. I'll go by myself."

"We're going to be evacuated, Hannah. You don't have to worry." Griff said.

Hannah sighed and took the book from Griff. She limped down the aisle toward the exit. With each step, dull pains shot through her feet and up her legs. Her blue nightgown brushed against her calves as she pushed past hospital workers and patients being carried outside.

When Hannah stepped outside the tent, the mid-morning sun stung her burned skin. She saw patients being lifted into ambulances and armed migrants filling rovers with women and children. No one seemed to notice Hannah.

About twenty feet away, sitting in the shadow of an adobe building under construction, was a two-seated rover. With the book tucked beneath her arm, her adrenaline racing, Hannah hurried toward the rover ignoring her pain. She jumped into the driver's seat, slammed the door and pushed the button to start the engine. The rover rose off the ground and hovered in mid-air.

"Hannah," Griff banged on the window. "Stop. Where are you going?" He ran around the front of the vehicle, opened the door on the passenger side and climbed into the rover.

"Don't be afraid," he said. "They're going to evacuate us. Where do you think you're going? "

Hannah pushed forward on the steering wheel. The rover began moving through the bustling camp. Platoons, preparing for battle, hurried toward the outskirts of the stronghold. Anxious women, with packs on their backs and children in tow, gathered in groups waiting for instructions. Hannah pushed the accelerator. Floating a few feet off the ground, the rover lunged forward and raced through the village, past the outer border of the community and headed north into the mountainous wasteland.

"Hannah, go back. Turn around." Griff's voice quivered as he spoke.

"Get out if you don't want to come with me," Hannah said and accelerated the speed again. The small rover rumbled and vibrated as it adjusted to the excessive speed.

"Can't you just tell me why you're doing this? Maybe I can help you, Hannah."

"It's the book, Griff. It's evil and I'm going to bury it," Hannah said. "There's a bluff over there and I'm going to bury it at the foot of the bluff. No one will find it." Salty tears rolled down her face.

"This book killed Bobby." She spoke as she guided the rover toward the plateau. "Bobby tried to get my backpack because he thought my book was in the backpack. Griff, strangers want this book, but I can't give it to them. I don't know what to do any more."

Hannah looked at Griff, the boy with the old man's eyes. She swallowed her tears and began to tell him about the book, her grandmother and the attic.

Griff listened as the rover moved deeper into the wilderness. Hannah told Griff about the march, her mother and the escape. He continued to listen as the rover flew over the rocks and lifeless earth.

Gunfire, explosions and shouts sounded in the distance. Bullets whizzed past the rover which jolted and slowed. Sensors, devices to prevent collisions, were embedded in the rover and adjusted the vehicle's speed when objects were near.

Soldiers in corporate uniforms ran across the rover's path, their weapons shouldered. Bullets chased the soldiers, flying over their heads, slamming into the ground and into their backs. Some men fell to the ground and other running men tripped over them.

The rover, in the center of the stampeding soldiers, hung in the air, twisting and turning as the fleeing men charged past. Bullets fell like lead confetti piercing dirt, rocks and humans. A spray of bullets skipped across the ground in front of the rover and a bullet pierced the hood. The rover twisted and jolted as though in pain, dropped to the ground as the engine clanged, sputtered and then went silent.

Hannah sat stunned, not moving until she realized she was not injured. She took a deep breath and looked at Griff. His face was pale, his hands shook, but he threw his door open and climbed out. Hannah crawled across the seat, grabbed the book and jumped out of the rover. She and Griff were sandwiched between a steep side of the bluff and the rover. They sat down and huddled together against the bluff until the stampede of soldiers thinned. Some stragglers continued to run toward the bluff, but most were now ascending the slope leading to the top of the ridge. Gunfire followed them, but the intensity of the

assault was slowing. In the panicked stampede, the disabled
rover was ignored.

"We have to get back to the migrants," Griff said.

"Not until I bury this book," Hannah said. "You go on."
Hannah scrapped her fingers against the hard-pan earth and
then tried hitting the ground with a rock.

"You're a crazy girl," Griff said. "I saw a ravine back a
ways. Maybe we can head back there and throw the book into
the ravine. Maybe we can meet-up with the migrants again. .
.what the. . ?"

Hannah looked toward the sky where Griff's attention
was focused. A cigar-shaped missile flew through the air like a
silver arrow, making a whistling sound as it sailed over their
heads, and exploded on the top of the plateau where the army of
soldiers had gathered.

"Now's our chance girl. Let's go." Griff jumped up and
pulled Hannah to her feet. He gave her a push and she stated to
run. Holding the book against her chest, Hannah hobbled across
the ground where the stampede of corporate militia had taken
place. Fallen soldiers writhed in agony. Others lay still, their
faces ashen. Blood painted the lifeless desert.

Griff was far ahead of her, but Hannah saw him stop and
turn around. He waved for her to hurry. Hannah caught up with
him, stopped to catch her breath and started running again. This
time, Griff stayed beside her.

As they ran, another missile sailed through the sky and
an army of migrants appeared in the distance charging toward
the plateau. Hannah felt hot blood surging through her veins.
She scanned the mountainous terrain looking for a place to hide.
The migrant army was surrounding the plateau and was
beginning to scale the steep sides beneath a barrage of gunfire.
Bullets rained down from the top of the plateau.

Two corporate militiamen, each with a weapon slung
over his shoulder and one with a bloody bandage wrapped

round his head, appeared from behind a hill. Before Hannah could dart away, the injured officer grabbed her and swung her up in his arms. Hannah attacked him with her fists and with the book, but he trapped her arms in his embrace making it impossible for her to move.

"I'm on your side. I'm trying to save your life," the soldier said as he ran with Hannah in his arms, back toward the hill from which he came. The other officer had caught Griff and was pulling him in the direction of the hill.

The injured soldier carried Hannah around the hill where a land rover with four children inside came into view. A woman leaned against the outside of the rover. The soldier placed Hannah on the ground beside the vehicle. Griff appeared walking beside the other militiaman.

"They're defectors," Griff said. "They're on our side."

Hannah's adrenalin slowed, but she was still frightened.

"My name is Rebecca," the woman said. "This is Officer Gage and Officer Bryant. We're not going to hurt you." Hannah looked into the woman's eyes and sensed kindness and honesty emanating from her spirit.

"My name is Hannah."

"Hannah?" Rebecca said. "Are you Hannah Merrick? Were you in the train wreck?"

"Yes. How did you know?" Hannah noticed Rebecca and the injured soldier glance at one another.

"We've been looking for you," Rebecca said and put her hands out. "May I see your book?"

Hannah stepped back and took a deep breath. Her feet throbbed and she wanted to sit down. She looked at the exhausted children huddled in the rover and at the two militiamen with assault weapons in their hands ready for use. She looked again at Rebecca and smiled. The gunfire on the mountain faded and the words of Hannah's grandmother came back to her.

"There will be many people who will come to you and try to take this book, but you must only give it to the person who will use it correctly. When that person comes, give it to that person and no one else. It is the secret hidden inside this book that people want and nothing else."

Hannah looked into Rebecca's face and sensed a strength and goodness. "You will know," her grandmother had said.

The sound of gunfire grew louder as Hannah handed the book to Rebecca.

Hannah felt peace.

CHAPTER TWENTY-TWO
The Beginning
The Mountain

Gage and his party of children and deserters sat trapped behind a rocky knoll while the battle for the plateau raged less than a mile away. To move from their sheltered position, Gage realized, would put them in the crossfire of both the migrants and the corporate militia. They had no choice but to stay where they were. No doubt, they could be seen by those on the mountain top, but Gage knew from experience that noncombatants were of no concern to soldiers fighting for their lives.

Missiles sailed over the heads of Gage's small group and slammed into the corporate troops on the top of the mountain. In the past, he had launched guided missiles from his gunship, but these missiles, now falling from the sky, decimated their targets with precision and with what seemed like no source of origin. As a veteran of many battles, Gage knew the fighters on the mountain were doomed.

Sitting with his long legs bent at the knees, leaning against the hill, his weapon across his lap, Gage watched the four children playing with small stones. Still dressed in their school uniforms, the three boys in blue shorts and white shirts and the girl in a dark-blue dress sat within the shade of the rover moving rocks around and piling them in front of one another. The two teenagers, Hannah and Griff, rested in the rover, the doors open for ventilation. Rebecca sat beside Gage while Bryant paced in front of the rover.

"Relax, Bryant," Gage said. We're stuck here for now. Those hills are full of migrant snipers and as long as those snipers are in combat mode, our World Tech rover is a prime target. We're going to have to abandon the rover and walk out of here when things calm down."

Gage looked at Rebecca holding the book in her lap. "So, you have your book. Now what?"

Rebecca looked at Gage and sighed. "Now our adventure is just beginning, Joe."

Gage drummed his fingers on his weapon. "You're with The Eight, Rebecca." He felt a sense of relief. He was defecting to The Eight and he no longer belonged to the kings. He felt free, both body and soul.

Rebecca smiled and nodded her head. "Yes, I am with The Eight. And so is my father."

"And you couldn't have told me any of this?" He looked at Rebecca as he spoke.

Rebecca shook her head. "Joe, you wouldn't have come and we needed you. We need pilots and good ones, but more than that, we need pilots who will be loyal to our cause."

Rebecca paused and tightened her lips. "Joe. I'm not the one who chose you." she said. "You were recommended by. . .well. . . someone who thought you could be trusted. We had to be sure before we told you the truth. I couldn't tell you about me because I had to keep my cover." Rebecca held his arm. "Joe, I had to keep pretending. I wanted to tell you, but I couldn't. And of course, we wanted you to choose pilots you could work with and trust. Men you have formed bonds with. You will be working close with your men.

Gage took a cigarette from his pocket and held it in his hand without lighting it.

"We need people who will fight for something more than just money," Rebecca said. "Who will fight for ideals."

"No one fights for ideals, Rebecca. We only fight because we want something." Gage crumbled the unlit cigarette in the palm of his hand. "Sometimes that something is our lives. Like those poor fools on that bluff up there." Gage waved his arm in the air. "Neither side has any choice but to fight. Those with the corporations are being paid. Without that payment, they become migrants and migrants have to fight to keep from starving." He looked away from Rebecca.

"The migrants once looked to the corporations to feed them," Gage continued. "But, they got thrown into the desert when the corporations were through with them. Now, they have nothing and no one cares. They have no choice but to fight."

"And why do you think I am here?" Rebecca said. "Instead of enjoying orange juice and cinnamon behind the walls."

"You, Rebecca?" Gage ran his finger down her cheek. "You are more than orange juice and cinnamon. An indifferent husband. A childless marriage." He shrugged. "Maybe other women could live with that. . . be a pet in a gilded cage. . . but not you, Rebecca. Your mind has an energy that can't be contained in a box. You need adventure. You can't be content to just explore the world." He winked at her. "You need to explore the universe."

"And what about you, Officer Gage? Why do you fight?"

"I'm tired of fighting." Gage stopped speaking and listened to the sounds of the battle. "I've killed enough for my time. I just want it to stop." He looked at Rebecca. "And now, Rebecca. Tell me about what you really want with me and my men. Why does The Eight need us so badly?"

Bryant quit pacing and sat on the ground in front of Gage and Rebecca. "You told me the migrants needed pilots," Bryant said. "I was ready to defect anyway, but there's more going on here, isn't there?"

"Yes." Rebecca took a deep breath and faced Gage and Bryant.

"Go on," Gage said. "Tell me everything."

Rebecca wet her lips and began. "Hannah's mother discovered this book in some boxes in a museum basement where she worked. The cover was torn reveling a computer chip hidden inside the leather book covering."

Hannah sat up in the rover seat and leaned toward Rebecca.

"Only the elite had access to the technology that could read what was contained in that ancient chip. So, Maddie, Hannah's grandmother. . ." Rebecca looked at Hannah and nodded, "contacted Patricia, who was at that time a servant to a corporate senator behind the third wall in Oakbourgh. Patricia was also a member of The Eight and she was able to get a note to me asking for help. I immediately took her into my employment."

Rebecca sat up on her knees and held the book in front of her. She told how she and Patricia accessed the information on the old chip. They discovered the entire plan for project Blue Eden, including precise instructions and steps used in the terraforming process.

"We replaced the chip in this book and repaired the cover." Rebecca ran her hand across the front of the book. "And we gave it back to Maddie, Hannah's grandmother, for safe keeping. When Robert showed up with two other chips and this wild story about finding some secret place beneath a mountain. . .well." Rebecca put her hand on Gage's arm. "I've been there, Joe. I've seen the inside of the mountain. There's. . .I saw spacecraft there."

Gage felt a wave of excitement surge through his body but he shook his head and laughed. "Really? Spacecraft?"

Bryant leaned forward, his face intent.

"Yes, five spacecraft. And those other two chips. . ." Rebecca took a deep breath. "Patricia has a chip that contains blue prints for those ships and instructions for taking them to the moon. The chip contains maps of the Milky Way. I have the third chip." Rebecca patted her hip. "I sewed it to an inside pocket of this skirt. The chip I'm holding has the blue prints to a space station on the moon and to three spaceships that will carry passengers from the moon to Mars. . .Blue Eden."

Gage leaned toward Rebecca. "So, you need me and my men to fly spaceships?" He tapped his weapon with his fingers. "Where are these ships?"

"There're close," Rebecca said. "The ships were found in a secret place in the mountains and now the ships belong to The Eight. We, The Eight, will use those ships to take us to the moon, and from the moon, we will travel to Mars. You Joe will be one of the co-pilots."

Gage's mind raced with a sensation of curiosity and adventure.

Rebecca sighed and glanced at Hannah "We need all three of those chips," she said. "And now we are almost there. Of course, we didn't know Hannah was going to run away and take the book with her."

"So, how did Hannah know to give you that book?"

Rebecca looked at the book as she spoke. "We in The Eight call it the third eye. Some have it, others don't. Hannah has the third eye." Rebecca looked toward Hannah. "Those with the third eye have the ability to connect with other people, to see into other people's character and to feel other's pain and happiness."

"Wait a minute," Bryant said. The shooting stopped."

Gage stood up, walked to the other side of the rover and looked toward the bluff. He turned back toward Rebecca and Bryant. Four armed migrants appeared on the top of the small knoll that sheltered Gage and his party. They pointed weapons at Gage ready to fire them.

"Put your guns down slowly and your hands up," one of the armed migrants said.

"It's okay," Gage said. We're migrants too."

Gage dropped his weapon, put his hands in the air and turned around. A migrant soldier, holding his weapon ready to fire, stood before him, skin and eyes black as pitch. A grizzled beard covered his face and a stench emanated from his filthy, ragged clothes.

"We've got orders to bring you all in." He waved his weapon in a tight circle. We've been watching you. Good thing you stayed put during that fight. We would not have been able to protect you."

A few hours later, Gage stood beside a spacecraft, examining the ship's massive fuselage as workers lifted crates of supplies into an open cargo hold. Others scurried throughout the shuttle, making final checks. Their voices hummed and echoed throughout the vast depot chamber. Gage stood in one of the five hangars, each holding a spacecraft. Within a few hours, Gage would be aboard one of the five shuttles traveling to an unexplored world and Rebecca would be with him.

When Gage and his party of children and defectors arrived at the hidden sanctuary called the Farmhouse, members of The Eight gave them food, a hot bath and clean clothes. Gage's combat boots were replaced with a pair of rubber soled shoes with a canvas covering. His wound was cleaned and bandaged. The militia uniform, that in the past had guaranteed him his livelihood and at the same time brought him so much pain, had been destroyed.

"Joe Gage." A women's voice spoke from behind him. When he turned around, a young woman stood a few feet from him. She wore gray, course cotton pantaloons and a long sleeved top that came to her knees. Her reddish-brown hair fell in braids across her breast. She wore wire-rimmed spectacles over a cut and badly bruised face.

"I'm Annie Miller," she said. "We need to talk." She motioned for him to follow her. Curious, Gage walked with her to a room set up like a classroom and adjacent to the hangar. Chairs were lined up facing a white board and a desk stood against one wall. A row of windows filled the wall between the room and the hangar through which Gage could see the shuttle. Gage entered the room leaving the door open and stood at the front of the room facing Annie.

"I guess I should get right to the point." Annie said. She looked down for a moment and then looked him in the face. "Joe, I'm your sister."

Gage stepped back. He swallowed a pain that formed in his throat. The memory that had haunted him like a specter came to the forefront of his mind. The child with the outstretched arms.

"My sister is dead." Gage shook his head and turned to walk out of the room.

Annie took his arm. "Don't leave. Please listen to me. Joe, I only know what my mother told me," Gage saw tears form in Annie's eyes as she spoke. "I don't remember the pirates. They left my. . .our mother for dead. I guess I was so small, they didn't bother with me." Gage felt Annie's hands tighten on his arm. "Maybe they thought I would just die. But that didn't happen. Our mother was strong. She survived. She had a sister in Oakbourgh and her sister's family took us in. That's where I grew up. . .in Oakbourgh." Annie, her hands still on Gage's arm, leaned closer to him.

Annie's voice became soft. "Mom always believed you were alive and she believed that someday you would be found." She took her hands away from his arm and began to fiddle with the end of her braid.

Gage looked into Annie's face and his stomach muscles tightened.

Annie spoke to him in a gentle voice. "When I joined The Eight and worked at the gun factory, I came across your name. Joe Gage. My maiden name was Gage. My brother was Joe Gage."

"You came across my name?"

Annie nodded. "You know I was a spy. I worked at night in the headquarters of the World Tech gun makers. Of course, I had access to a wealth of information. I sifted through all kinds of paperwork, even filing cabinets and computer files. I picked up anything I could find whether it seemed useful or not. Joe, you worked for World Tech. Your name came up on some military lists."

"So, you gave my name to The Eight so I would be on this mission?"

Annie's eyes flooded with tears and she nodded her head. "You believe me don't you?" she said.

Gage stepped closer to Annie and placed his hands on her shoulders. For the first time since the pirates came, tears filled his eyes. Annie leaned into him and they held each other. This was his baby sister, the girl with the outstretched arms. He felt the truth and he knew it was real. "I never forgot you," Gage said. "You were always in my dreams. . .in my memories. Even when I tried to forget, I couldn't." So many lost years without my family, Gage thought as he held his sister. A long silence ensued before Gage spoke.

"We have a lot to talk about," Gage said. "I want to know everything. We have time to talk. We will be flying through space together toward Blue Eden."

Annie pushed away from him. "I'm not going," she said.

"I don't understand. I thought. . ."

"You thought wrong," Gage watched Annie walk to the open door, stop and face him. "I know. I've been elected the leader of this expedition," She said. "But I can't accept. I'm tired.

I just want to be with my husband and my children." Annie smiled and Gage felt a sense of peace flow from her.

"We will spend time together and talk, but for now we have work to do. I see some people in the hangar you need to meet," Annie said, her voice soft. She took her brother's arm and led him into the hangar.

Standing beneath the wing of the shuttle was a slender dark-haired woman with brown eyes and fine even features. She was talking to a man Gage had seen but they had not been introduced. The two looked up as Gage and Annie approached.

"Joe," Annie said. "This is Grace. She will be the pilot of your ship and you will be her co-pilot." Annie turned toward the young man standing next to Grace. "And this is Ray. He's been learning how these ships work. He will be going on your ship."

Gage shook hands with Grace and Ray.

"We have five shuttles," Annie said. "We need five pilots and five co-pilots. Our pilots have been training out here for six months, now. Not long, I understand, but Joe, a lot longer than you will have to learn. You and the four new co-pilots will have on-the-job training. You will have to learn fast."

"From what I understand," Gage said. "We only have four co-pilots. Diego and Johnson are here at the Farmhouse and have been briefed. Young Bryant is here. Counting me, that's four."

"We brought in another co-pilot," Annie said. "A man named Zack. He was picked up in the city with the train wreck survivors. When we registered him in the stronghold, he checked the box stating he had been a pilot. Now, excuse me," Annie said. "I will leave you three to discuss the mission." She nodded and walked away. Gage watched his sister step into the elevator and the door slide closed.

"Our mission is pretty straight forward," Grace said, breaking Gage's focus. "Each of these shuttles carries one hundred passengers plus ten crew members. The first stop is the moon. It will take us two earth days to get there. These shuttles are using three rocket stages to get us to the moon. Officer Gage, you'll see how that works later."

"Each of us pilots has already taken the shuttles up. . .not to the moon. . .just up into space and back. We've repaired the runway outside the hangars. It's a little over 12,000 feet long, but we've discovered the shuttle really only needs about 8000 feet to land if we use full brakes, drag chute and spoilers." Grace shifted her stance and rubbed her fingers across her mouth.

"According to the information we have, there's a space station up there on the moon, but we don't know what condition the station is in. We may have to make some repairs, maybe not." Grace smiled. "It will be safe to live there, underground, because we can easily be sealed off from the hostile environment"

"And if we can't?" Gage said.

Grace shrugged her shoulders. "Well, we can live in the shuttles for a month. That will give us time to seal the space station on the moon."

"In the early twenty-first century," Ray said. "A reservoir of water was discovered beneath the Moon's surface that has the same concentration of water as some reservoirs in the upper mantle of Earth. That water can be tapped to sustain a food supply and support human life. We can use that water and the food supply we're taking with us to survive for a while aboard the shuttles." Ray ran his hand across the top of his head.

"At this point," Ray said, "There are three ships orbiting the moon. Well, there's supposed to be three ships. They are. . .well, from what we can understand, they're like flying hotels. We plan on leaving a small crew on the moon and the rest of us will take the three ships to Mars."

"And we're going to be flying those things?" Gage asked.

"That's right." Grace nodded. "With the help of Ray and his team of scientists."

Ray's eyes opened wide and his body moved with an animated energy. "It will take three weeks to get from the moon to Mars in those ships."

Gage shot him a disbelieving look.

"No, it's true," Ray said, waving his arms around as he spoke. "We're using a device called PPAR, short for Photon, Plasma, Accelerator, Regulator."

"Keep talking," Gage said.

Ray took a deep breath. "The PPAR uses an entirely new state of matter, a matter that actually slows down the speed of light and was first observed at the end of the twentieth century," he said. "The idea of this new kind of matter was first proposed in 1924 by Albert Einstein. According to Einstein's theory, atoms crowded close enough in ultra-low temperatures would lock together to form a single glob of solid matter which would produce waves that behave like radio waves." Ray held his hands up, clenched and unclenched his fingers.

"Laser beams moving at the normal speed of light collide with atoms. As the atoms absorb particles of light. . .photons. . .the atoms slow down, thus slowing down the speed of light. Einstein's theory of relativity placed an upper, but not lower limit on the speed of light. "

Gage shook his head. "I thought the idea was to move faster, not slower."

Grace laughed. "Yes, and no," she said. "Traveling at the speed of light is great for vast distances, like moving across the galaxy, but it is not desirable for short distances. When traveling short distances and at high speeds, the ship would never have time to slow down and stop. It would crash almost instantly into a planet. You see," Grace said, "light normally travels from the Moon to Mars in less than two minutes. We need to slow that speed down so we can have better control."

"Exactly," Ray said. "Using Einstein's theory, experiments were conducted that eventually allowed humans to regulate the speed of light and to use that beam of light to move large masses with small amounts of fuel. Ray moved closer to Gage, unable to curb his excitement. "The PPAR was invented. The PPAR device initiates an explosion, and a plasma beam similar to light is produced which kicks the ship forward," Ray explained. "It's like how a soccer player can control the speed of a ball by using his feet to kick the ball. As the player runs across a field kicking the ball, the player is using his feet to propel the ball at the same speed he is running. Then the player can kick that ball ahead of him toward the goal and the ball now is moving at a faster rate than the player.

A week before reaching Mars, a slowing process will take place. An alternate beam is generated, acting like a break that slows the ship to a desirable speed. The trip should take about three weeks to reach Mars from the Moon."

Gage listened with fascination.

"Hey, Look," Grace said. "We pilots have been briefed on how this PPAR device works. Ray and his team are going with us. All of you co-pilots will be learning from them about how this plasma beam moves mass through the void of space. In order to minimize the effects of G force, the acceleration process takes about twenty to twenty-five minutes, depending on the mass, to push the spacecraft to the desired speed. After that it's smooth sailing until we start to put the brakes on." Grace smiled at him. "This is only the beginning."

Gage was elated.

"Annie, I know you didn't plan on going on this first voyage, but our people need you to lead them to Blue Eden. Then you will return to earth to help me. I will be here when you return."

Annie felt Robert's fingers dig into her shoulders, his breath warm against her face. "This is a perilous but critical trip," Robert said. "These pilgrims need you, Annie. They trust you and they believe in you."

Annie pushed Robert away from her. "Robert, I have waited with the children for three years. Three years to be with you. Why can't you come with us? I need you. The children need you." Tears burned her eyes.

Robert threw his hands in the air and walked in circles. "Damn you, Annie, stop it. You talk like we're factory workers behind the walls."

Annie sat down on a sofa in Robert's private office and buried her face in her hands. Robert stood across the room from her, his face pale.

"I've spent the last three years in this mountain, planning this mission," Robert said, his voice strained. "But you're the real leader, Annie. I'm Espiritu, the invisible man no one sees. I have vision, yes, and I know exactly what has to be done. But, you Annie. . .you have a special energy that connects with the people." Robert walked across the room and stood in front of her.

"Sometimes one can almost see that energy it's so strong. Annie, I have to use other people to move my ideals. I use Ivan, and yes I use you. But you," Robert waved his hands in the air. "Annie, you can light a room with your energy. I can't do that. I need you for that. You'll be back here in eight months or maybe a year."

"And what about the children?" Annie asked.

"The children will remain on Mars until it's safe to come back."

Annie stood up and walked away from Robert. She turned to face him, her fists clenched. "When is that going to be? How much longer?"

"We just won our first battle today." Robert spoke just above a whisper. "We took back our outpost from World Tech and we took the plateau in less than an hour." Robert moved a few steps closer to Annie. "We captured one hundred and ninety-three prisoners, Annie, and Mullans was captured trying to sneak away. The revolution has started." Annie took a deep breath.

"Look," he said. "We migrants have been getting away with a lot because the corporate kings had a huge weakness that they no longer have. That weakness was arrogance." Robert started to pace and then stopped. "To the kings, we migrants are considered so inferior, we are to them more like mindless machines or some type of rodent. To them, we're trainable most of the time, but the kings believe we are lacking in real intelligence. We migrants have never been taken seriously by the kings." Annie noticed Robert's clenched fists and his muscles tighten.

"The Eight has worked that weakness to our advantage," Robert said. "Believe me, when someone thinks you're stupid, they let their guard down. But the kings won't let their guard down anymore. Next time, the corporate kings will come better prepared. "Listen to me Annie. You have to leave here and you have to take the children with you. We're planning an attack on Oakbourgh."

"But, Oakbourgh. . .?" Annie said.

"Yes. Yes. Yes." Robert waved his hands in the air. "The water's running out and the corporations are going to abandon it. I know. But we are going to take it before they leave. There is a lot of wealth there and we are going to take it. We need to put the kings on the defensive before they come for us. Take our children where it will be safe. Annie, we need to get those shuttles out of here as soon as we can."

Robert placed his hands on each side of Annie's face. "Those corporate kings have always lacked the ability to wield their power with wisdom and compassion. They have always used fear and lies to hold dominion over the masses. Proving the existence of Blue Eden will weaken the kings' power and transfer that power to us. Annie, I trust you to take those pilgrims to Mars. Get the colony started. Promise them a democracy, Annie." Robert laughed.

"People love to build new things, Annie. Building new things, creating new projects, spreading new ideas is exhilarating. The people will work hard to build a new democracy in a new world. The idea of a new democracy on a new world will fuel our revolution, but you must bring those shuttles back to earth again." Robert held Annie's face between his hands and kissed her.

Hannah sat down next to Griff, buckled her seat belt and draped a thick blanket over her legs. There were one hundred people on the ship, not counting the crew, and Hannah recognized only a few of them. Rebecca and Patricia were on board and so were some of the survivors from the train wreck. Dennis and his family were on another shuttle and Zack was a co-pilot.

"Isn't this exciting?" Griff said as the shuttle began to move out of the hangar and onto the runway. Griff sat next to the window, but he leaned back so he would not block Hannah's view of the outside.

"I guess," Hannah said, leaning back and closing her eyes.

"Well, aren't you scared?" Griff said. "Aren't you excited?"

Hannah opened her eyes and looked straight ahead. "Maybe a little," she said.

Once outside the hangar, the shuttle stopped.

"Good," Griff said.

"Good?" Hannah turned toward Griff. "You want me to be scared?"

"I want you to feel something, Hannah. If you can't feel joy or excitement, then maybe you can feel fear. That's a start. At least fear will start your emotions working again. You know Hannah, the worst danger is during take-off."

Hannah adjusted her blanket and seat that were designed to reduce the pressure of G force during take-off.

"Are you scared?" Hannah said, her voice soft.

"Yeah," Griff said. "I'm a lot scared."

The shuttle started to move.

"I'm mostly scared about being alone." Griff looked straight ahead as he spoke.

Hannah looked at Griff sitting straight, covered in his blanket, his hands gripping the arm rests. She touched his hand with her fingers and felt his muscles relax.

For two minutes the fuselage shook, but Hannah could not hear the sound of the engines inside the shuttle. She had been told that the solid rocket boosters would drop off and the ride would become smoother after another two minutes.

Gentle warmth radiated from the window and Hannah knew from listening to the other passengers that this heat was caused by the high speed of the shuttle creating friction with the atmosphere. The air outside was hot enough to melt the metal of a spacecraft that was not built to withstand the temperatures.

Hannah squeezed Griff's hand. He smiled but did not move his head. During the last four minutes of the take-off, Hannah felt a pressure across her chest so strong she feared she could not catch her breath. And then she was floating. Her seatbelt kept her in place, but she was floating without the sensation of water on her skin. Her legs and arms moved about with the slightest amount of effort. Gasps and giggles filled the cabin, but a few children screamed in fear.

Hannah looked at Griff. He no longer looked afraid. Hannah laughed and Griff laughed with her.

During take-off, Annie put her arm around Michael and placed her face close to his. Michael belonged to her now. Tanika was dead, and Annie had promised that if anything happened to Tanika, she would raise Michael as her own child. Annie meant to keep that promise.

Michael screamed with surprise as weightlessness lifted him in the air. He bounced in his seat and within the constraints of his seatbelt. Her daughter, Greta, sat next to Rebecca and squealed with delight as the shuttle took them into the weightlessness of space. Annie's sons, Gilbert and Alex, their faces glowing with joy, looked across the aisle at Annie for reassurance.

"It's okay," Annie told them. "A new experience," she said and the boys laughed. Annie laughed with them.

Take the boys to safety, Robert had said. Build a new government. Build a world that is safe and just. You can do that, Robert had told her.

Annie looked at her children, so young and innocent. She would start a new world for them, but what would they do with it, she wondered. Would they get tired of the work a democracy required and hand their world over to the kings to run? The future belonged to the young, Annie knew. She would give her children a seed and teach them how to make it grow. It would be up to them to nurture that seed to full bloom.

Annie smiled. Her heart lifted.

Gage felt no sense of motion at all. He seemed to be suspended in space while the earth rolled by below and the moon fell toward him. Excitement burned through his veins and yet a sensation of serenity shielded him from fear.

"This is just the beginning," Gage's voice was a whisper.

"Did you say something?" Grace spoke to him from the pilot's chair.

"What?. . .I guess I did," he said. "This is amazing. I can't explain the feeling."

Grace laughed. "I know that feeling of awe and wonder and even adventure. But, we have a mission," she said. "It took us eight minutes to get from the runway into space. We had no problems" Grace said. "Our engines launched fine."

Gage shifted his eyes to the control panel.

"Flying in space is different from flying on earth, Officer Gage," Grace said. In space, you don't have air mass to help you fly. Instead, you need to remember Newton's Law."

"And that is," Gage said, "for every action there is an equal and opposite reaction."

"Exactly," Grace said. "The shuttle has attitude control jets on its nose, tail and wing tips. When the shuttle needs to turn left, a jet fires a tiny squirt of gas pointed to the right and the shuttle moves to the left.

Since there is no air in space, there is no friction, so a push this way can put the ship into a spin. To prevent that, it is necessary to fire another small gas jet pointed in the opposite direction to make the shuttle stop when the turn is complete. It takes practice, Officer Gage. So now, the controls are yours." She nodded at him.

Gage sat up straight and placed his hands on the controls. With his mind and senses alert, Gage looked out into the Milky Way and guided the ship forward. Today was the beginning of a new future.

EPILOG
THE MAKING OF BLUE EDEN

Scientists of the late 20th and early 21st centuries discovered that Mars was about half the size of Earth and in some ways was like Earth. Mars is the 4th planet from the sun, Earth the 3rd. Mars rotates in 24.6 hours and tilts on its axis by 24 degrees almost the same as Earth, which meant that Mars has seasons like Earth. Its orbit wanders toward and away from the sun as much as Earth's, giving Mars a range of climates similar to Earth though much hotter and colder.

On average, the temperature on Mars is about minus 80 degrees F (minus 60 degrees C). In winter, near the poles temperatures can get down to minus 195 degrees F (minus 125 degrees C). A summer day on Mars may get up to 70 degrees F (20 degrees C) near the equator, but at night the temperature can plummet to about minus 100 degrees F (minus 73 C). Frost forms on the rocks at night, but as dawn approaches and the air gets warmer, the frost turns to vapor and there is 100 percent humidity until it evaporates.

It takes 1.88 Earth years for Mars to orbit the sun. Mars has two moons. The Martian sky was found to have clouds and is generally butterscotch in color, except for the pink or red of sunset and sunrise. The ground, as seen from our earth's telescopes, changes colors during the 687-day Martian year.

Geologists found Mars to be almost alive. It has volcanoes, dune fields, ice sheets and dust storms. Mars has traces of a magnetic field, an oxidized surface, as well as an iron core and a silicate mantle, large river valleys and glacial and pre-glacial landforms. Scientists have found evidence of running water in the past and a surface covered with basalt boulders.

Martian river valleys have been found to be fed not by rainfall as on Earth, but carved in two different ways: sudden outbursts of water after volcanoes or impacts from asteroids melted the permafrost, or slow melting of permafrost during climate changes related to Mars's orbital cycles. Water-altered minerals found in Mars' bedrock, verified the theories that an ancient ocean once covered the northern hemisphere.

The Martian magnetic field recorded in rocks of the southern hemisphere shows crude strips in polarity, like those on Earth's seafloor. Some have thought that Mars once had the kind of plate tectonics that creates the strips on Earth. But by the early 21st century, there was no other evidence of plate tectonics. The crust on Mars is thick.

Mars has ice caps both at its North and South poles. The largest volcano on Mars, Mount Olympus, is three times higher than Mount Everest, standing 78,000 feet high. Mars also has one of the largest craters ever discovered, about 1,300 miles wide. At the later part of the 20th century and the beginning of the 21st century, Mars had a very thin atmosphere made mostly of carbon dioxide.

Since Mars has less mass than Earth, the Mars surface gravity is less than the surface gravity on Earth. The surface gravity on Mars is only about 38% of the surface gravity on Earth, so if you weigh 100 pounds on Earth, you would weigh only 38 pounds on Mars.

During a fifty year span, scientists on Earth began preparing Mars for human habitation. Mars has all of the ingredients necessary for life. It once had an atmosphere thick and warm enough to allow for the flow of liquid water on its surface – the prerequisite for life. Scientists knew that once there was again an atmosphere that would allow the existence of liquid water, there would be life on Mars again.

Terraforming, as the scientists called the creating of an atmosphere on Mars, was first a restoration project to return the cold, dry planet to a more life-like period in its geological past.

Terraforming Mars began with a warming up and thickening of the existing atmosphere in order to make Mars habitable for the micro-organisms that can prosper in a carbon dioxide rich environment. This process has been termed leucopoiesis from the Greek meaning fabricating or producing an abode or dwelling place. The process of leucopoiesis on Mars requires the transformation of three things: the soil, the atmosphere and the water. These play a large role in the organization of the future biosphere and in turn, are changed by the living matter within them. There were four terraforming steps used in the beginning of the 21st century to transform Mars.

The first step: Large Mylar mirrors were placed a hundred thousand miles from Mars and used to reflect the sun's radiation and heat the Martian surface. These mirrors have a diameter of 250 km (155.34 miles) and cover an area larger than Lake Michigan. Once these mirrors were in place and directed at the polar ice caps of Mars, the surface temperature of the planet began to rise and the polar caps began to melt. As the ice caps began to melt, and over a period of several decades, carbon dioxide that was trapped inside the ice was released. Greenhouse gases, such as chlorofluorocarbons were released and the warming of the planet accelerated.

The second step: Hundreds of light weight, solar-powered, greenhouse gas – forming factories were produced on earth, transported to Mars and dropped to the surface of the planet. Their sole purpose was to pump out methane, carbon dioxide and other greenhouse gases into the atmosphere. At the same time, machines that mimicked the natural process of plant photosynthesis, inhaling carbon dioxide and emitting oxygen were also placed on the planet.

The third step: Scientists of the early 21st century also created factories that utilized fluorine – based gases, composed of elements readily available on the Martian surface that were known to be effective at absorbing thermal infrared energy. They found that a compound known as octafluoropropane, that is a chemical formula C3F8, produced the greatest warming while its combination with several similar gases enhanced the warming even further.

The researchers found that adding approximately 300 parts per million of the gas mixture in the current Martian atmosphere, which is the equivalent of nearly two parts per million in an Earth – like atmosphere, sparked a runaway greenhouse effect, creating an instability in the polar ice sheets that began to evaporate the frozen carbon dioxide on the planet's surface. The release of increasing amounts of carbon dioxide lead to further melting and global temperature increases that then enhanced atmospheric pressure and restored a thicker atmosphere to the planet.

The fourth step: In addition to the mirrors and the factories, huge ammonia-heavy asteroids and those made of ice were guided, with care, toward the planet by rockets. The rockets would shut off, allowing the 10 billion-ton asteroids to fall to the planet where upon impact exploded, releasing 130 million megawatts of power. Over a period of 30 years, four of these explosions occurred raising the planet's temperature to 12 degrees Celsius. The sudden raise in temperature of the planet melted trillions of tons of water, including the ice asteroids. That created a body of water covering 25% of the planet. Since Mars is a salt rich environment, much of the water became saturated with brine, much like earth. Yet, the runoff from the melting icecaps also created fresh water streams and lakes.

After a while biological plants, which breathed in carbon dioxide and emitted oxygen, were introduction into the inhospitable environment. Life took hold and began to flourish. Next, seeds were transported to Mars and spread in abundance across the planet. Fish, such as salmon, bass, trout, shrimp, lobster and cat fish were released into the oceans and streams. Animals of every species such as rabbits, horses, cows, squirrels, goats, wild boar and deer and birds of every variety were released into the forests of this waiting paradise.

QUESTIONS FOR BOOK CLUBS

Why did they build walls? Were the walls successful in their purpose?

Have the Ditchings existed in the past?

What was the significance of smoking cigerettes?

What was the secret of the Blue Eden?

Did Gage change and if so, why?

What was Annie's conflict?

What did Hannah's youth represent?

Was there a difference between El Espiritu and the corporate Kings?

What was the importance of returning to Earth from Blue Eden?

Would you have gone to Blue Eden?

What was the McGuffin?